BRACING the BLUE LINE

LINDSAY PAIGE

This is a work of fiction. Names, characters, places, brands, media, and incidents are either the product of the author's imagination or are used fictitiously. The author acknowledges the trademarked status and trademark owners of various products referenced in this work of fiction, which have been used without permission. The publication/use of these trademarks is not authorized, associated with, or sponsored by the trademark owners.

Copyright © 2014 by Lindsay Paige
Editing by K² Editing
Cover Design by Damonza
Print and eBook Design by JT Formatting

All rights reserved. Without limiting the rights under copyright reserved above, no part of this publication may be reproduced, stored in or introduced into a retrieval system, or transmitted, in any form, or by any means (electronic, mechanical, photocopying, recording, or otherwise) without the prior written permission of the above copyright owner of this book.

Printed in the United States of America
First Edition: July 2014
Library of Congress Cataloging-in-Publication Data

Paige, Lindsay
 Bracing the Blue Line / Lindsay Paige – 1st ed
  ISBN-13: 978-1500636791

BLUE LINE (NOUN):

Either of two blue lines that divide an ice-hockey rink into three equal zones and that separate the *offensive* and *defensive* zones from the center-ice *neutral* zone

Winston

DAMN, THAT GAME was brutal. Going up against one of the best teams around will do that to a defenseman. I'm nearly too tired to head to the bar with the team, but I'm going anyway. It's better to go and deal with it than to hear shit about me going home early. So I tag along and by the time we get to the bar, I'm not as tired. I'm probably going to regret going though because it's a three game week with one today that we just finished, tomorrow, and Saturday.

We take up two booths and I, along with a couple of other guys, pull a chair up to the table for all of us to have a seat. A pretty waitress walks over with her low-cut white t-shirt and red bra underneath to take our drink order. She knows us because this is where we usually come to hang out after a game when there isn't a party. Her smile is friendly and flirtatious, particularly aimed at one of my teammates. They have this weird non-relationship, but almost a relationship thing going on.

"What time do you get off?" Vincent Taylor, another defenseman, asks her.

"Around the time you all end up leaving."

Vincent grins and subtly nods. "Good."

"Who I go home with, if anyone, is debatable."

His smile quickly disappears, and her comment obviously pisses him off. They insist on this cat and mouse game it seems. I have no idea why. Once she walks away, I look up from my phone and am about to open my mouth to say something to him when arms wrap around my neck. Who the fuck is this?

"Winston Brooks!" a voice that I haven't heard in a long time squeals in my ear. Her voice immediately makes my stomach drop and my heart rate increase.

I turn in my seat as her arms loosen to see my best friend's baby sister and my sort of ex-girlfriend. "Maddie? Wow, you look..." my voice trails off. This girl doesn't look anything like I remember. She looks even better. Maddie was always pretty, but wow. She's wearing tight, olive green skinny jeans that, in combination with a skin-fitting black top, shows off a figure I never knew existed.

"Hot as hell, right?" she grins. Did she cuss? Wait, she's smiling at me? I can't believe she would even come up to me. Not after what happened, not after what I did to her.

"Who's this?" Grant Faison curiously asks. He's our goalie, a junior like me, and rarely goes out with us. He likes to study too much, but tonight, he decided to come.

Before I can introduce her, Maddie sticks out her

hand. "I'm Maddie, a friend of Winston's from back home."

A friend. We were way more than friends, but only we knew that. It almost hurts that she called me an old friend. It shouldn't, especially not after how I hurt her. They shake hands before she brings her attention back to me.

"What are you doing here?" I ask, slipping my phone into my coat pocket.

She laughs. "Haven't you talked to Dave lately? I go here now."

Dave Evans is her brother and my best friend, who goes to another university. "Yeah, but he never mentioned it. Here," I say, sliding out of my seat so she can sit down. Once I grab another chair for myself and sit next to her, she leans over to hug me.

"I've missed you! I kept hoping I would run into you. How have you been? Dave only talks to me like once a month, and you're never on Facebook, so I've been out of the loop."

"I've been good. What about you?" I ask, trying to get my brain to catch up from the girl I left behind to the girl she is now. She's small, probably only five feet tall, a stark contrast to my 6'1" height. She used to be heavier, something her brother teased her about endlessly. She was gorgeous, still is. Not to mention that she actually seems happy to see me. Maybe Maddie didn't hold a grudge.

"I've been great. It's fun making new friends, going to parties, and exploring this place."

"You've been going to parties?" I question with disbelief. "What parties? What happened to you?" I joke. According to Dave, Maddie never went to parties when we were in high school, although we were a little older than her and she did go to one, but only briefly. His baby sister was too good for that kind of thing. If he only knew.

Before she can answer, Neil Lawson, our captain and a senior, saddles up next to her, laying an arm around her shoulder. He's grinning one of those smiles that always makes girls want to go home with him. It makes me want to punch him because that smile doesn't need to be directed at Maddie.

"Who might you be?" he asks.

"Maddie." She smiles, but turns to me, effectively ignoring him. "We should catch up sometime. We're still friends, right?"

And there it is. The first acknowledgement of our past together has softened her voice, showing a vulnerability I'm responsible for, and it makes me want to fix things between us. Not to get back together, but to right a wrong. I never truly apologized.

"Yeah, of course," I struggle to say.

Maddie doesn't notice, though. She smiles and almost looks relieved before reaching into my coat pocket for my phone like she has the right to stick her hand into my pocket and retrieve whatever she wants. She used to do that all the time, so her action doesn't completely surprise me. While she does whatever with her eyes on the screen, she adds, "We can get to know each other again." She glances up at me with her brown eyes and smiles.

Just then, a guy walks up and says, "Here you are." Maddie beams a smile at him, one I used to get all the time, but before she can even say hello, he kisses her in greeting. And not just a simple peck on the lips. I'm talking about a full blown, tongue-filled kiss. That definitely formed the inside to make it more comfortable when she did go there. You could almost forget what type of building you were in. I knew, as Dave's best friend, his sister was off limits. That was completely fine until Maddie started turning into someone who was more than a friend to me.

We were nearly inseparable, as much as we possibly could be while keeping our relationship a secret. I knew all too well how Dave saw his baby sister, and I didn't want to lose my longest friendship. So we didn't tell anyone. I thought I loved her. God, I had to have. She was everything to me. I wanted to call her with good news or to recount a good or bad day before anyone else. I kissed her first. I touched her first. I made all the big moves first. I wanted to give her everything.

Except the one thing she ended up wanting the most.

Maddie wanted to go out on dates with me in public instead of sneaking an hour away. She wanted to be able to hold my hand and kiss me without caring who saw. I wanted that too, but not enough to tell her brother. Dave and I are close. We know nearly everything about each other and we always have the other's back. I couldn't risk losing him. Losing his friendship would make my relationship with Maddie even harder. I just knew that I would lose them both and in turn, lose the family I had come so close to after all these years.

Dave was dating some chick and was out with her one night. My parents were out of the house, attending some fundraiser. Maddie snuck over and one thing led to another, and we slept together. I was her first. I was happy that she trusted me, loved me, and believed in us enough to give me that part of her.

It only made things worse in the end.

The next night, Dave and I were at a party. It was a big one, because summer was only three weeks away and this was our last high school party before we left for college. Maddie and I had been arguing about her wanting to tell people we were together. She, for the first time, showed up at the same party as us. Things would have been fine if she hadn't walked over to us, standing next to me.

"What are you doing here, Fatty Maddie?" Dave had asked her, using his own personal nickname for her. She wasn't overweight, but she was a little chunky and he liked to tease her about it. His stupid nickname caused some of the guys to laugh. It wasn't funny and hasn't ever been funny, especially not when I found out how much it bothered Maddie.

"Same thing you are." She took the cup of beer from my hand and took a swallow before handing it back to me. When we were alone, she was always doing that. Taking a sip of my drinks, eating from my plate, taking my phone from my pocket if hers was dead.

"This is for seniors. You don't need to be here. And it's a beach party. People wear bathing suits to these things," he told her as a girl walked by in a skimpy bikini. He was right. Everyone was in a bathing suit except Maddie. She wore shorts and a tank top instead. There wasn't even a bathing suit beneath her clothes. She was probably too self-conscious because of Dave's fucking comments. "Maybe if you lose some weight, you can go to your own senior party. Go home, Fatty Maddie."

My free hand balled into a fist by my side. Since Dave picked on his sister, one of the other guys made fun of her too.

"Yeah, no one wants a fat girl here."

Dave didn't say anything. Not even an 'I'm the only one who can pick on my sister'. Maddie glanced up at me with glassy eyes. She waited for me to defend her, to stand up to them, to put her and her feelings first.

I hated myself before I shrugged like I didn't even care and added, "They're right. You should go."

That's when things ended between us. Until tonight, Maddie hasn't spoken to me since. I tried to apologize to her later, tried to call her, text her, talk to her through every method except the one that mattered the most. I wouldn't go to her house and make her talk to me. I couldn't risk letting Dave know about something that no longer existed. Now, Maddie's going to the same college as me and she's skinny. I can't help but wonder if there's a reason why she lost weight.

"I'm heading out. I have an early start tomorrow," Grant says, bringing my attention back to the table.

"Yeah, I think I'm going to go too," I add, wondering if Dave knows about Maddie's boyfriend. She's on my mind the entire way back to where I live off-campus with Grant, Neil, and Bo, another teammate of ours and a senior as well. After I've changed, I power up my laptop and start a FaceTime call with Dave.

His face pops up almost immediately. "How'd the game go?" he asks.

"Good. They were a tough team, and I'll probably be sore tomorrow, but good." After a pause, I blurt out, "I saw Maddie."

"Really? Where? I forgot to tell you that that's where she decided to go."

"Yeah, I was surprised when she came up to me...in a bar."

Dave's eyes widen. "Seriously?" I nod. "She probably saw you go in and wanted to come say hi. Hey, you need to send your schedule to me again, so I can pick a weekend to come up. I accidentally deleted the first one, and I don't feel like searching for the schedule online."

I laugh. "Lazy much?"

"Lil bit." Dave's eyes flick to something behind his computer as I hear a door open and close. He grins, looks down at me, and says, "Gotta go." I would bet five bucks that his girlfriend just walked in. The call ends, and I close my laptop.

A glance at the clock shows that it's almost one. The game wore me out, so I start to change into pajama pants and get ready for bed. As I pull back the covers, there's a knock on my bedroom door.

"Winston! I have a present for you," Neil yells from the other side. What the hell is he up to? With a sigh, I walk over, open the door, and look down to find Maddie standing next to Neil. What is she doing here? Neil gives me a grin before walking away.

"Hey, Winston." Her eyes survey my bare torso before coming back to my face. "This is sort of a long story. Can I come in?" She gives me a hopeful smile as she rocks on her heels.

"Of course," I answer, moving aside for her. It's not like I can say no to Dave's sister, especially if she needs something. Hell, it's not like I can say no to *Maddie*. Period.

"You still wear something on your head all the time?" she asks, glancing around my room before taking a seat on the edge of my bed.

I reach up and feel the fabric of a beanie on my head. I'd forgotten I was even wearing it. "Why? Does it bother you?" Sitting down next to her and feeling slightly awkward having her in my bedroom, I take off my beanie and drop it in her lap.

Maddie reaches over and ruffles my hair, laughing softly. "No, it doesn't. It was only an observation. I'd almost forgotten that you have perfect, dark brown hair underneath it." Her hand falls back into her lap. "Ready for my long story?"

I scoot back on my bed to lean my back against the headboard and spread my legs out behind her. Once I clasp my hands behind my head, I say, "Okay, I'm ready."

She takes a deep breath, but ends up mumbling, "Boys are stupid."

Laughing, I tell her, "That's the best you got? Stupid? Wouldn't idiotic jerks sound better? Or what about insensitive jackasses? Or should we go with something like, boys are mindless morons who don't know how to keep a girl happy? I thought you were more imaginative than that, Maddie."

That makes her smile. "Are there any guys who actually know how to keep a girl happy?" She cuts her eyes over at me, probably remembering that I failed her too.

"Only a few." I pause, wondering if I should ask, but then decide I should. "Are you okay? I mean, you're not going to burst into tears, are you?"

Maddie laughs, shaking her head. "No, I'm not. He didn't do anything worthy of tears. I ended up here because my boyfriend broke up with me over something stupid, and my roommate decided to lock me out for a couple hours. I went back to the bar, saw your teammates, and thought we could go ahead and catch up. Neil showed me the way, so here I am." She slips off her shoes, turns to face me, and sits with her legs crossed in front of her.

"I was about to go to bed," I point out.

She seems to think about that before she says, "Well, isn't there some sort of rule that you should be extra nice to me because of Dave?" There's no bitterness with his name, no mention of what we once were. Like we didn't ever happen.

I force a chuckle. "Maybe when we were younger, but not anymore."

"Oh, c'mon, Winston. I thought we were friends too. Humor me. Please," she pleads. Maddie decides to not wait for a response. "How's hockey? Looks like you're doing well, considering you're on the team and all. I didn't know you wanted to play after high school. Do you want to try for the NHL?"

"Don't we all? That's the ultimate dream, to play professionally. I'd love to be good enough for the Olympics one day too. Hockey is good, though. The game tonight is one reason why I was about to go to bed."

Maddie rolls her eyes at my feeble attempt to get her to leave. "I don't know how you do it. I've been ice skating before, and I'm more likely to fall flat on my ass, much less try to play a game."

I raise an eyebrow at her, reaching over to steal my beanie back from her hands and put it back on my head. "Since when do you have such a vulgar mouth?" This is what I really want to know. "And since when do you go to bars and make out in public? I told Dave I saw you in a bar, and he thought you saw me and only went in to say hi."

"He would," she laughs. "A cuss word here and there doesn't mean I have a vulgar mouth either. Are you really that surprised?" Why does she pick and choose when to acknowledge what happened? It's driving me crazy and confusing me on how I should respond.

"I guess not. It's just that all Dave has ever said about you is that you're like an angel, and that was all I could think about. How he would be stunned to see you tonight. I mean, Dave is the bad apple, so to speak. He's the one who needed rules, and you were the responsible one. Don't know if I'd go as far as to say you were an angel, though."

Maddie smiles. "I feel like I have everyone fooled without even meaning to. Not sure how they all came to that conclusion about me."

"Then how come they never saw this side of you? You weren't as...proper, I guess, around me."

"I don't know. Maybe because I know how they expect me to behave, so when I'm around them, that's how I behave."

I nod, satisfied with her answer. "Why did you decide to come here for school?"

She shrugs. "It's a great school with great programs. I think my parents were hoping I'd go to the same university as Dave, but I didn't want to. They think I'm naïve, don't they? That's what it feels like sometimes when they talk to me."

Dave thinks she is. I've heard him say it plenty of times before. "I don't know," I lie.

Maddie seems to accept my answer. "Do you like it here? The school and all, I mean?"

"Yeah. There's a lot of good people here, and I have a

great coach."

"What about a girlfriend? I know Dave has his string of girls. Someone isn't going to barge in here and be disappointed when they see you have company, are they?"

I laugh. "No. Lost the girlfriend over the summer, and your brother doesn't have a string of girls. He has a girlfriend at the moment."

She seems to think about something, but when she speaks again, it's about hockey. "How did you ever start playing anyway? You never told me."

I smile and a large sense of gratitude washes over me. "For my fifth birthday, Dad took me to a game. That was my introduction to hockey, and I was hooked. I begged my parents for weeks to start me on lessons, but we lived in this small ass town, and there weren't any rinks nearby. Mom said I threw a tantrum when they told me I couldn't, and I gave them the silent treatment. A couple of weeks later, I remember Mom and Dad sitting me down.

"They said that if I really wanted to play, I could, but we would have to move, and I would have to give up my friends. I didn't care. I wanted to learn how. Turns out, my dad asked for a transfer at work to move closer to a city where I could learn. Three months later, we moved. As I got older, I realized how much my parents gave up, just so I could play, even when I was a five year old brat. Haven't stopped since."

Maddie smiles. "That's when you moved in next to us?"

"Yeah, you were three, so I doubt you remember that. Now, I just want to be a good enough player to make them proud and know their sacrifices were worth it."

"I'm sure you have done that already, Winston." She

stops, but adds, "I feel selfish, you know."

"How so?" I couldn't see her being selfish, but what do I know?

"Your parents did all that for you and you want to make sure you do your best because of it. I, on the other hand, tend to do the opposite of what they want for me or what they think I should want for myself. Not all the time, but often enough. I just try to ignore their dreams. I mean, I have to make sure that it's what *I* want first. After hearing that, it makes me feel selfish."

I nudge my knee against her thigh. "That doesn't make you selfish, Maddie." It's almost like we're back to being us, but there's still an awkwardness between us whether she accepts it or not.

She takes a deep breath and nods. "I guess I should let you go to bed now. Thanks for letting me come by." Maddie starts to stand to leave.

"How do you plan on getting back?" I ask. Dave would kill me if I let his baby sister catch a bus back to campus this late at night. Hell, I wouldn't want her to leave this late, but I can't very well say that in those words.

"My car. I followed Neil here."

Damn it. I'm screwed either way. "Why don't you crash here tonight? I can sleep on my couch." I lift my chin in the direction of where it sits across the room from my bed. It's old and probably needs to be replaced, but it sleeps pretty well.

Maddie glances at the piece of furniture and then back to me. "It's okay, Winston. You don't have to make a big fuss about this. I'll be fine."

"Dave would murder me if I let you leave this late at night. Don't argue. Stay and say thanks."

I watch as she debates it in her mind for a moment before she agrees. "Thanks, but you don't have to sleep on-"

"Don't be ridiculous," I interrupt. Standing, I walk to my little closet and pull out some blankets. I ask her to toss me a pillow and begin making a makeshift bed. Maddie excuses herself to the bathroom and once I've finished with the couch, I get comfortable.

She comes out, but stays near the door. "Um, I hate sleeping in jeans. It's like the most aggravating thing ever. Do you have something I could wear?"

"Seriously? I'm like a foot taller than you, Maddie."

"Shut up, and find me something. A t-shirt, gym shorts, anything. Or I'll leave." She folds her arms over her chest, knowing that she has me right where she wants me.

Huffing, I walk over to my dresser. Maddie softly laughs over her achievement, and I shoot her a mean look. I shuffle through the clothes and glance at her figure a few times. No way in hell any of my shorts will stay on her hips, even with help from the drawstrings. Her waist is too tiny.

"You're fucking compact, Maddie. I could probably stuff you in my suitcase. Looks like it'll be a shirt."

As I toss her one, she says, "If you were ever online, you'd know that they call people like me fun-sized now."

I burst out laughing. All I can picture in my head is a little bar of Snickers and comparing that to Maddie. She mumbles something under her breath as she returns back to the bathroom to change. I go back to the couch and lay down, rolling over to face the wall. Seeing Maddie in only a t-shirt isn't something I want to see.

Even if she does look good.

Her soft footsteps make their way across the room as

I listen to her climb into my bed and get comfortable. Right before she clicks off the lamp next to my bed, she says softly, "Night, Winston. Thanks for letting me stay."

"Night, and you're welcome."

The light goes off, and we're thrown into darkness. I close my eyes and attempt to ignore she's here until I fall asleep.

THE FIRST THING I notice as I awaken is a female body against me. One bare leg is thrown over my waist, and I can feel bent arms pressed against my chest. Hot air hits just above them in even intervals. The leg tightens around my waist, pulling the body closer to me, and my dick hardens as she brushes against me. I glide my hand down her back, my fingers hitting the soft fabric of her panties thanks to her shirt being hiked up.

Wait.

There's a girl in my bed?

My eyes pop open, and I look down to see Maddie's blonde hair. Fuck! Faintly, I can remember that I slept like shit on the couch, kept waking up, and decided that I would sleep in my own bed. I thought we would be able to stay on separate sides of the bed, but I guess not. Shit, this is bad. There's no way to get away with her wrapped around me like this. I slowly move my hand off her bottom and up to her back. For a moment, I'm distracted by her sleeping position. I mean, her leg is wrapped around me. Who the hell sleeps like this?

Focus, Winston! You're in bed with your best friend's baby sister, your secret ex-girlfriend, *and* she gave you a fucking hard-on! Maddie stirs next to me, and my eyes quickly close. That's the best thing I can think to do. The scent of coconut floats by my nose, probably from her shampoo. It sort of reminds me of the beach. Damn it, I need to stop thinking like this.

Her leg falls away from my waist, and I figure she's still asleep when she doesn't say anything or make a move to get away from me, so I open my eyes to decide on how to get out of this bed. Only, a set of hazel eyes are squinting at me in confusion.

"What are you doing?" she whispers curiously. "Why are you cuddling with me?"

"I'm not-" I start.

"That's what it feels like," Maddie interrupts.

"My point was that it's not a me thing. *I'm* not. *We* are. But, uh, I wasn't sleeping well on the couch, so I got back into *my* bed." For some reason, I feel like if I emphasize that it's my bed, then it'll somehow be her fault for being in it in the first place.

"Oh, well that makes sense. But why are we still laying here like this?"

Right. Maddie scoots back away from me as I roll over and then move to the couch.

"Sorry," I offer.

"It's no big deal. I did invade your room last night. I'll just get dressed and head on back." She slides out of bed, holding my shirt close to her thighs so she doesn't show too much. It's kind of useless because of how long it is anyway.

Maddie disappears into my bathroom with her clothes. I lean forward and bury my face in my hands. Please tell me that this is all a dream, and I wasn't momentarily attracted to her. Again. It's morning, and I was half sleep, so it doesn't matter, right? Maddie probably has had her fill of catching up, so I won't have to worry about it anymore. Just because we have a past and just because she's grown into a more gorgeous girl than before doesn't mean I'm about to act on it. I messed up, ruined things for us, and I won't do it again.

"Winston?"

I lift my head to see her standing directly in front of me.

"You okay?"

"Yeah," I reply, rubbing my eyes a little. "Still a little tired, I guess."

She laughs. "I'm going to head back. Thanks, again." Maddie gives me an innocent kiss on the cheek in gratitude before heading towards the door. She opens it, but turns around before walking out. "Do you have a game tonight? I'd really like to see you play at least once. I feel bad that I've never seen you play."

I shake my head in affirmation. "Get there at six to get a good seat."

And just like that, Maddie leaves. God damn it. I lean back onto the couch and glare at my crotch, where my dick wants to come out and play. Thank God Maddie didn't notice. I'd be in deep shit trying to explain that. This was a one time thing, no big deal. Groaning, I get up to take a cold shower. It's going to be a long fucking day. I can ignore a gorgeous girl, especially when she's Dave's little sister and the girl I hurt so badly three years ago.

NEIL

GRANT, WINSTON, BO Harris, and I all live off campus together in a house my parents used to rent out. Once I decided to come here for college, they said that I could live here if I wanted to. Of course I did. I invited the guys to live with me too. Grant and Winston just left, one off to study, the other to the gym, so when there's a knock on the door, I'm half expecting it to be one of them for some reason. Instead, I answer the door to a Hispanic girl in sweats and a hoodie that are entirely too big for her. Her dark brown hair is in a ponytail, and she seems extremely nervous. She kind of looks familiar too, but I can't place her face.

"Can I help you?" I ask, an uneasiness forming in my stomach the more anxious she looks.

Her shoulders sag with disappointment. "You don't

remember me, do you?"

Uh, oh. That probably means I've fucked her before. I shake my head. "Do you have any piercings, tattoos, or birthmarks to jog my memory?" I'm actually trying to be helpful, even if it doesn't sound like it. She obviously wants me to remember her, and that's my way of helping.

She doesn't like what I said, though. Her jaw tenses right before she sighs and turns around. Mystery girl lifts her shirt just high enough to show me her tramp stamp of a bunch of flowers. Slowly, the memories come back. I slept with her at the end of last semester. We were at a party, and I ended up spending twenty four hours with her, drinking, having sex, and sleeping. I can't believe I forgot about her.

"Right," I nod, wondering why the hell she's here. Her face hardens as I ask, "What's your name again?"

"Audra Garcia."

How could I forget a name like that? I probably didn't ever ask her what her name was or I was too drunk to remember when she did say it. "Can I help you, Audra?" I repeat.

"It's probably best if I go ahead and spit this out, isn't it?"

I nod, although I don't know what 'this' is. Audra grabs the hem of her hoodie and lifts to show me a little, swollen, light brown stomach. That can only mean one thing. It instantly sends pings of pain to my heart. No, this can't be happening. I stare at her belly until she lowers her shirt, forcing my eyes back to hers. My heart is beating so fast I wonder if I might faint. I'm feeling quite lightheaded, and I'm not so sure I have legs anymore.

"Could we go somewhere private to talk?" A rummaging sound comes from behind me, and Audra adds, "Preferably away from your friends?"

"Bo!" I yell. God, do I need my best friend and left winger right now. "Come in," I tell Audra. "Trust me. You're going to want him here."

Reluctantly, she steps inside and follows me into the living room. She takes a seat on the couch while I begin to pace. Bo still hasn't come yet. What the hell is he doing?

"Bo!" I yell louder.

He strides into the living room, looking agitated about my interruption. It fades when he sees we have company. I keep pacing, unsure what will happen once I stop. This can't be real. I don't want it to be real. Things that are real bring only one thing.

Pain.

"What's going on, Neil?" Bo asks cautiously.

"He's freaking out because I showed him I'm pregnant."

"Don't say it!" God, her saying it out loud just makes it worse.

"Whether I say it or not, the fact is still the same," she says evenly. Audra must be getting warm because she takes off her hoodie, leaving her in a white t-shirt.

Bo stares at her stomach. No, this can't be right.

"How far along are you?" I ask. There has to be a mistake. I'm not the father, surely.

"Five months."

Shit. No, no, no. I can't be a dad. That's absurd. I don't need this. I can't have this happening. This is too much to handle, and I find myself blowing up at her with panic and unwanted memories surging forward. "How do you even know it's mine? I don't know you, and if you've slept with me, then you could be a fucking whore for all I know!"

"Neil," Bo warns. That's why he's here because I'm freaking the fuck out.

Suddenly, Audra starts crying, burying her face in her hands. Shit. If there are two people I can't stand to see cry, it's old women and pregnant women. I look to Bo with a pained expression. He needs to help me. Bo shakes his head, and then nods towards Audra. He wants me to comfort her? Damn it!

I sit down on the couch next to her and pat her back. I feel like Sheldon from *The Big Bang Theory* when he says, "There, there." After a deep breath, I do my best to make her stop crying.

"Look, I'm sorry, Audra. Even though what I said is reasonable, I probably shouldn't have said it like that."

Bo glares at me, but Audra makes a mangled laugh sound. See? She appreciated my attempt.

"Sorry, I've been a bit of an emotional mess." Audra wipes away her tears. "If you want a paternity test, that's no problem. It is completely reasonable because I know how it might look, but it's yours. I wasn't sleeping with anyone, um, like six months before and then after," she pauses with a glance at me, "I was ashamed when I slept with you, so I took a break from sex. Then I found out I was pregnant."

"Ashamed? What? I'm a fucking great lay!"

Bo cuts his eyes over at me. Right. Not what we should be discussing. "Why did you wait so long to come tell Neil?" Bo asks.

Audra glances at me and thanks to her watery eyes, mine are drawn to them as I notice that they are dark brown. "Because it took me this long to get the courage to come find him."

For a moment, a sliver of a second, I feel for this girl. It has to be scary as fuck to be where she is, and I don't even know her. But I don't have to know her to know what she's feeling unfortunately.

"Have you thought about what you're going to do? Like are you keeping it or putting it up for adoption?" Her eyes widen and her mouth parts. However, I think it's more because I've asked than the question itself.

"I've thought about adoption, but I haven't made any decisions." Her hands move to her belly protectively.

"I think you should put the baby up for adoption," I spout quickly.

"Neil!" Bo says exasperated.

"What? You seriously want me to want that for myself? To put myself through that? No way in hell!"

He opens his mouth, but Audra distracts him with her nonchalant, "Okay." She grabs her hoodie and stands, stepping in front of me to head to the door.

"Okay?" What does she mean by that?

Audra turns around to face me. "That's why I came here, Neil."

"For me to tell you what to do?"

"No, the only reason I'm here is because I thought you deserved the chance to make a choice. You've made it." With that, she turns and walks out the door.

That's it? It was that easy? When I look at Bo, he's pissed. What for? Problem solved. I'm out of the equation. He gets up and bolts out the door. Where the fuck is he going? I take a deep breath of relief at the bullet I dodged. That could have ruined my life in so many ways, but now, it's all over and done with. I don't have to worry about it anymore.

"What the fuck was that?" Bo asks angrily as he walks back into the room. "Neil, that could very well be your kid she's carrying and the best you could do was freak out and tell her to put it up for adoption? You have a responsibility!"

His words stir me to stand up and begin to pace again. "She said she was considering it anyway, Bo. I don't need that responsibility. I have enough as it is."

"Then you should have kept your dick in your pants!" he explodes.

I ignore that. "What did you do when you went outside?" I ask.

"I apologized for your dumb ass." His voice turns eerily calm as he continues. "You can't do this, Neil. You know better from the first time."

"Don't even go there, Bo! I will beat the shit out of you without a second thought." He will *not* bring that up. Not now and especially not when that girl doesn't mean anything to me. There is no comparison.

"Then do it," he challenges. "You know, I'm glad you knocked her up because I'm sick of you fucking everything with tits, which has only put you back in the very situation you were-"

"Stop!" I yell. My pulse can be felt everywhere, throbbing in my fingertips, my neck, and my forehead. My hands are clenched in fists by my side. Bo is walking in dangerous territory, and he damn well knows it. "I'm warning you. Open your mouth one more time, and I'll rip you to pieces."

He stares at me, waiting for me to break, and it makes me want to punch him that much more. I've never wanted to hit him as badly as I do right now. He's my best friend, but at this very second, I don't give a flying fuck. I turn and walk out the front door, slamming it hard enough that the windows rattle. Then I get in my car, and I leave.

Fuck him.

I drive around aimlessly, eyeing the gas needle before finally deciding to stop and fill up. I can't believe Bo would bring that up. It's not something we talk about and the only time we acknowledge it is on Sundays.

"Fuck," I mutter, kicking my tire halfheartedly. This isn't what I want to think about. Not at all. Thinking about it means bringing back memories I don't want to have and an awful pain reminding me that it was all real. Regardless of what Bo says, I like my life the way it is. If I want to sleep with three different girls in one weekend, then that's my decision. If I want to party and have fun, then so be it. If I want to put myself first and foremost to keep history from repeating itself, then who is he to tell me I can't?

History has already started to repeat itself though. I've made the choice. I'm not going to change my mind either. I do not need nor want a kid or a baby momma. Sighing, I eventually go back to the house to grab my things for practice. We've got a game tonight, and I need to focus on that and nothing else. Being the captain of the Salem University hockey team requires me to be at my best because when I'm off my game, it travels to my teammates.

But being on the ice doesn't bring me comfort today. Not in the least. I'm making snide comments to everyone, almost hoping to piss them off too. I'm being selfish and a terrible leader, but all I can think about is the way Audra looked when she said she had to gather the courage to come find me. Winston was smiling earlier in the locker room, and it's pissed me off. If I'm not happy, then neither will he.

Winston

"WINSTON!" NEIL YELLS. "Get your head out of your ass and focus!"

That's the third time he's yelled at me in less than ten minutes. Coach keeps making us run the same drill over and over and apparently, Neil thinks I'm the reason why. Regardless that it's not all me, I nod and grunt as we resume our pre-game practice, knowing I don't need to say anything back to him. Something has put him a sour mood, and I'm his target. Neil seems to be one of those happy go-lucky guys, so if he's pissy, there's usually a good reason for it. Letting him harp on me to get it out of his system is fine.

Once again, he crawls down my throat for no good reason. My jaw tenses as I debate saying something. Neil's face is protruded in anger with him standing right in front of me. It almost seems like he wants me to start something with him. He's that angry. There's no way in hell that I'm about to hit him or make things escalate.

"Calm the fuck down, Neil. I don't know who pissed you off, but you need to chill."

His shoulders relax slightly, and Coach Nixon skates over to us.

"We're done, boys. Go relax before the game," he orders, looking at Neil.

He glances at him. "Yes, sir," he says before skating off the ice.

"Do you know what's bothering him?" Coach asks.

"No, but you know Neil. It won't be long before he fixes whatever it is," I answer. That's the truth too. Neil doesn't let anything keep him down for long. We have about an hour before we have to be back to the rink, and I'm starving. Back in the locker room, I question, "Anybody up for some food?"

Bo, Vincent, and Grant opt in while Neil shakes his head. Bo says something quietly to him, but he shrugs him off. I just hope he snaps out of it before the game. If he isn't focused on playing his best and has his mind elsewhere, it's going to affect the rest of us. Not that it's happened often, but when it does, we all falter. That's like our Achilles heel.

Once we change, we get into Grant's truck, and he drives us to a restaurant where we can get something light and healthy to eat. As soon as we take a seat with our food, Grant nudges my elbow with his.

"I saw that Maddie spent the night."

"Oh? The short chick from last night? I saw her walking across campus this morning," Vincent adds.

I eye him for a moment as I take a swallow of water. "Does that mean your waitress girl didn't leave with you last night?" No way he would have been out and about this morning if she stayed over.

Vincent narrows his eyes at me. "Her name is Mary and no, she didn't. I don't know what the hell her problem is."

"It's probably you," Bo laughs.

Vincent throws his napkin at him. "And when was the

last time you got laid?"

Before he can answer, Grant says, "I thought she was dating that guy." He raises an eyebrow, waiting for me to say something.

"They broke up, and I slept on my couch. That's all." I look at Bo. "What's going on with Neil?"

He shakes his head. "He'll be ready come game time," he answers, effectively ending that conversation before it starts. We begin discussing the upcoming game as we eat and then we're heading back to the rink.

THE ENTIRE TIME I was standing across from Winston, my anger kept rising. It was irrational, but the rage was real. I kept thinking I shouldn't be in this situation with Audra. Then all the times I've fucked a girl without a condom started filtering through my mind. I silently pled that he would punch me. Just once, so I could hit back and let out all my anger. I desperately wanted to start something. Between Audra and Bo, I wanted to beat the shit out of someone.

When Coach walked over, I couldn't believe what I wanted to happen. I wanted to fight my *teammate* because I'm pissed at myself. We're playing a damn good team tonight and starting shit with my guys will ensure we'll lose. Bo's quiet conversation with me before they left to go eat replays in my mind. There was no way in hell I was going to be around them, so I declined. I need time to cool down before the game.

"Forget about this shit for a while, so we will actually have a chance tonight, Neil. Although, you're going to have to face it soon," Bo mumbled under his breath before he left.

He wants me to forget it and come back in a good mood? Fine. I will do what he wants, and really, it's what I want, because I don't want to jeopardize our chances to win. Gladly, I can do exactly as he wishes.

But I need to get laid for that to happen.

I scroll through my contacts as I walk out of the building and towards the parking lot. On a few girls, I pull up their contact to get a better look at their saved picture. Sex with me has no bounds, so there is a diversity of girls to choose from in my phone. I decide to call Ginger, a thin, limber white girl with blonde hair and blue eyes.

It rings five times before she answers. "Neil?" She sounds hopeful, but surprised that I'm calling her.

"Hey, I need a little good luck sex before tonight. Think you could meet me in twenty minutes at my place?"

"Really?" The surprise seeps through her voice again. "I mean, yeah, of course. I'll be right over."

"Good. See ya."

I hang up and head to the house. By the time I get there, Ginger is pulling in behind me. There's no need to wait for her because she'll come on in anyway. Seconds after I've stepped inside, she's behind me. I grab her hand and tug her to my room. There, I take a moment to glance over her body. She's in tight jeans and a fitted shirt. Not for long.

"Good luck sex, huh?" she says as she shimmies out of her clothes as I do the same.

"Yep."

"Never heard of that before."

"That's because I've never called you for it before. Now, stop talking." I move forward and lay us down on the bed.

She begins to stroke me as I reach for a condom off my nightstand. There's an entire box sitting on it. I push everything out of my mind with every kiss to her lips, jaw, neck, and shoulders, and then I fuck her until she's screaming my name.

When I show up before the game, I have a big ass grin on my face. Ginger was exactly what I needed. Bo shakes his head when he sees me because he knows what I just did. Not my problem. Coach said to relax, and Bo said to forget about it. That's all I did. On the ice, my happy mood gets mixed with my mood from earlier. It's not a bad mixture for hockey.

My head isn't in it though. Somehow, I manage to play well, but in the back of my mind, I'm thinking about Audra. She's the last person I want to think about. This whole thing has déjà vu written all over it, and I refuse to go within a hundred miles of it. That can't happen again. It seems like Audra has it all figured out anyway. She doesn't need me.

And I don't want her to.

CHAPTER 3

Winston

SURE ENOUGH, NEIL is smiling when he shows up. His mood has changed entirely, which puts us all in a great mood. That mindset is fantastic going into a game. When we step out onto the ice for warm ups, determination is pulsing through each of us. The team we're playing tonight talks trash like no other. They love trying to get under our skin every chance they get. That's exactly why we try to dominate as much as possible.

Grant is on his A-game and Vincent and I do our part. The long, tough three periods are full of energy. Contagious energy that carries over to the entire team and our fans in the crowd. Without a doubt, there'll be a party afterwards to celebrate our win. College parties are the best. I don't drink, but I people-watch. I'm probably one of the few people at the party who won't take a sip of alcohol all night.

The only thing I drink is water with a soda here and there. I'm too much of a health nut for anything else. I want to be in the best shape possible, and that's the only way to do it. So I stand in the corner and watch the people around me. My shoulders sag when I see Maddie. What is she doing here? Is she following my every move now? No, that's ridiculous. It looks like one of her friends is here with one of my teammates, so that's probably why.

Maddie spots me, gives me a smile, but keeps going in the direction she was headed. Good. My eyes scan the room. There's a game of beer pong going on to my left, which is drawing quite the crowd. To my right, a couple people are flirting or making out. In the midst of all this, everyone is mingling. No one is particularly interesting tonight, but just as I decide to head back to the house, my eyes catch sight of Maddie again. It's been like two hours since she showed up, and I hadn't seen her since then.

I still don't understand how she could be so gorgeous after only three years. Maddie's eyes are focused on something across the room. She's slightly frowning with her arms crossed over her chest. As I follow her gaze, I see her crappy ex-boyfriend making out with some chick. What a jackass. But then, I sure am one to talk. Pushing off the wall I was leaning against, I walk over to Maddie.

"Hey," I say as I come to a stop in her line of vision to her ex.

She tilts her head back a bit to look at me, granting me a small smile. "Hey, Winston. That was a great game. Are they always like that?"

"Like what?"

"Intense, fast-paced, fun, and filled with that crazy energy?"

"Pretty much. Does this mean you're becoming a fan?" I ask.

"I like watching you, if that's what you mean." Maddie gives me a coy smile. Before I can question it, someone bumps into her, pushing her into me. I catch her stumble and wrap my arm around her to steady her. The top of her head just reaches the middle of my ribcage.

I glare at the apologizing guy who ran into her and rest my hands on her shoulders as she takes a step back. "You okay?" I question, looking down at her, noticing that her hand is still on my side.

"Yeah. He probably didn't even see me because I'm so short. He should have seen you with your freakish height, though."

My laugh is cut off thanks to her former boyfriend grabbing her elbow and spinning her to face him.

"What are you doing?" he accuses her.

Maddie yanks her arm away from him. "I'm talking to someone, obviously." She steps away, probably intending on leaving him, but he wraps his fingers around her arm and yanks her so hard back to him that she almost crashes into him.

"Hey, let her go." I take a step closer to Maddie. He shouldn't be touching her like that, and I'm not about to watch him manhandle her.

"Winston, right?" he says as his fingers tighten around her arm.

This jackass is seriously about to piss me off. I take a step closer to him as Maddie tugs on her arm. From the corner of my eye, I see Neil stand, waiting to see if he needs to come break something up.

"You're being a jerk, Brad. Let me go." Softer, she adds, "You're hurting me."

He flicks his eyes to her and releases his hold. There may be hope for the bastard yet. Gently, I place my hand on her lower back. "C'mon, Maddie. Let's go."

She lets me lead her away from him and outside. "Sorry, Winston. He's an idiot."

"Why are you apologizing to me?"

Maddie laughs. "I don't know. Where are we going?"

"I was going to walk you to your dorm," I answer, removing my hand from her back. She frowns. "What?"

"It's still pretty early. I don't want to go to my dorm, and you've taken me away from the party, so-"

"Do you want to go back?" I ask with an incredulous tone. Surely, she doesn't.

"No." Maddie shakes her head. "I just don't want to go to my dorm either." When I glance at her, she adds, "Don't worry. I don't need you to babysit me." Maddie reaches into her back pocket. "I'll text one of my friends to meet me."

Babysit her? Since when have I ever done that? "Aren't we supposed to be catching up? Getting to know one another again? Isn't that what you said? Why do you want that anyway?" I ask quietly. We walk up to a bench, and I sit down, reaching for her hand to make her sit next to me. Once we sit though, I release her hand. It feels too familiar.

Maddie crosses her legs, stuffing her hands into her coat pockets before she says anything. Her knee bounces. It's clear that she's nervous about something. She looks down the way we came, away from me. "I remembered how things used to be and spoke without thinking. I didn't want to always be seen as his little sister to you."

"But you are," I say, confused. It's the one thing that can't be changed.

She sighs in frustration. "Yeah, but that's not all I am, Winston." She looks over at me. "I thought you knew that, but I guess not. You never saw *me* anyway, not without thinking about how I'm his sister."

I hate that she's still hurting after all this time. I don't get the chance to say anything before my phone starts vibrating in my pocket with a FaceTime call from Dave. Damn it. I swipe the bar and his face appears.

"Where the fuck are you?" he says.

Maddie's face swivels towards his voice, and I lay my hand on her thigh, hoping she'll stay quiet. "I'm outside. Just left a party. Why are you so damn nosey?"

Dave laughs. "You look weird on my screen. How'd the game go?"

"We won, hence the party."

"I hope y'all win when I come up. I'll be pissed if I came all that way for y'all to lose." Dave chuckles at his comment. "Have you run into Maddie again? I doubt she'd be at a party, though."

For some reason, I was hoping he wouldn't ask about her. "Well," I trail.

Maddie leans over so her face is in view of the camera. "Hey, Dave."

His mouth falls open with shock. "Maddie? What are you doing? Why are you with Winston? Were you at the party?"

"Do you have to know all that, Dave?" she smarts back. "Winston is being nice by walking me back to my dorm since it's so late at night. He'll call you later." Maddie reaches out and ends our video call. "He's going to be pissed about that, isn't he?"

"Probably."

"Why didn't you want him to know I was with you?" she asks softly.

"You saw his reaction. It would be easier if he didn't know. Less explaining, I guess."

Maddie nods as she looks down at her knees. As her words run through my mind again, I feel a little bad because in a way, she's right. I never saw her quite the way she wanted. Dave has always been attached to her.

"I'm sorry-" I start, only to have her cut me off.

"Can we forget it, please? Once and for all?" She rests her elbows on her knees and covers her face with her hands.

I try to pull her hands away, but she won't budge. "Maddie, don't make me go to the extreme." I need her to look at me.

"What extreme?" she mumbles through her hands.

I tug again and when she doesn't move, I grab her waist and move her tiny body into my lap, tickling her sides. When they were younger, Dave used to practically torture her by tickle attacks.

"Winston!" she screeches, wiggling in my lap. "Stop! Please," she breathes through a fit of giggles. "Fine!" she adds.

My hands freeze, resting on her hips, as I watch her try to regain control of her breathing.

"I can't believe you would stoop so low, Winston."

"I warned you."

"Yeah, well, it's going to cost you a box of Gobstoppers."

"Gobstoppers? You still eat those things?" I'm surprised the girl didn't get sick from all the candy she ate. Maddie was, and apparently still is, addicted to munching on those.

"I have five boxes in my dorm, so yeah, I still eat them, but only when I'm stressed. They help me focus when I'm studying or doing homework." Maddie moves back to her seat next to me.

"I'm really sorry about everything, Maddie. I wish you would have talked to me, but I understand why you didn't. If I could go back and change it, I would in a heartbeat."

She abruptly stands and looks down at me. I should have left it alone because she's closed me out now. Any hopes of fixing things go out the window as she says, "You know what, my dorm sounds pretty nice right about now."

For a moment, I debate on if I should say anything or not to try to make her stay. Might as well walk her there, if that's what she wants. I stand, swinging my arm out for her to lead the way. Maddie gives me a fake glare, but starts walking.

"Just so you know, you were so much hotter when I didn't have your attention."

I laugh, faintly noting that she thinks I'm hot. "Would you rather I ignore you?"

"No," she answers softly. After a moment, she adds, "You know what I hated the most about us? You were this give-it-all kind of guy with everything and everyone but me."

Maddie has been careful not to look over at me,

which is okay because I keep glancing at her. "What do you mean a 'give-it-all' guy?" What the hell is that?

"Well, like hockey, for example. I never saw you play, but anyone with eyes and a brain could tell that you were dedicated, passionate, and you gave it everything you had to do your best and be your best. You do that with school, with Dave, and you love your parents like that too. That's the way you are and always have been with everything in your life that means something to you."

That's the way she sees me? Wow. I try to process what she says, noting how the wording of her last sentence excluded herself. I want to say something, to reassure her that I was that way with her too, but I can't because she's right. There was one thing I could have done to prove that to her and I didn't do it. We come up to the door of her building before I can think of anything worth saying. Maddie turns towards me, that awkward goodbye air surrounding us. She lifts her head to look me in the eyes.

There's so much I want to say, but I don't. Instead, I unthinkingly yet slowly lean down to kiss her forehead, and murmur, "Night, Maddie." Standing upright and rigid because of my gesture, I quickly get away from her and her wide, green-brown eyes without waiting for a response.

The entire way back to the house, I mull her words over and over in my head. I try to forget that I kissed her forehead, something I used to do all the time. We can't go back there. Nothing has changed. Dave is still clueless, and I'm still not willing to tell him. I just need to stay away from her.

I change and fall into bed, resting my arm behind my head while staring up at my ceiling. Everything she said repeats on a loop in my head. The only reason I'm thinking about this as much as I am is because I'm attracted to her, even more so than before. How Maddie does or doesn't feel or how I feel is irrelevant now. All that matters is keeping my focus on school and hockey. I don't need to hurt her all over again.

CHAPTER 4

Grant

WE SKATE ONTO the ice for warm ups, and I find a spot to stretch before taking my place in front of the net. I notice a girl with shoulder length, black hair taking pictures of us. Even from a distance, I can tell that her camera isn't just a digital camera. It's bigger and covers most of her face. She stands out amongst the crowd that has gathered for our game.

"Hey, Neil." I catch the attention of our captain. "Why is a girl taking pictures of us?"

He looks over to the girl. "I don't know. Go ask and then get your ass in the net." He chuckles before leaving me to continue warming up.

I'm glad he's in a good mood again today. My curiosity is piqued, so I skate over. I go behind the net as she snaps away at the players in the opposite direction.

"Hey," I say. She lowers the camera, and I'm face-to-face with the most beautiful bright, blue eyes. "What are you doing?"

Her pale cheeks flush, as if I caught her doing something she wasn't supposed to do. "Oh, I'm a, uh, sports photographer for the school paper, and they want more hockey coverage this season, so here I am." She looks uncomfortable and holds up a badge that confirms what she says, along with her name.

Lucy Kennedy.

"Grant!" I turn my head at the sound of Bo's voice. "We don't have all fucking day!"

I face the girl, smile, and say, "Nice to meet you, Lucy."

Finally, I take my spot as the team practices shooting, and then warm ups are over. Our coach gives us his speech, and it's game time. Being the goalie, a lot weighs on my shoulders. I take my spot seriously. Focus is required to ensure that very few, if any, goals are allowed past me. If I'm having a bad day, my team has to work extra hard, and I do my best to not have any bad days.

This team is aggressive and pucks fly at me throughout the game. However, today is a one where I'm having a really good day. I get my first shutout of the season. The guys come up and congratulate me, bumping their helmet with mine. We head to the locker room for Coach to talk to us. Afterwards, I see Lucy the photographer standing just outside the door with her camera hanging from her neck, looking nervous. What is she doing now?

I'm naked above the waist, having already taken my pads off, but I go to her. When I open the door, she looks startled.

"Can I help you with something?"

"Our usual reporter left early tonight, and he sent some questions for me to ask some of the players." She rocks on her heels, and I wonder if she's a nervous person in general, or if I'm making her nervous.

"Who do you need to talk to? I can go ahead and get them out here, so you can get done quicker."

She pulls out a folded piece of paper from her pocket, reading the names off to me. "I'm supposed to talk to Neil, Bo, Vincent, and you."

"Okay, I'll get them." I'm about to open the door, but she stops me.

"Wait! Here are all the questions." She shoves the paper at me. Her voice is shaky. "Could you take this and ask them for me?" Must be nervous in general. "I only take pictures." Lucy holds up her camera for evidence.

"I'm only a goalie," I tell her before I can stop myself. Her eyes beg me. "Fine. Do you have a pen?" I want to tell her that next time the school reporter should show up, so I don't have to do this shit, but I don't. She looks uncomfortable as it is. After I get a pen from her, I return to the locker room and call out for the guys.

"We're getting famous, boys. The school newspaper is expanding their coverage on hockey, and it starts with you answering some questions."

"You're a reporter now, Grant?" Neil asks, getting laughs from the other two.

"Shut the hell up." I go through the questions, scribbling down everyone's answers, and then answer the questions for myself. When I go back into the hallway, Lucy is leaning against the wall, looking down at her camera.

"Here you go."

She jumps, but takes the paper from my hand. "Thanks so much."

And then she walks away, disappearing around the corner. She's pretty, but way too jumpy.

"LOOK AT THIS shit. You made the front page, Grant." Neil throws the school paper on the table. It slides across, nearly crashing into my bowl of cereal, and I pick it up.

On the front is a damn good close-up of me from the shoulders up from our game, but it was from Thursday night. I must have missed her before. Somehow, that girl snapped a picture like that and managed to get a decent shot of my face. I must have been facing her direction when she took it. I scan the article, my eyes zooming in on another picture of me making a save. There are a couple more, smaller images from the game as well as a link to where you can see all the photos taken on the school website.

"Damn. She's good," I say with a bite.

"Yeah, she managed to make you look presentable." He laughs. "Who is she anyway?"

I read the end of the caption, even though I already know. "Photographs taken by Lucy Kennedy."

"Doesn't ring a bell," he says as he rummages through the pantry.

"This coming from the guy who doesn't ask what their name is before sleeping with them."

"Hey, your captain has needs." Neil laughs.

"Let me see," Winston says, sitting across from me. I hand him the paper.

"You said Kennedy?" Neil adds, seeming to think about something.

"Yeah, why?"

He turns to face me with a box of poptarts in one hand. "I wonder if she's the little sister of the Kennedy brothers. You know them, right?"

Everyone on campus knows that trio. Patrick is a junior, Jonathon is a senior, and Corey graduated last spring. They are all football players and some of the best in the college league, although Corey was injured in his last season and can no longer play. I vaguely remember hearing that they are crazily protective of their baby sister. I nod in acknowledgement to Neil.

"That may be who she is then."

"Who who is?" Bo asks, walking into the kitchen.

"Lucy Kennedy, the girl taking pictures yesterday. We think she's the sister of the Kennedy brothers," Neil informs him, going back to find something else.

"The football players? I wouldn't know. I don't like football." Bo shrugs.

"Well, I need to study and do homework, so I'll catch you guys later."

Even though, Neil and Bo leave the house on Sundays, I still go to the library to study. I want A's, and that's where I can focus the best. Plus, Mom will kick my ass if my grades slip. Dad cares about hockey. Mom cares about my education. Well, they care about both, really. It's just Mom gets on me about school, and Dad hounds me about hockey. So instead of partying it up all night, I'll spend most of my time at the library.

I wrap up things here and head to the gym. Exercising is one of my favorite things to do. I love the burn, the sweat, and the satisfied feeling I get after a grueling workout. I even love the semi-cold shower I take afterwards to cool my body down. Sometimes, I think there's nothing better in this world than that. My free time is basically divided between being on the ice, in the gym, or in the library. I end up being there for a couple hours, finishing in time to shower and go grab a late lunch.

After that, I walk across campus to the library. The guys would murder me if they found out exactly how much I like to read. People will assume I'm working on something for school if I'm in the library. Plus, it minimizes the distractions. I need silence to read and study. The library is perfect for both. I find a table in a corner, knowing the foot traffic will be minimal there and take a seat.

My backpack sits unopened next to my chair, slouching against a leg of the table, as I crack open my historical fiction book. Those are my favorite with an occasional memoir. I lean back in my chair, rest the book in my lap and against the table, and begin to read. Roughly two hours pass while I'm lost in a WWII battle when I hear the slightest clicking sound. My eyes flick up, searching the area for the source of the distracting noise. There's no one in front of me and nothing but rows of books.

I hear it again and turn my head to the left, looking down the aisle. My eyes land on the only possible source. A camera lens is focused on me, a pale and slender finger on a silver button, pressing down. Familiar black hair falls over her shoulders as she crouches. If she was next to me, she would be eye level with the table.

What the hell? Why is she taking pictures of me? As if she now realizes I'm looking, the camera slowly lowers to reveal fiery red cheeks and large, surprised to be caught, blue eyes. Lucy stands upright with all the confidence she can muster and walks over. My mouth stays shut as she takes a seat next to me and fidgets. I watch her, wary because she was sneaking pictures of me for no good reason.

"I'm sorry," she says in a library appropriate voice. The camera sits in her lap, the black strap hanging from her neck to hold it in place. Although, it's pointless because her hands never leave the damn thing. "You were perfect for a shot, and I couldn't resist. I take pictures of people all the time, but they never really notice. Do you want to see it?"

The pale blue shirt she's wearing makes her eyes look even brighter. Lucy glances down at the camera, pressing buttons. I still don't say anything because I don't know what to make of her taking pictures of me. Is she some crazy chick or something? But then she holds up the camera, turning it to me so I can see the image on the screen.

There I am, slouched in my seat, one hand at the top of the spine. She caught me biting my nail, something I didn't even realize I was doing. Even though it's a side shot, you can tell that I'm focused on the book.

"I can delete them if you want," she adds, bringing the camera back to her lap.

"Them?" I question, finally speaking. "There's more than one?"

Lucy looks guilty as a blush flashes on her cheeks again. She presses another button and shows another photo of me, but this time, I'm looking at her. It was when I turned to find out what was making the subtle noise. Her thumb presses again, and there's another of when I lifted my head.

"How long were you there?" I ask.

"Not long. I think there's only two more shots, but those are from over there." She lifts her hand and points to where I first looked. "I moved to try a different angle. I was going to tell you afterwards, though," she rushes to explain. "If I had interrupted you, then the shot would have been messed up. People change if they know they are having their picture taken. I'm sorry," she repeats.

"It's okay, I think." I frown, caught off guard that I was her subject today. "Do you always carry that around?" I glance at the camera.

"Of course," she answers like I should already know this. "I'm a photography major. I love taking pictures, so of course I have it with me all the time."

Right. "Well, you're good. I saw the pictures from the game in the paper this morning. They were amazing."

Lucy smiles wide at the compliment, bringing attention to ruby lips and white teeth. "I think I was lucky with those. I'm more accustomed to baseball and football, so I was worried to move into a new sport."

"Looked good to me." Since she brought up football, I add, "Are you related to the Kennedy boys on the football team?"

She nods with a smile. "Do you know my brothers?"

I shake my head. "Know of them, but that's it."

"Oh, well, I should go and let you get back to your reading. Do you want me to delete the photos? If they show up anywhere, it'll be an assignment or my personal portfolio. Never know when images that aren't sports-related might be helpful."

My brow bunches with a bit of confusion. "Aren't sports-related?"

Lucy laughs softly. "Sports photographer, remember?"

"Right. You can keep them, I guess."

"Thanks."

Just as she goes to stand, someone calls her name. Lucy grins, looking happy with adoration. I turn to see one of her brothers, the youngest of the trio. He glances at me with a frown, walking over to us.

He sticks his hand out. "Hey, I'm Patrick Kennedy, Lucy's brother. You would be?"

I shake his hand firmly, deciding to go with the flow. "Grant Faison, Lucy's test subject apparently."

Recognition flashes in his eyes. "You're the goalie for the hockey team, right? Lucy showed me some of the pictures she got of you at the game last night."

"That would be me," I confirm.

Patrick turns to his sister, his interrogation over. "Ready? Corey is going to meet us for dinner."

Lucy lets out a quiet squeal of excitement, and Patrick shakes his head goodnaturedly. "Good. I miss him."

"Do you want to join us, Grant?" Patrick asks. It almost seems like there's a challenge in his question.

"Patrick," Lucy chides. "Leave him alone. I've traumatized him enough for today. Let's go. Corey's going to be upset if we're late," she tells him before turning to me. "Thanks again, Grant."

"No problem, Lucy."

She walks off with her brother as he puts a protective arm around her shoulders. Lucy doesn't seem to mind how her brothers are with her. But that's based on a very short encounter. What do I know? I rub my hand over my head, feeling the soft, quarter-inch, light brown hair beneath it.

What the hell just happened?

I shake my head, deciding to let the ordeal go, and start reading again. My stomach growls a couple times, but I ignore it as I switch to studying. I'll grab something to eat when I'm done. After I hit the books, I even manage to write some papers. I hate typing. My fingers never move as fast and efficiently as I would like. So I'll handwrite my papers, go home, and use one of those talk-to-text programs to type for me.

It's been a long day thanks to these past few hours studying, but I think I may go to the rink. I love skating. It's a good thing I'm a goalie because I'm slow as hell. Much slower than all the other guys, at least. The only place I have speed is in the net, but that doesn't take away from my natural love to skate around the rink.

I love the movement of my legs, the burn I feel, and my overall body motion. Being a lean 6' and 180 pounds, this is a completely different kind of workout than being at the gym. I'm not on the ice five minutes when I find Lucy looking nervous by the benches.

"I'm sorry for interrupting," she offers first. "I didn't think anyone would be here."

"How did you get in?" I ask curiously because I locked the entrance behind me.

"I borrowed a key for tonight from your coach."

The sound of my skates on the ice as I glide over are loud and almost echo around us. "Did you have a good dinner with your brothers?" I question. As an only child, her relationship with her brothers and seemingly love even for their overprotectiveness has me very curious.

Lucy smiles, the fondness clear on her face. "Yes, I did."

I nod. "What are you doing here?"

Her smile falters a little. "I can come back at another time, Grant. I really didn't mean to interrupt."

"You aren't, depending on why you're here."

She holds up her camera that's hanging around her neck. I don't know how I overlooked it. "I wanted to get comfortable here if I'm going to take more pictures."

I cock my head to the side to examine her. "What do you mean?"

Lucy rocks on her heels slightly. "Well, I'm used to the football field or the baseball field. I feel at home there, almost. The rink is relatively new to me, so I thought I could get some generic shots, get a better feel for the place, and my shots will come out even better."

"Well, come on. Be careful or you'll fall." I start to skate backwards, away from her. "And yell if I get in your way."

"Thanks, Grant."

From the corner of my eye, I watch as she slowly walks along the boards to behind the net. She tilts her head as if thinking about what she wants to do. Lucy shuffles her way in front of the net. She squats down, and it looks like she's taking a picture of the pole itself. I skate around this side of the rink, watching as she takes shot after shot.

"Grant," she calls out when I'm standing in the middle of the ice. She's crouched behind the net, her camera already in place. "Come this way, please. I'll tell you when you're out of the way."

I start to skate towards her, and she calls out as promised. I keep going because this is a picture I want to see. She takes a bunch of different ones while I lean against the boards before she pulls away. Without paying me a lick of attention, she stands, reviewing what she took and nodding in approval as she turns to the left.

Lucy lifts her head and jumps when she sees me. She's so startled that she loses her balance. I quickly reach for her elbow to steady her.

"Sorry, I didn't mean to scare you." Her cheeks burn with embarrassment, so I decide to move on to why I was back here. "Can I see?" I remove my hand and point to the camera.

"Of course." Lucy looks down at the camera, finds a shot she's happy with, and I skate around to look over her shoulder. Wow. The outer edges is the netting, but the center of the shot is the other net across the rink. "It needs some editing," she murmurs.

"That's an awesome picture, Lucy."

"Thanks. I'm going to get some of center ice, if that's okay?" She turns her head to look up at me over her shoulder.

"Yeah, sure."

She slowly makes her way over there. She's so absorbed by what she's doing that even though I can't take my eyes off of her, she doesn't notice me at all. I'm fascinated watching her. At one point, she lays on her stomach to get a better angle at whatever she's wanting to take a picture of exactly.

"Hey, Grant?"

"Yeah?" I ask as I skate towards her.

"This was a bad idea."

I glide to a stop in front of her and bend down. She's resting on her elbows with her camera firmly in her grasp. "Why is that?" I ask, confused.

"How am I going to get up without messing up my

camera?"

A laugh easily falls from my mouth. That was the last thing I was expecting. Lucy frowns at me. "Do you want me to hold the camera for you or just pick you up?"

"You can take the camera. Be careful with it, though."

My fingers brush hers as I grab it with one hand and slide my other hand up the strap to lift it over her head. Damn, her hair is ridiculously soft. I clear my throat as my gaze drops to her revealing chest thanks to how she's laying and her v-neck shirt. As she goes to stand, I do the same, tense and ready to spring in case she loses her footing again.

"Thanks," she says, reaching for her camera. "I think I'm done for tonight. Laying on the ice before I was done wasn't my best idea," she mumbles, looking down at the wet spots on her clothes.

I chuckle. "Probably not."

I follow her to the bench because I'm done for tonight too. Once I sit down to take off my skates, I realize that she's waiting for me.

"Could I ask a huge favor?" she questions nervously.

"You ask a lot, you know. First, you make me play reporter, then you sneak pictures of me at the library. Next, you crash my skating. Now, you want a favor?" I tease. Her cheeks turn bright red, and it makes me feel bad. "I'm just messing. What is it?"

She shakes her head, changing her mind. "Thanks for letting me invade. I'm going to go."

When she turns to walk away, I joke, "Want me to walk you out? It's pretty late, and a murderer could be out there."

Lucy immediately tenses and slowly faces me. "That's not funny," she says quietly. "I'll be fine."

And then she gets the hell away from me. Her reaction seemed too severe. That's the second time in less than five minutes that I've said the wrong thing. Maybe she just scares easily. It would explain how she seems extra nervous sometimes. I shake my head, lock up the rink for tonight, and head home. Winston is in his room, and I can't say I blame him. It looks like Neil is back in his pissed off mood. What the hell happened to set him off today?

CHAPTER 5

NEIL

EVERY SUNDAY, BO and I make the hour trip to have dinner with Mr. and Mrs. Lanier. We've been having this dinner since the summer before I started college, which was about four years ago. I didn't want to go alone, so I made Bo tag along, and he hasn't missed a dinner yet. But right about now, I wish I had left him at the house. And it's not because he bitched at me this morning for sleeping with a girl last night. Apparently, I should be celibate now.

When I walk into the house, Alice, their six year old daughter, rush up to me, jumping into my arms.

"Neil! I've missed you! I'm glad you came," she squeals excitedly.

"I always come, Alice." I pick her up and she hugs me tighter.

"Don't let go, Neil," she warns like usual. "It's a long

way down."

I laugh. "I won't. Where are your parents?"

"Setting the table. Oh, hey, Bo," she greets like she just now noticed him. Bo has always been a second thought for Alice. I'm her favorite visitor after all.

As we walk into the dining room, I ask her, "How's school? Are you in high school yet?"

Alice giggles. "No! I'm in the first grade, Neil."

"Oh yeah, you just grow so much every week. I keep forgetting." Mr. and Mrs. Lanier smile at me as we walk in. "Hey," I greet, kissing Mrs. Lanier on the cheek and dipping my chin in a nod at Mr. Lanier.

After we start eating, things go south, thanks to Bo. Conversation was flowing smoothly like normal. Mrs. Lanier was asking about school and hockey and plans after college. It's nearly the exact same conversation every Sunday. She likes to keep tabs on me to make sure that I'm doing well. They both do, which is why I come. And because of Alice, too. Although, sometimes, it's hard to see her family's resemblance in her. Plus, the Lanier's are like second parents to me. In all honesty, I care more about what they think than I do my own parents. So I come each week, giving her answers that will make her happy, even if they aren't always true. Next, she asks the question I always dread.

"Have you met anyone?"

Just as I'm about to answer, Bo blurts out, "He's gotten a girl pregnant."

God damn it! Slowly, I turn towards him in my seat. He better be so fucking happy that I don't have a knife in my hand because I'm sure I would stab him. Why the fuck would he say that to them? He has the nerve to simply shrug.

Alice gasps. "You're having a baby like my teacher? She's pregnant too. Mrs. Perry says she'll bring him to class for us to see one day."

All the words that I could possibly say to these people, to this little girl, disappear. My vocabulary has been wiped clean, and my mouth is parted with no hopes of speaking.

"Oh, Neil," Mrs. Lanier says.

God, I hate Bo so much. With a deep, controlled breath, I face her again. However, Bo opens his giant mouth, and I want to punch him so many times that he has to get it wired shut for it to heal.

"He told her to put it up for adoption."

I drop my fork and put my fisted hands in my lap. This isn't for him to share, and it damn well isn't his place to tell them.

"What's adoption?" Alice asks.

"Sweetie, why don't you take your plate into the living room and watch cartoons?" Mr. Lanier suggests. Alice squeals with excitement and takes off as fast as she can while being cautious. He then turns his attention to me. "Neil, please tell me that you had a lengthy conversation with her before you two came to that decision."

"Nope. She was a one night stand, and she came over to tell him. Then he told her to put it up for adoption. We haven't seen her since," Bo happily answers.

I'm going to fucking murder him. I'm not that guy to them, and he has showed them who I am when I'm not here on Sunday. He had no business telling them about Audra, and he's going to pay for it when we leave.

I see Mr. Lanier shake his head from the corner of my

eye, but I'm looking at Mrs. Lanier. I don't want to break her heart again. There's a sad expression on her face. Bo put that there, the bastard. She reaches across the table with her palm up. Reluctantly, I put mine in hers.

"I know you're only twenty-two, but you are too old to behave like that. You need to find her and have a conversation with her, no matter how much you don't want to. You need to do the right thing, Neil. We know first hand that you're capable of that."

My heart shreds at her words. My throat feels like it's closing, and I hate it. This is exactly why I didn't want them to know. Slowly, I nod my head.

"You're smart, Neil," Mr. Lanier starts. "And you're a good man. Don't forget that. Remember, we're here for you too. My wife is right. You need to do the right thing. I'm sure I can talk to my brother-in-law and get you a job. It won't be great, but then you'll have some of your own money coming in."

All I can do is nod. They ask me to keep them updated, to call if I need anything, and then I tell them that we need to go. They seem to hug me extra tight before we leave. Alice wants me to stay longer and play with her, but I tell her I'll play twice as long next time. The rage is boiling my blood and if Bo gets close enough, I'm going to knock the motherfucker out. We're not a mile from their house when he speaks.

"I'm sorry, but I knew you would listen to them. You respect them too much not to."

"You had no fucking right, Bo! It wasn't your place, and they didn't need to hear that shit," I yell, my voice entirely too loud for the enclosed space of my car. "No. Fucking. Right!" My knuckles are white as I clench the steering wheel, fighting for control over my emotions. I feel like he just betrayed me to my parents, except Mr. and Mrs. Lanier aren't my parents. He did betray me though.

"Someone had to get through to you," he starts.

"Not them! They are the last people on this God damn earth who you should have told that I knocked a girl up! You should know better, Bo. You had no fucking right to bring that up to them. None. And you didn't just say she was pregnant, you had to add that she was a one night stand, and I threw her out the moment she came to me. And in front of Alice? God, you're a fucking bastard."

"Neil," he tries.

"No. You stay the hell away from me." I throw my car into park and get out, storming into the house. Every door I reach gets slammed shut. The front door, the cabinet door, my bedroom door, if it's a door, I force it closed as hard as possible. Let the damn things break, I don't care. I go to my room, blast some music, and lay on my bed.

What am I going to do now?

Every drop of blood in me is telling me to *not* do the right thing. It isn't worth the risk, and I don't want that life. Yet, on the other side of the argument is Mr. and Mrs. Lanier and Alice. How am I going to face them every week if I don't go hunt down Audra and be there like I'm supposed to be? I can't do that. It would be worse to do nothing and face them than stepping up to take care of my responsibility. Either option sucks.

How am I even supposed to make it work? My future only goes as far as tomorrow with the exception of possibly getting signed this year. God, do I even want to try to figure this out? Because if I do, then I'm going to have to find Audra. If I find her, then I'm going to have to face the reality. I sigh, burying my face into my pillow.

This is all Bo's fault. If he hadn't said anything to them, then I could have gone at least another month without worrying about a guilty conscience. I'll give him a couple more days of grief before I let him know what I've decided. I just hope I'm ready for my world to turn completely upside down.

For now, I'm not thinking any more about it. There's homework I need to do because if I expect to keep my scholarship, I need to keep my grades up. I can't focus, though, so it takes three times as long to complete than normal, which makes sure that I stay in my foul mood. When I do leave my room, I slam the doors and see that Grant is back.

"Stop with the slamming," Bo calls from the living room.

"Fuck off, Bo," I snap.

Grant seems confused, but he's smart and doesn't say anything. I grab something to drink from the fridge and stalk back to my room. With my laptop in front of me, I try searching Facebook for Audra, but I don't come up with any results. Either she doesn't have one, or she has it so people can't find her. It's a problem for me because I'm not sure how to get up with her now.

I think I've had enough of being awake for one day.

I STAY IN a bad mood with Bo for another day before I decide he's had enough. I'm out of ideas on how to find Audra, so it's making me antsy. How can I do what's right if I can't find her? Bo is lying on the couch, watching an NHL game on TV when I go into the living room and begin to pace.

"If I ask what's wrong, are you going to bite my head off?" he asks.

"No, but if you ever do something like that again with the Lanier's, I'll kill you." Bo nods. "I've tried searching for Audra online, but nothing shows up. Any ideas on how to get up with her?"

"Yeah, maybe."

I stop pacing and sit in the recliner. "Well?"

Bo leaves before returning and handing me a slip of paper with a phone number on it. "There's her number."

"Why do you have this? How do you have it?" I ask, staring at it. The nerves have taken over, but I'm trying not to freak out again. Calling her will have me cornered and will start a new journey in life, one that I already don't want to be on. Not to mention everything that could go wrong.

"When I went outside after her, I told her not to make any decisions for a week or so and that you would come around. I asked for her number, so I would have it when you were ready. You're welcome."

I sit in silence for a few moments. The rat bastard has had her number all this time? He knew that I would change my mind? That partly pisses me off, but I'm relieved too. Bo doesn't deserve an answer, so I go back to my room to call Audra, wearing the carpet down while I wait for her to answer.

"Hello?"

"Hey, Audra? It's Neil."

She sighs. "What do you want?" Well, that wasn't what I was expecting.

"Could we meet and talk? Please?" Audra doesn't say

anything for the longest time, but I know she's there because I can hear movement in the background. "Please, Audra," I beg.

"Okay. I get off work in two hours, and I'll have a little time before my class tonight. You can buy me dinner. Do you know where that little pizza place is near Ladybug Road?"

"Yeah, I do. I'll see you there in two and a half hours?"

"Right. My break's over. Bye, Neil."

She hangs up without waiting for a response. Audra is working and going to school? That must tire her out, especially now that she's pregnant. With time to spare, I call Mr. Lanier, knowing that I'm going to need an income as well.

"I'm glad to hear about this, Neil. You're making the best decision. I'll talk to him and he'll call you. Now, it's most likely going to be a graveyard shift, but it's better than nothing. You'll still be able to play and go to school too."

"Thank you, sir. I'm grateful for any opportunity," I tell him truthfully. The graveyard shift will mean I'm going to be tired as fuck all the time, but I'm sure I can make it work. He tells me more about the job, which is a janitorial position, cleaning the building spotless at night in preparation for the following workday.

Before he gets off the phone, he says, "Don't forget that we're here for you. Call us if you need anything. Have you spoken to your parents yet?"

"No, sir. I will soon enough. I'm actually about to go meet with Audra now and talk to her."

"Good. We'll see you Sunday then."

I hang up and then I'm on my way to meet Audra. I can already tell how the next few months are going to go. My stomach is in knots, so I'm going to be nothing but pure, wild nerves on the edge. Part of it is because I have no control over this situation, Audra, or this baby, and I damn well know it. Audra has the upper hand, so to speak. I can't make her do anything or not do something. I kind of feel like I'm in a war with nature, helpless to make much of a difference.

When I walk into the delicious aroma-filled restaurant, my eyes immediately land on Audra. She's looking down at the table, ripping up a napkin.

"Can I help you?" a middle-aged woman who looks eerily similar to Audra asks.

"I'm here to meet someone," I answer, pointing over to Audra.

The woman's lips set in a firm, unhappy line. She nods and steps aside so I can go over to her. Audra finally looks up as I pull my chair back. She doesn't smile either.

"Hey," I say.

"Hey, Neil. I already ordered my favorite, but I didn't know what you wanted to drink."

A waitress promptly comes over to take my drink order. Once she leaves, I start apologizing and explaining.

"I'm sorry about last week. If you'll let me, I'd really like to go through this with you as much as I possibly can. Maybe we should try to get to know each other a little better. Do you know much about me? I don't know if you've heard things around campus or not."

Audra narrows her eyes at me. She has indeed heard things. "You mean the fact that you'll sleep with anything with a pulse, so you're basically a man-whore? The kind of guy I don't want anywhere near my baby because she deserves better than that for a father."

She.

All I can do is stare at her because she said 'she'. My heart feels still as it soaks in that we're having a baby girl. There's a bite of pain, a feeling that this isn't right because I don't love Audra, and the awful, bad taste of memories screaming, 'what could have been.' But I ignore all that with a clearing of my throat. "It's a girl?" I say quietly, needing her to confirm.

Her eyes widen slightly, and I'm guessing it was a slip of the tongue. She barely nods. "I found out this morning."

I lean back in my seat as the waitress walks over and sets the pizza down on the table. For a few seconds, I watch Audra. Today, she's in all black from work at a retail store, but her clothes fit her better than when she came to see me. Audra is very pretty, obviously. If I didn't find her attractive, I wouldn't have slept with her in the first place. Suddenly, I'm trying to picture my baby girl with her features. The words of adoption that I spoke about before pass through my mind, and I sit up. If I'm going to do this, I need to do it right, all the way.

"You haven't made any decisions since the last time I saw you, have you?" I ask as she takes a bite of the pizza. I wish I had timed my question better because I have to wait for her to finish now.

"Actually, I have," she answers seconds later. I hold my breath while she takes a swallow of water, wondering if she's already decided on adoption. "But you don't get to know," Audra sighs like I'm personally exhausting her.

"What are you talking about?" I breathe just enough to ask those five words.

"You made your choice, Neil. Honestly, I think the only reason you're here is because of a guilty conscience. After a few weeks, you'll probably change your mind again, and I don't have the energy to deal with that. Being pregnant is enough without having to deal with you too."

My mouth hangs open. "You can't be serious, Audra. I freaked out because you showed up at my house and lifted your shirt. That was all panic, and you are going to make me stick with my stupid choice?"

"Is everything okay?" The woman who I saw when I first walked in has come to our table, but her question is for Audra.

"Yes, Ma, we're fine." Ma? The lady nods, sends me a glare, and then leaves. "Sorry, this is my parents' restaurant, and she's been watching us like a hawk ever since you sat down." Audra takes a deep breath. "Why should I believe that you're sincere, Neil? You have until I finish this slice because I have to get to class."

So while she eats, I make my case. I know I could say one thing to make her believe me, but I'm not going to do that. I don't know her that well yet. Besides, it might piss her off more than anything.

"For one, I think I deserve a chance because you're deciding this based on something I said while I was trying to fully understand what you told me. I've had to do some serious thinking and what happened that day wasn't the right thing. All I want is to be there for my daughter and you while you're carrying her. You shouldn't try to deny that to me anymore than you already have," I finish in a low, well-controlled voice. I'm hoping that last sentence will be the push she needs. She waited all this time to come tell me. I've missed all these doctor's appointments so maybe that will get through to her.

Audra is quiet for a moment before she gasps softly, quickly looking down at her belly.

"What is it? Are you okay?" I rush with panic.

She nods, placing a hand on her lower right side. "Yeah, she kicked and caught me by surprise, that's all," she murmurs.

"Can I feel?"

Audra's head snaps up at my question. She's looking at me like I grew two more heads, but she subtly nods. I scoot my chair closer to her and reach my hand out. Audra takes my hand and places it where hers was. At first, I don't feel anything. She moves my hand a little, my eyes trained on it as if I could feel on sight alone. It's barely there, but I finally feel the smallest of movements.

I look to Audra. "That was it, wasn't it?"

"Yeah, that was it," she whispers. She seems as mesmerized as I am. For a moment, I don't ever want to move my hand because I want to feel it again and again, but I have to pull it away. "You're right, Neil, about what you said. I knew you were, but I was still pissed. I know that I'm capable of taking care of her, which is why I decided to keep her. Not to mention that if I didn't want to be faced with such a decision, then I should have been more careful."

Air leaves my body in relief. I was worried that I had missed my chance. That partly surprises me.

"We have a lot of work ahead of us in the next few months, but today is not the day to start. I have to get to class before I'm late." Audra manages to look even more serious as she adds, "Don't make me regret this, Neil."

"I won't."

CHAPTER 6

Winston

FOR A FEW days, I managed to go without hearing, seeing, or running into Maddie. Dave never asked anything more than if his sister was bothering me. Of course, she wasn't. I wish she hadn't been at the party, though, because all it has done is bring back all of those memories. I successfully managed to put it all behind me and focus on this week's games.

Neil seems to be in a better mood, so everything is back to normal. Well, sort of. Turns out, he got a job, but works like six hours every night. I can't say that this fact doesn't have me a bit worried, because it does. The exhaustion is obvious with all the yawning he does. I don't even think he's fucked a girl this week. When would he have the time? He's either in class, doing homework, working, catching up on sleep, or playing hockey. I asked him why he got a job to start with, but he shrugged off answering me.

Practice just ended, so I'm walking out to the parking lot. Before I left, Vincent said something about going to see his girl who isn't his girl. I shake my head at the thought of those two. I don't get what their problem is with each other. Something keeps holding each of them back, but damn if I know what. Vincent doesn't share much about their relationship.

"Winston!"

Shit. I turn around to find Maddie jogging towards me. She's wearing a sports bra with tight capri exercise pants, and her hair is up in a ponytail. What the hell does this look like? A park with a jogging trail? And it's fifty degrees out here! My eyes are drawn to her bouncing breasts until she comes to a stop in front of me, and I force my eyes to hers. Maddie's hair is swishing back and forth as she alternates kicking her feet up to keep running in place. I didn't know she ran.

"What's up?" I ask.

She stops jogging, rests her hands on her hips, and takes a few deep breaths. "How have you been?"

"You stopped to ask how I've been?" Maddie nods. "I've been great. You? Has that guy bothered you since the party?"

"Not really. I've been good."

When she doesn't add anything, I raise my eyebrow at her. "That all?"

Maddie's lips fall into a small frown. "Yeah, I guess so." She shifts her weight to her left foot and decides that that isn't all. "Actually, there is something else. You can totally say no, and there won't be any hard feelings. I promise."

"Spit it out already, Maddie," I order gently. I don't like watching her squirm with her words. Whatever she wants to say, she should say it. It's only us here.

"Promise me one thing first?"

"What's that?" What does she want to ask me?

"Don't call me a baby or anything of the sorts?" She tilts her head back a little to get a better look at me.

"Promise."

"Could we hang out and watch a movie or something? I'm feeling a little homesick, but I don't want to call my parents and say so. You're the closest thing to home I have here."

"Go," I drag my eyes over her body one more time, "change and drive over to my place. We can watch a *Madea* movie or something. Text me with what kind of sub you want, and I'll pick it up."

Suddenly, Maddie hugs me. "Thanks, Winston. It'll be like an hour from now. You're the best."

"Yeah, yeah. I'll see you later."

And then she's off, running back the way she came.

I wish she would stay away from me, but I know what it's like to miss home. There's no way I was about to tell her no. I run to the sub shop before going home with her preferred choice, some 6 inch sub.

A knock on the door brings me out of my thoughts. Maddie gives me a sheepish smile as I step aside for her to come in.

"Hey, Winston."

"Hey. Food is in my room." We head that way.

"Thanks. I'll have to repay you somehow."

I wave my hand at her dismissively. "Don't worry about it. After we eat, I need to do a little homework, but you can start the movie then anyway."

She nods, takes a seat on my bed, and unwraps her sub. I go to the couch. We don't say much as we eat, but I watch Maddie. She blows my mind, nibbling on her food, though she eventually finishes it.

"You won't tell Dave that I missed home, will you?" she asks after taking a sip of her soda.

"No. Why are you worried about that? Everyone gets homesick every now and then. It's nothing to be ashamed of."

Maddie crisscrosses her legs. "I feel like I shouldn't. Like I'm too old. I'm in college and after a bad day, I wanted to go home to my own room and be around people who love me."

I return my focus to my last bite after saying, "You sound pretty normal to me, Maddie."

She doesn't say anything as she hands me her trash, so I can go throw it away. Once I return, she goes to start the movie, and I grab my books to do a little homework. I could've done it yesterday, but I pushed it off until today. Maddie ended up being an unexpected surprise, so I'm having to work around her presence. Every time Maddie laughs, a little loudly, I end up peeking a glance at her. She's sitting with her back against my headboard as she watches the movie while I'm on my couch. Usually, a loud laugh irritates me, but Maddie's and how she looks when she laughs is cute. Maybe it irritated me before because it reminded me of her. After about thirty minutes, I lose my concentration completely.

"Done already?" she asks as I slam my notebook and

textbook close.

"Yep," I lie, setting them down on the cushion I previously occupied before moving over to the bed to sit next to Maddie and watch the movie.

The only sound we make is our laughter. When that one is over, Maddie puts in another. As she slips the disc into the DVD player, she looks over her shoulder with gratitude. "Thanks, Winston."

"No problem."

She crawls back into bed on the side closest to the wall, laying on her side, careful not to touch me. I slink down further to get more comfortable, stifling a yawn. My phone vibrates with a FaceTime call, but I reach over and silence it, turning off the lamp as well. I don't really feel like talking tonight. What a crappy friend I'm being to Maddie. She's missing home and the best I can do is try to stay awake. But this is what she wanted to do, watch TV, so it's okay, I guess.

Without the light, though, my eyes are getting heavier and heavier.

MMM. I INHALE a coconut, beach-y smell as I bury my nose in her hair. She makes my senses go on full alert. Fuck. Again? I open my eyes to see Maddie laying next to me on her stomach. My arm wrapped tightly around her waist while I lay on my side, enjoying the scent of her hair. My other arm is underneath her neck and I swear it's about to fall off, it's so numb. We used to lay like this all the time. Why does she have to turn me on? What is it about her that still does?

The smell of her shampoo? How her small, short self

almost gets lost next to me now? How good and easy this is? How familiar she feels?

With that thought, I move my hips away from her a bit, so she won't feel my erection. The slight motion wakes Maddie up. She stretches her legs out and lifts her head to look at me with a small smile, which makes my own lips lift in return. Maybe it's that small action, that simple smile first thing this morning.

In that moment, she's not thinking about anything other than waking up securely in someone's arms, leaving sweet dreams behind, and seeing a familiar face next to her. Her eyes seem to be darker or browner than usual. Stray strands of her blonde hair stick out around her face and the wrinkles from my pillowcase are imprinted on her cheek. Her lips are the perfect shade of pink, drawing my eyes down to them. An insane, ridiculous, raging need to kiss her is nearly uncontrollable. Just as I go to lean forward, Maddie laughs softly.

"I'm becoming a pain in the ass, aren't I?" she whispers.

Her words jar me from the stupid act I was about to commit, leaving me temporarily dumbfounded by her words. "What?"

"You're always so nice to me, letting me hang out with you, and I repay you by sleeping over in your bed. Again."

"Uh, yeah," I mumble, distracted by my thoughts. "Real pain in the ass." I lay my head back on the pillow, but Maddie doesn't attempt to move, so I don't remove myself from her. She's watching me though. I look up at the ceiling, anywhere away from those eyes and that pretty face. "I was about to kiss you," I breathe in honest disbelief. What in the hell is wrong with me?

"You were?" Maddie's eyebrows are perched high. "Why?" She sounds more curious than asking as if that was the most confusing thing ever. And the fact that she doesn't sound upset or disgusted that I would go there, but instead slightly surprised with wonder, makes me want to kiss her that much more.

"Fuck if I know," I grumble. She frowns, and I quickly add, "Not that kissing you would be terrible. You're in my damn bed, Maddie. Look at us." As if that explains it all. "You're fucking gorgeous too. That doesn't help," I confide.

She props herself up on her elbows with a smile like she's remembering something. "You used to kiss me all the time. I could be in the middle of telling you what happened that day and you'd interrupt me with a quick kiss, saying that you loved listening to me." Her eyes lock onto my own. "Do you still like me, Winston?" There's almost a light, teasing tone in her voice.

Turning my head to look at her, I set her straight. "No, I do not. That's come and gone, Maddie. I wanted to kiss you for a moment. That's all."

"Then do it."

"What?" She can't be serious.

"Do it," Maddie repeats. "Kiss me." It's a softly ordered demand. A *demand*. Oh, fuck.

Without another thought, I cup her cheeks as she moves to lay on me, eliminating all space between us. I stare into her eyes, searching for some sort of sign to stop and not to go a step further. All I see is a familiar desire. I move forward until only a breath separates us, our noses brushing against each other slightly.

Our breathing intermingles, and I'm sure I can feel Maddie's heart beating against her chest. Her tongue slips out of her mouth to run over her lower lip, brushing against mine in the process. She quickly presses her lips to mine, and I feel her move to straddle me, her fingers grasping my sides just above her knees. Maddie parts her mouth and mine automatically does the same. A groan from deep in my throat unleashes into her mouth as she slides her tongue against mine.

My hands glide down her back until I cup her ass. The kiss turns a bit frenzied as we attempt to devour each other. I want to pull her closer and closer until absolutely nothing separates us. I lift my head every time she slightly pulls away, always drawing her back to me. Our teeth clash, which makes me focus a little more than I was a second ago.

"Stop," I murmur, closing my eyes and leaning back into my pillow. Maddie begins to kiss along my jaw, choosing to partly ignore me. When her fingers begin to dance up my torso, I struggle to remember why I wanted her to stop in the first place. "Damn it, Maddie! Stop," I say more forcefully.

That catches her attention. She sits up and stares at me, waiting for me to explain. All I want to do is bury myself inside her, but that can't happen. Not now, not ever. I'm taking too long to say something, though, because she leans forward to rest her lips over mine. She's not kissing me, but she knows that when I go to talk, I'm going to have no choice but to feel that soft mouth.

"You're Dave's sister," I quietly mumble the most pathetic excuse.

That's all it takes for her eyes to harden and for her to

move off of me. Maddie stands, grabs her phone from the nightstand before walking over to the door, and slips on her shoes. "I can't believe that's all you can think about! After all this time, you *still* don't care enough. I don't know why I thought things would have changed. I don't know how I could be stupid enough to put myself back in this position. You said you would change it if you could, but I guess that was only a line to feed me, huh? You know what? You won't have to worry about me being around anymore."

"Wait," I protest as she starts to walk out the door, wanting to take the blame. It's my fault after all.

She glances at me over her shoulder. "Bye, Winston." And then she practically runs out of my room.

Damn it. I swing my legs off the bed and run after her. "Maddie! Wait," I call out.

She looks over her shoulder at me from the front door and groans. "Don't make this any more embarrassing than it is already, Winston. I won't bother you again, I promise." She goes to leave, but I reach for her elbow to stop her.

"You don't have to do that. If you ever need anything, you can still call me, okay?" That has to be the lamest thing to ever leave my mouth. It's not what I want to say, but it's all I can force out.

"Yeah, okay," she says.

I have a feeling that I won't see her for a long time. Before she can go any further, I kiss her forehead and release her elbow. Her lips are far too tempting, but I needed to kiss her, even on her forehead, to let her know that I care about upsetting her. Maddie quickly walks out the door, leaving me staring after her. What the fuck just happened? And why the hell do I want to bring her ass back here and make things better? Why did such a simple, innocent kiss feel like an apology and a goodbye? Sighing, I turn around, intent on going to my room when I hear Neil laugh.

"What the fuck was that?"

I flip him the bird before returning to my room. I'm horny and frustrated, which is not a good combination. After a cold shower, I decide that what I need is to get laid. Surely being sex-deprived is the cause of all this shit with Maddie. My shower ends up being pointless because I decide to go to the gym to workout before practice. Dave has texted me a few times, asking what happened after Maddie disconnected the call. When I finally reply in-between exercises, I tell him I walked her to her dorm. That's all.

"Winston?" a female voice says.

I lift my head with a smile in hopes that this goes how I want. "Hey, Paula. How have you been?" I ask my ex-girlfriend.

"Good. You? You seem to be playing well. You certainly look good."

Grinning, I nod. "Yeah, you too. Are you seeing anyone?"

She shakes her head, and my smile grows. "Why are you looking at me like that?" Reaching for her hips, I tug her closer to me. I slip my thumbs underneath her tank top. Before I can speak, she shakes her head. "Winston, no. No, no, no, no."

"Oh, c'mon." I pull her into my lap and she comes easily. As I begin kissing her neck, she wraps her arms loosely around mine. "Just once, right now."

"You're a dick," she breathes, and I know I've hooked

her. Paula can't resist a kiss to her neck. "Why do you want this so badly anyway? We both know you're choosing me only because I'm right here and I won't come crawling after you when we're done."

Maddie flashes in my mind, but I shove her back out. "Yes or no?" I ask, ignoring her question.

"Answer me and it's a yes. You aren't the only one wanting something."

We stand. I take her hand and begin leading her to a private bathroom one floor up. "I need to get laid, Paula. I'm sick of being so damn frustrated."

"Who is frustrating you?" She asks as I pull her into the room, locking the door behind her.

I don't even answer. Instead, I tug our shorts off and within seconds, I'm inside her. It's quick, but I feel so much better once we're done. As we redress, I mumble a thanks.

Paula laughs. "Don't make this a habit, Winston. Might as well go after the girl."

I groan as I open the door, just as Maddie walks by. Her eyes widen with surprise, but she gives us a tight smile and keeps on walking. What in the hell? Is she going to show up everywhere now?

"That her?" Paula whispers.

"Go to hell."

Her laughter follows me as I go back downstairs to finish my workout. It doesn't matter that Maddie saw us or could figure out what we were doing in the bathroom together. I can do whatever I damn well please.

Grant

"THAT WAS A shitty shot, Neil," I taunt. He's been trying to score on me for the past ten minutes, and he hasn't yet.

"Shut the fuck up." He nods to Bo and a couple of others before they all come at me at once.

There's no way I can block them all and they laugh as I scramble in an attempt to do so. Practice ended thirty minutes ago, but a couple of us stayed back to hang out for some relaxed fun.

"Those were some shitty saves, Grant," Neil mocks as he laughs.

I shrug. "Don't worry. I'm leaving. You have an empty net and nothing but your bad shots to keep you from scoring."

He glares, sending a puck my way hard and fast, but I glove it and grin.

"Bastard," he mumbles.

Feeling satisfied, I skate off the ice, calling see-you-later's out over my shoulder.

"Hey! Wait up. I'm coming with you," Bo yells from behind me.

We walk to the locker room, change, and then head out to my truck. Bo is in the middle of a joke when we hear a pissed off male yell, "Grant Faison!"

We stop and turn around. I immediately recognize Patrick. He's with a guy who has to be his other brother, Jonathan. What do they want from me? It's been a few days since I've seen Lucy, not that I would run into her, and I don't know why her brothers would want to talk to me. They walk up to me, folding their arms over their chests, and I hope they don't mean to intimidate me. I mean, Jonathan is a big football player while Patrick is still built, but smaller. That's what it feels like they are trying to do though. It doesn't help that they both look pissed.

"Hey, Patrick. Jonathan, I'm assuming?" I look towards the taller of the two, and it's clear they are related. They share the same black hair, although their eyes aren't blue like Lucy's.

Jonathan nods curtly. "What did you say to our sister?" He's accusing me of something, but I don't have a clue what he's talking about. Bo stands next to me awkwardly.

"Excuse me?" I question, confused.

Patrick rolls his eyes, clearly annoyed with me. What the hell is their problem? "What. Did. You. Say. To. Her?" He pronounces each word slowly like I've taken too many pucks to the head.

Jonathan chuckles, amused with his brother, and it pisses me off. "Saturday night. She came here and ran into you. What did you say?"

"Not much. Why the hell does it matter?"

That pisses them both off, their nostrils flaring almost simultaneously. Patrick is the one to speak though. "Because you said something to upset her, only she brushes it off. Look," he starts, losing his aggressive stance and looking like someone who is worried, "I'm sure you've heard how we are with her. And it's true. We're overprotective with very good reasons. We normally don't confront people who upset her because she can usually handle herself. But she won't tell us what you said, which worried us.

"That's why we're here. Lucy's silence speaks loudly, and it's rarely a good thing. She was supposed to ask you a favor. Did she?"

My anger at them fades when I can see that they, or Patrick at least, really is concerned. Which makes no fucking sense because I didn't say anything terrible to her.

"No. She was going to, but I joked that she asked a lot of me, and she changed her mind. I offered to walk her outside, made another joke, and then she declined. She was in a hurry to leave after that, but I didn't say anything mean to her whatsoever."

Jonathan shakes his head, not believing me, and again, I wonder about their sibling relationship. "What was your other joke?"

I sigh, aggravated again. "I told her that she should let me walk her out because there could be a murderer outside."

"Fuck," Patrick curses under his breath and I'm at a

loss once again. "Thanks, Grant," he says for my cooperation. "Let's go, Jon."

They go to turn around, but I stop them because I'm curious. I want to know what was so wrong with what I said, but I decide to go with the next best thing. "What was her favor?"

Patrick walks backwards as he answers, "She wants to learn about hockey. She's the main photographer for it now, and she wants to understand it. You're the only person Luce knows that plays."

Oh. "Tell her to see me after the game Saturday."

Patrick nods and then they disappear around the corner.

"What the fuck was that all about?" Bo asks from next to me.

"Hell if I know."

"Are you really going to teach her about hockey?"

We finish the walk to my car. "Yeah," I answer simply. I kind of feel bad that I upset her, but I don't understand why a few stupid comments upset her so much that she wouldn't even tell her brothers. She clearly has a close relationship with them. Now I'm too curious not to find out more. Let's just hope my curiosity doesn't bite me in the ass.

"Is Neil working again tonight?" I ask. Bo nods. "Why did he get a job anyway? We don't have rent and his parents give him a monthly allowance. Why does he need more money?" It doesn't add up to me. Something is off. Or maybe Neil wants extra money to save for something. Who knows.

Bo shrugs. "He's got some stuff going on. That's all I'm allowed to say."

"And this won't affect his play? Working nights?" It's not but like six hours, I think, but still. He's always catching up on sleep and homework. So far, it doesn't seem like it's affected him too much.

"No, but there are more important things than hockey, Grant." Bo sounds irritated, so I stop asking questions. It's not really my business anyway.

God. Look at me. I'm so freaking curious about everyone's damn lives. At least I can say that I don't gossip. I like to listen and learn, not discuss it with the world. All curiosity is pushed aside once we arrive back at the house. This week, I'm studying like crazy for one of my classes. Somehow, I managed a B on one of my papers, so I'm trying to make sure I get an A next time.

That's pretty much how the week passes leading up to yet another intense game. I have a love/hate relationship with games like tonight. I love the energy, love having to put forth all that concentration to make sure I play my best, but afterwards? Not so much. I'm exhausted, physically and emotionally. Unfortunately, we lose, our first loss of the season. Thankfully, that means no party tonight. I'm in no mood for any of that.

I'm one of the last to leave, and Lucy is waiting outside the locker room for me. I completely forgot about her. She lifts her head at the sound of the door opening and immediately starts talking.

"I apologize for my brothers, Grant. You don't have to teach me because they forced you into it. I can learn on my own. That's all I wanted to say."

She goes to turn away, but I stop her when I laugh. "Your brothers didn't 'force' me to do anything." Her brows come together. "Do you really think they could make me do something if I didn't want to?"

Lucy looks a little embarrassed. "Well, they can be intimidating when they want to be. I shouldn't have assumed they were, I guess."

"Do you want to learn hockey?"

She nods. "I've watched a few games on TV, but it's hard for me to follow."

"If it's okay with you, you can come over to the house tomorrow, and we'll watch one there." It's subtle, but her eyes widen. "Starts at noon," I add. Is she scared of me? Or scared of being alone with me? Maybe she's just nervous about it.

"Yeah, okay. Thank you." Lucy nods one too many times like she reassuring herself this is what she wants to do.

"Could I have your number? So I can text you the address? It's not too far from campus."

Lucy spits out her phone number while I enter it into my phone. "Is anyone else going to be there?"

"Do you want there to be?" My question is simply a means to find out what she needs to be comfortable, and I think she can tell. She wasn't expecting me to ask though.

"Um, no. I was just wondering. I'll get Patrick to take me. Thanks again, Grant."

Lucy starts walking away, but I hurry to walk next to her. "I'm sorry," I offer, suddenly feeling like I need to apologize for whatever I did to upset her last week. The confusion flits across her face as she glances at me before opening the door to the outside, so I add, "For what I said that upset you."

She waves me away. "Oh, don't worry about it. It didn't really have anything to do with you, Grant. I'm sorry you felt sorry," she laughs softly. For a moment, I wonder if there's anything loud about her. She's not loud, her laugh isn't either. The only thing that raises its voice for attention is her beauty, and even then, that's soft too.

"Do you want me to walk you?" As soon as it's out of my mouth, I see Patrick walking over to us. I have a feeling that somehow, he's going to be a pain in my ass.

"That's why I'm here," he answers for her. Lucy turns around at the sound of his voice, a smile was already forming. The girl loves her brothers. That much is clear. "Sorry I'm late, Luce." He gives her a one-armed hug.

"It's okay. Grant was keeping me company." She turns back to me. "See you tomorrow around noon?"

"A little before noon," I correct.

Lucy nods and then they say goodbye and are walking away. It seems like all she does is walk away from me. That's crazy because she's usually only leaving to go somewhere else, but the thought passes my mind anyway.

EVERY SUNDAY, NEIL and Bo head somewhere together, but I don't know where. They don't say, and I don't ask. There's an unspoken air around them that clearly states not to question them. Winston is off at the gym again. It seems like all he's been doing since Maddie stayed the night is working out. That leaves only me at home. The knock at the door finally comes just as I wonder if she's going to be a no-show. That can only be one person. I open the door to find Lucy, camera around her neck, and notice Patrick giving me a hard look before he starts backing out of the driveway.

"Cutting it close, aren't you?" I step aside so she can

walk it. It's 11:57.

"Patrick doesn't understand the concept of time," she mumbles as she looks around, taking in the place.

"Planning to take pictures while you're here?" I ask, closing the door.

Lucy looks down at the camera clutched in her hands. "Just in case. Is anyone else here?"

"No. C'mon, the game is about to start."

We go into the living room on the left and sit down on the couch, me at one end, Lucy far away at the other. The volume is low enough not to be distracting, but loud enough that we can hear it. As the game begins, I start telling her about face-offs, zones, puck possession, and penalties as they happen. At the end of the first, I ask Lucy how she thinks this is going.

"Ugh! Forget this! I give up. Sports are just not my thing." Lucy is clearly frustrated that she's not comprehending what I'm explaining.

"What do you mean, 'sports'? You don't understand football and baseball either?"

She cuts me a glare. "Baseball is easy. One, two, three strikes, you're out. Nine innings, hit the ball with a bat, and make it home. Football is a little harder and this," she waves her hand at the TV, "is just ridiculous. I don't understand how my brothers possess so much athletic talent, but I can't even *understand* the stupid games."

"But you take pictures for the paper. How haven't you picked up on what's happening?"

"Can I borrow your laptop?"

It's so out in left field that all I can manage to do is comply. I get up, go to my room, get my laptop, and come back. After I place it on the coffee table in front of us, Lucy moves to the middle of the couch to sit next to me, powers it on, and starts explaining.

"I don't see the game like you do. Players see the rules, regulations, and what their job is while they are playing." Lucy takes the memory card from her camera and inserts it into my computer. She pulls up all the pictures and starts searching. "I see emotions and moments. That's why I love taking pictures. They capture seconds in time that can make all the difference without needing to look at the big picture."

She pulls up one from the game last night. "This was right before he scored his third goal of the night. He already knew he was victorious before he even did it. You can see it in his face, the determination in his stance as he skates towards the net. This guy is desperate to stop him, still hoping there's time before he shoots the puck forward."

She moves to another picture of a face-off. "This guy right here is brutal during whatever they are doing."

"Face-off," I interrupt.

"Anyway, he almost always comes away with the puck and he's super fast. I've tried to get a decent shot of right after the puck drops, that split second before it lands on the ice, but the pictures don't come out as well as I want. I have a few ideas on what to tweak during the next game, though."

I lean back onto the couch. "Sounds to me like you already know the game. Just not in the same terms as I do." Then I sit back up, resting my elbows just above my knees on my thighs, and nod towards the computer. "Show me some more."

Lucy begins to scroll through the images, commenting on the emotions she believes the players are having based on their current action. Slowly, I start seeing more and more pictures of me. She glances at me with a blush before explaining the same things to me, but about me. She's pretty spot on too. When she starts to skip some, I realize that she takes a serious amount of photos of me. Lucy starts to speak before I can question her.

"I take multiple shots at a time to have a batch of photos for one particular moment so I can pick the best shot. With yours, I can't decide on the best. There are things I like about all of them. That's why there are so many of you. You're very photogenic, Grant." Her blush darkens when she sneaks a peek at me before looking back to the screen. "You are my favorite person to photograph. I hope that doesn't sound creepy or anything."

A little bit. This is for her schooling, though. It's not like she's following me around and keeping secret photos of me. Her comment about me being her favorite stands out the most. I'm not quite sure why though. Before I can answer, Lucy gasps and grabs my knee.

"They're fighting! Are they allowed to do that? Why are they fighting anyway?" Her eyes are glued to the TV now.

I eye her hand and then look up to her as she glances at me. "It's an intense game with lots of hits and emotions run wild. Not to mention how physical some players are." I missed what happened to cause this fight, thanks to Lucy. She seems captured by the punches being thrown by the players. Suddenly, as my knee gets warm underneath her hand, I blurt out, "Would you like to go to a game?"

Lucy quickly turns to look at me, the players heading to their respective boxes. "What?" she questions, bringing her hand back to her lap.

"Do you want to go see a game in person?" I repeat.

"With you?" Her voice is a mixture of surprise and skepticism, which makes me laugh.

"Yeah, who else?"

Lucy's lips form a perfect O. "Right, duh. That would make the most sense, huh? You caught me by surprise, sorry." She takes a deep breath. "That sounds like fun, though. I would love to go." Her phone dings and she apologizes as she reads a text. "It's Patrick checking in," she says with a roll of her eyes.

"Checking in?" I ask, wanting to ask about their relationship with such a perfect opportunity.

"Yeah. He worries, and apparently, you aren't well-known on campus other than the fact you play hockey, so he doesn't know much about you. That's why he's checking in, sorry." She blushes a little. "You probably didn't want to know that."

"Actually," I begin. This is my chance to satisfy my curiosity. "I would like to hear about your brothers."

"Why?" Lucy seems genuinely confused.

"I'm an only child," I explain. "What was it like growing up with three siblings?"

"Oh, well, it was great." That adoring smile is back on her face. "They are seriously the definition of protective older brothers, but they are the best. We are really close, too. Um, let's see." Lucy seems to think about how she wants to describe them to me. She subtly nods her head, scoots back from the edge of the couch, and turns towards me a little while tucking her legs underneath her.

"Patrick is like my best friend. I'm closer to him than Jon or Corey. He always puts my best interests in mind and he's practically on stand-by if I ever need him. I could call him right now and he'd be in here in ten minutes, no matter what he's doing. I'm not as close to Jon or Corey, but they would both drop anything if I called them and needed them.

"Jonathan much rather I call Patrick because he just doesn't know how to be helpful, sometimes. He always answers his phone by the third ring when I call, though. I think he would rather play bodyguard or something. Corey is the worst, overprotective-wise. He wants what he thinks is best, which isn't always what is best.

"Oddly enough, when it comes to something concerning me, Patrick has the final word between the three of them. It doesn't matter that he's the youngest. They all know that he knows me best, so they'll listen to him. Does any of that make sense?"

I shrug. "You make it sound like they are protective because there is something serious you need protecting from and not normal brother stuff. Have they always been that way? Is your dad that way with you too? You don't mind how they are?" I spout off all the questions I've been dying to ask.

Lucy frowns and her eyes sadden immediately. This look doesn't fit her. I hate that I've somehow upset her again. "It's all I've ever known, and I don't mind it at all. Actually, I wouldn't change anything about my brothers, even if they can be a pain sometimes. Let's watch the rest of the game."

She turns back towards the TV as the third period starts. The longer she stays silent, the more Patrick's words repeat in my head. If she's quiet, it's not a good thing. I nudge my elbow against hers.

"You okay, Lucy?"

She smiles at me and those bright blue eyes look more happy than sad now. "Yeah, I'm fine. When are you thinking about going to a game?"

"We can look up some upcoming ones and pick right now, if you want." Lucy nods, so I bring my laptop to my lap and pull up the website to order tickets. "It'll have to be during the week, most likely." I bring up the schedule and silently narrow it down based on my own schedule. "Okay," I start as Lucy leans towards me to look at the screen, "what about this Wednesday or next Thursday?"

"This Wednesday works for me." Her nose wrinkles and her eyes squint as she looks at me. "Is this a date?"

"Based on the look on your face, I hope not. God, Lucy, way to make me feel pathetic. I didn't know a date with me sounded so terrible." I frown. I hadn't thought of it as a date, but it doesn't feel good to know that she wouldn't want it to be. Talk about hitting my ego.

Lucy gasps. "I didn't mean it like that," she apologizes quickly.

"Oh, you so did." I laugh at her response. "Don't worry, Lucy. I want to take you as my new friend. Unless," I drag the word out to tease her, "do you secretly want this to be a date? I mean, you do take an awful lot of pictures of me."

That seems to loosen the tension for her as she giggles softly. "I don't even know how to recover from that."

The front door opens, causing us both to turn and see Neil and Bo walk in. They stop when they see Lucy.

"Guys, this is Lucy Kennedy. Lucy, that's Neil and Bo, though I'm sure you knew that already."

She waves her hand in hello. They walk into the living room, and Neil sits down next to Lucy. A little too close, probably. He gives her a big grin.

"You are the photographer girl, little sister to the Kennedy brothers, right?" he asks.

Lucy nods and smiles. "Do you know them?"

"No, I don't," he answers. "If I had known that you looked like-"

"Neil, I'll kick your ass. Don't start that shit with her," I interrupt suddenly. They both look at me surprised.

"Yeah, her brothers are fucking crazy. You should have seen them confront Grant the other day," Bo says, shaking his head at the memory.

"Hello," Lucy waves her hand in a circle, "I'm right here. And my brothers aren't crazy." Her lips fall into a frown. "What did they say to you?" she asks me. "You said they didn't force or intimidate you."

"They didn't. They were half pissed, half concerned, and they tried to be intimidating, but they weren't. Maybe you should tell them that I am not stupid, though."

Lucy looks confused, but Bo laughs. "Yeah, they talked to him slowly at first like he had taken too many hits."

"I'm sorry," she mumbles. "They can be crazy, I guess."

"Don't worry about it."

A horn honks from outside, and she groans. "That's probably Patrick." She takes her memory card from my computer and puts it back in her camera. "Thanks for today," she says, looking back up at me. "I'll see you Wednesday, then?"

"Yeah, I'll text you."

Satisfied, she stands and is out the door in seconds.

Both Bo and Neil are watching me, waiting for me to explain further. I don't make any move to do so. Lucy is none of their damn business. They seem to be the opposite of her, and that makes me want to keep her safely away from them for some reason. I start looking for good seats, but Neil can't handle the suspense.

"Well?"

"Well, what?" I answer without taking my eyes away from the screen.

"What was she doing here? What's Wednesday?"

"He's teaching her about hockey," Bo answers. The mention of that makes me realize that we didn't even watch the end of the game. "I'm assuming that's why she was here anyway."

"Yeah, that was why," I confirm.

"And Wednesday?" Neil pushes.

"When did you get so damn curious?" He stares at me and waits for me to answer. "I'm taking her to a game. As her friend," I clarify as I purchase our tickets.

CHAPTER 8

Winston

UNFORTUNATELY, I DON'T run into Paula anymore, and I'm above texting her just to have sex. She was right. That doesn't need to become a habit. After the horrible loss, I spend most of the weekend at the gym exercising since I'm not getting laid. The entire week has been shit with dirty dreams I don't want to have, the loss, and completely forgetting about an assignment. It's made me cranky. I'm still in a pissy mood when Dave FaceTimes me Sunday evening as I'm leaving the gym. It doesn't help at all that he looks so cheery.

"Make it quick," I greet.

"What the hell is wrong with you? This is like the third day in a row you've been like this."

"What the hell is wrong with you? Why are you so

fucking happy?" I ask with as much irritation I can muster.

Dave glares at me, knowing as good as I do that I'm being ridiculous. "I was going to ask for a favor, but I think I'll wait until you're in a better mood."

A favor? I raise an eyebrow at him. "What kind of favor?"

Somehow, I manage to withhold a groan as he answers, "I called Maddie for my monthly checkup, as per my parents. She mentioned something about needing to study more for one of her classes, one I'm pretty sure you took and aced."

"What do you want, Dave?" I grit.

"Calm down. It's not like I'm asking you to give her a kidney. I'm asking you to help her study and make a better grade than what she's doing right now."

"Why does it have to be me? She can go get a tutor or form a study group. That's what you should have told her to do." Not make me be around the girl invading my dreams. If they weren't so damn good, I would call them nightmares.

"Because then you can keep an eye out for her. God knows what college guys could talk her into." He shakes his head like she's this innocent child.

"Get a grip, Dave. She's not five."

He glares at me. "Are you going to help her or not?"

"Yeah. You owe me big time."

Dave grins at his victory. "Thanks."

"Whatever. I gotta go." I end the call and finally groan. Fuck. Seeing Maddie is the last thing I want to do. I'm torn between wishing she chose a different university and hating myself for how I destroyed any second chance I had with her. Since I'm on campus, I might as well go ahead and see her now. The walk doesn't take long, and it isn't until I'm opening the door to the building that I consider the fact that she might not currently be in her dorm. Only one way to find out. I knock and wait. No answer, so I knock one more time before I give up.

"Winston? What are you doing here?" Maddie glances down the hall, like someone is going to notice I'm standing outside her room and actually care.

"Dave said you needed help with a class and I'm going to help. We need to figure some things out first though."

"Thanks, but no thanks." Maddie starts to shut the door, but my hand flies out to stop her.

"What?" She's turning me down?

Maddie sighs, but makes no further move to open the door back open. "I don't want your help, Winston."

Leaning against the doorframe, I fold my arms over my chest. "Why didn't you just come ask me for help yourself? I told you that-"

"Yeah, right." Maddie laughs harshly. "Like I would come ask you for anything." I don't realize my mouth parted until she reaches out and pushes my jaw back up. "Go home, Winston."

I'm surprised and a little hurt, but more disappointed in myself that I caused this reaction from her. I lose my defensive stance and plead with her. "C'mon, Maddie. At least let me come in, so we can talk."

She watches me for a moment as she decides. "There's nothing to talk about, but if you want to waste your breath, feel free." She turns around, going back into her room, and I follow her. The other bed belonging to her roommate is empty and made. We take a seat on her bed,

Maddie up by her pillows and me at the foot with our legs folded as we sit across from one another.

"Can't we be friends, Maddie?" I ask. "Let's focus on that."

"Let's forget that anything ever happened between us basically?" she says, but there's no anger or annoyance in her voice. Only sadness. "I can't believe you would want to pretend we never happened, secret or not."

"I don't want to forget, Maddie. I couldn't if I wanted to. All I meant is I want us to be friends now. I can help you with your class and we can still hang out some if you want. Maybe then you won't get homesick again. You could meet more people that way too."

"I get it, Winston. That sounds great." I don't think she really means it though.

My phone beeps from my pocket and I pull it out. It's a text from Grant asking if I want to go with him and Lucy to a game Wednesday and that maybe I could ask Maddie to go too. He'll explain more later, but he thinks Lucy will have more fun with other people there.

"Hey, Grant's inviting me to go see a game Wednesday with him and some chick. Want to go? I don't know why, but he wants people to go with them." I look up from my phone to gauge her reaction.

"Um, sure, I guess. I've never been to one before, so it should be fun. Do you know who the girl is?"

"Lucy Kennedy," I answer.

Maddie's eyes almost pop out of her head. "As in the crazy good photographer and little sister of the unbelievably hot, football superstars Kennedy brothers? That Lucy?" She almost sounds excited.

"Yeah, that Lucy," I deadpan to counteract her enthusiasm.

"Sweet. How about we study Tuesday and then game Wednesday? That sound good to you?"

"That works for me."

She nods. "All right. I would love to stay and chat, but I was about to head to the gym before you got here, so..."

"You want me to leave? So you can do what you want to do? Sort of like the other night when I wanted to go to bed." I perk an eyebrow at her, making her laugh. Part of me wants to ask when she started all this exercising, but I don't.

"Be the better person, Winston."

"Fine. Text me with a time for Tuesday and I'll let you know about Wednesday." When I stand to leave, I have a small urge to kiss her forehead, but I don't do that, of course. Instead, I smile and throw out a "catch ya later."

Being friends with Maddie will be easy. It's a familiar place, and much better than the tempting, bad alternative. This week will prove that friendship is exactly where we need to be.

NEIL

GOD, I'M EXHAUSTED. More spent than I've ever been, that's for sure. After spending time with the Lanier's, all I want to do is crawl into my bed and collapse, so I can fall into a deep sleep. Unfortunately, I can't do that. I almost want to stay here and figure out what the hell is going on with Grant and Lucy, but that's not happening either. Audra, who has done her best to communicate with me as little as possible this week, has finally invited me over to talk. She was clear that I better not "pull any shit" because she just finished her shift and wasn't in the mood to deal with my crap.

Without a word and with my keys in hand, I leave the house, following my phone's GPS to Audra's place. I knock on the door when I finally get there and note that it isn't the nicest of areas around. Audra gives me a tight-lipped smile and lets me in. Based on the looks of things, she lives in a small, one bedroom apartment.

"Hey, Neil. Can I get you something to drink or anything?"

"No, thanks," I answer.

"I don't really know how we should do this," she says as she takes a seat on the couch. Audra props her bare feet onto her wooden coffee table. She rests her hands over her belly and leans her head back with her eyes closed.

"How often do you work?" I ask. Suddenly, my fatigue doesn't seem so bad in the face of how tired she looks. "How are you sleeping?"

Audra peeks an eye open and tilts her head to look at me. Her mouth parts, but nothing comes out at first. "You genuinely care, don't you?"

"Does that surprise you?" My brows wrinkle at the thought. I'm not sure if it's because I do genuinely care or the fact that it surprises her. I wasn't always this guy. The one who would try to get rid of a pregnant girl like she was nothing more than leftovers that needs to be thrown away. I used to be the guy who would immediately, without any doubt, be by her side at whatever cost. For just a moment,

I wonder how I could have gotten so far away from that person. For just a moment, I want to be that guy again.

"Well, yeah, it does. I work as often as I can and I'm sleeping fine. How are *you* sleeping?" She reaches out to mess with my black hair, patting it down as if it was out of place. "Sorry, that's been bugging me since you walked in."

"It's okay." Audra looks at me expectantly and I realize that she's waiting for me to answer her question. "How I sleep isn't the issue. It's finding the time. I got a job, working nights," I finish in explanation.

Shock registers before she tucks it away and rests her head on the back of the couch again. "Well, why don't you tell me about yourself and how you're going to be helpful to me."

"Oh, all right." I look around the room as I talk. Audra's closed her eyes anyway. "Um, I'll go with you to the doctor's appointments and if possible, I would be grateful if you could schedule them so I don't miss class or hockey practice. I'll go to any classes you want me to go to. Basically, the exact same things as if we were in a relationship, going through this-"

Audra stirs next to me, so I glance at her as her head falls to the side and she slowly tilts until she leans on my shoulder.

"Audra?"

No answer. Her chest is moving normally, so she's probably just asleep. Poor girl. Can't even stay awake long enough to talk to me. Part of me wants to wake her up, but I really don't want to. If she's that tired, then I should let her sleep. Sighing, I relax into the couch, thankful the TV is on, and decide to wait for her to wake back up.

"NEIL?"

I grunt, feeling a terrible kink in my neck.

"Neil?" the voice says again.

My eyes flash open to find Audra standing in front of me. I yawn, wanting to stretch my legs, but can't until she moves. "About time you wake up," I grumble with my thick, just-woken-up voice.

She laughs. "You were the one sleeping. I need to eat. I'm feeling a little lightheaded."

I sit up and grab her hips. "Lightheaded? Why are you standing?" I guide her over until she's sitting down next to me. "What do you need? What do you want? I can run to the store. I-"

"Neil," she rests a hand on my arm, "calm down. I'm only a little weak. There's no need to panic." Her voice is soothing, which makes me relax a little.

"Right. Do you want me to fix you something to eat or go get something?"

Audra moves to stand, but I gently make her sit again. I do not want her passing out. She huffs and gives me a fake glare. "You don't have to do anything. I woke you up because I figured that would be better than you waking because of some banging around in the kitchen."

"Yeah, well, you stay here. Tell me what you want and I'll go fix it for you."

"Neil," she protests.

"Unless my name is about to be followed with what food you want to eat, then I don't want to hear it." I level my gaze at her until she sighs and tells me what she wants.

I leave Audra in the living room and start rummaging through her kitchen to find what I need. She wants chicken Alfredo. I have no freaking clue how to put all that together, but I'm sure I can figure it out. How hard can it be? She already has chicken breasts in the fridge, so I grab those.

"You're going to need-"

I spin to see Audra pulling out a chair at the kitchen table. "What are you doing?" I interrupt.

"I make it from scratch, and since you're so determined to cook, I'm going to tell you how."

So Audra starts instructing me on what I need to do and where I need to get the ingredients. I keep glancing at her to make sure she looks okay. Every time I look, she's scrolling through her phone, rubbing her stomach, or watching my every move. About halfway through, she gets up and walks over to me.

"Feeling okay?" I question as she peers into the pot.

"I'm feeling freaked out that you are in my kitchen cooking. And a little worried that you're going to burn my apartment down." Audra glances at me, causing me to laugh.

"Just imagine how I feel then, but I have things under control. You can go sit back down now."

"Please tell me you aren't going to be this way until the baby comes. That sounds even freakier than you cooking for me."

I laugh again. "We'll see." The thought that she's having a girl passes my mind again like it has many times since I found out. That terrifies me even more. A sweet, innocent baby girl. How fucking scary is that? I clear my throat as I stir. "Have you thought of any names yet?"

Audra shakes her head before walking back to her seat. "No. I wasn't ever one of those girls that had a list of names I liked or even really had a preference for names. I mean, I like mine and that's as far as it goes." She chuckles. Her voice turns soft as she adds, "I'm more scared than anything, if I'm being perfectly honest."

I look over to her, but she has her head down. "Yeah, me too." Scared is such an innocent, lighthearted word for how I feel.

"I never dreamed of having kids one day, much less right now. But ever since I found out, underneath all the fear, there's a bit of excitement too. I might not have wanted kids before, but I want this little girl." She laughs, but it's a disbelieving one. Audra lifts her gaze to me. "And you are just making sure you take care of your responsibility."

Her words are like a hard slap to the face. She's right. This isn't about whether I want that baby or not. I'm here because I should be. It's the right thing to do. Everything else is supposed to fall into place as we go along. I can't stand to look at her anymore, so I fill up a plate of the now done pasta and take it to her.

"Here you go, Audra. I'll catch up with you later. Call if you need anything."

This is the last place I want to be. Because now all I can think about is what if everything doesn't fall into place? What if by the time the baby comes, I still don't want her? What if she's born and I feel nothing but an obligation? A chore? A responsibility? What if my baby girl realizes this and it affects her as she grows up? Am I just making things worse for Audra and her?

I'm halfway to the door when Audra says, "Wait. Neil, I'm sorry. I shouldn't have said that."

I turn to face her. "Doesn't make any difference if you're thinking it already. I should go, though. I need to eat before I have to go into work."

"You just fixed dinner," she says like that is the answer to all our problems. "C'mon, Neil. Are you going to make a pregnant girl beg?" She gives me a subtle smile.

"Maybe," I smirk.

Audra laughs. "There's the Neil I know. Fix yourself a plate and have a seat. We never talked, so let's do that." Once I've done as she said and am sitting across from her, she tells me her plan in-between bites. "First, we obviously need to get to know each other better. If you're serious about being here, then we need to do that and be able to get along because we're going to be around one another for a long, long time."

"So what do you suggest for that to happen?"

"We meet two or three times a week to hang out. We'll have to figure out when our schedules can coincide for that, but it's possible. From there, we can learn how to make things work for us pre-baby and post-baby."

Great. Another commitment to add to my list of things to fit into my schedule, but this is important, so I'll have to find room. "I can do that."

Grant

I'M ALMOST POSITIVE that something is wrong with Lucy. Why? Because she makes me worry for no good reason. It's been days since she came over, and in a moment of panic with her question about if she would be alone with me or not when she comes to the house, I texted Winston Sunday to see if he wanted to go to the game.

Lucy seemed fine that day, but I kept thinking that she would be more comfortable if it wasn't just us. Plus, it definitely wouldn't feel like a date.

A smile finds its way to my lips at remembering Lucy's horror expression that it might be a date. Winston and I are on our way to pick up the girls from campus. They are supposed to be waiting in the parking lot closest to Maddie's dorm. Tonight will be a much welcomed getaway. Bo and Neil are bickering more than usual and it's not like Neil is at the house all that often. I don't know where he goes, but he's not at the house. His mood is all over the place, and I think it's largely from lack of a decent sleep. I'm definitely ready for tonight.

The girls are chitchatting, obviously getting acquainted with one another. Lucy laughs at something Maddie says and I kind of wish I could hear it. Once I put the truck in park, I take in that she looks pretty in jeans and a black sweater that really makes her eyes stand out. Eyes that have thin black eyeliner around them. Something seems different about her other than the makeup, but I can't put my finger on it. We hop out of my truck and say hello to them as they walk over to us. I open the passenger door for Lucy while Winston moves to the back seat with Maddie.

"Thanks, Grant," Lucy says with a smile over her shoulder before she climbs into the vehicle.

"Mhm." Then I walk around, get in, and we're on our way. Maddie and Winston are talking quietly, so I glance at Lucy. "Please tell me that you've had a good week so far."

She laughs, granting me the luxury to hear it. "Yeah, I have. Why do you say it like that?"

"Seems like everyone else isn't having a good one and

I didn't want you to be grouchy too." As an afterthought, I add, "Have you ever been grouchy, Lucy? I don't think I could imagine you being that way."

"Oh, I could so be that way. It's rare, though. I rather not have negative emotions." What she says totally fits because I couldn't see her with those emotions either.

"Hey," Winston pipes in. "Don't let him fool you about us. I haven't been pissy, only Bo and Neil. Are y'all excited for your first pro game?"

"Most definitely," Maddie says from behind me.

"Um, yeah," Lucy adds.

I chuckle. "You don't sound so sure."

"I feel kind of naked." My head swings over to her, and she quickly rushes, "I mean, I don't have my camera with me. I feel like I'm going to miss something and like I'm naked without it."

Ah, that's it. She doesn't have that camera hanging around her neck. That's why she looked different. "You'll be fine, promise. What did your brothers say about you coming with me?" I figure that they know, and I'm curious to hear their response.

Maddie leans forward until her head is between our seats. "Ooh, yes, let's talk about those delicious brothers of yours."

Winston groans and Lucy looks almost embarrassed to hear someone talk about her brothers that way.

"They don't know. They didn't ask, and I didn't offer." Lucy focuses on me with a hard look that I thankfully don't have to see for long because my eyes are back on the road. "Just because they look out for me doesn't mean that they run my life, Grant."

"I didn't mean it like that," I stumble, feeling like I've

been scolded.

She laughs. "Yes, you did. It's okay. A lot of people assume that."

Before I can offer an apology, Maddie starts peppering her about her brothers' relationship statuses. After disappointing answers that don't reveal much, Maddie starts picking on Winston. Apparently, they've been working out together and Maddie is a faster runner than him.

"Your short legs somehow manage to get you more distance, that's all," he brushes her off.

Lucy falls quiet as they continue talking. The arena isn't too far away and finding a place to park doesn't take long. As we begin walking to the building, Maddie and Winston are slightly ahead of us in their own little world, and Lucy takes in everything around us.

"Wow, there are a lot of people here," she whispers in awe with a touch of fear.

I reach over and take her hand. We haven't even walked inside yet. "Do crowds bother you?" Because there is about to be a more packed one.

"Not really, but don't let go." She squeezes my hand as we fall in line behind Maddie and Winston. Lucy rubs her arm with her free hand. "I thought this would be enough," she mumbles.

"I would offer my jacket, but..."

"You don't have one," she laughs.

"Come here." I can't let her stand there, cold. I tug on her hand until she's standing in front of me, still facing towards the front of the line. Releasing her hand, I run mine up and down her arms while standing close to her, hoping that will help. Lucy grabs my hands and pulls my arms around her as she leans into me.

"More warmth this way," she explains. Whatever you say, Lucy. I hug her closer, trying to keep her warm and cozy. "You have the tickets, right?" She turns her head to look at me.

"Of course, I do," I chuckle.

"How much do I owe you?"

"Nothing." Winston is the one who owes me since I covered his tickets.

Her cute, little nose wrinkles in confusion. "This isn't a date, so I should pay for mine."

"Then consider it a date," I shrug. That seems like an okay thing to say, right? She's not about to pay me for her ticket because I asked her to come, date or not. Lucy isn't happy with my answer, though.

"You can't do that." She turns in my arms, placing hers around my waist, a frown on her face. I'm tired of seeing that damn thing already and it only just appeared. "You can't make this a date so I won't owe you. That's not fair. What makes you think I would want to be on a date with you anyway?"

That, unfortunately, catches Winston and Maddie's attention during a pause in their conversation, and they try to conceal their laughter. The line moves forward, though, and I don't get a chance to respond as our turn in line arises. We make it through security before getting our tickets scanned. What is so bad about being on a date with me? I take her hand and lead her through the building. There are a ton of people in here. It's like rush hour without the cars. Lucy ends up walking behind me. I keep a firm hold on her hand, but I still feel her grab the back of my shirt. Like I'm going to release her hand and leave her alone to find her own way to our seats.

We go up the stairs until we reach the top level. Winston and Maddie lead the way to our section. Once we finally reach our row, Lucy lets go of my shirt, so I do the same to her hand. We sit with Winston and me on the ends and Maddie and Lucy in between us. They are both looking around and down at the ice, making comments to one another as the players warm up. As soon as there seems to be a pause, I grab Lucy's attention and ask the one question that is bugging the hell out of me.

"Why wouldn't you want to go on a date with me? That's like the third or fourth time you've said something like that." I make sure to ask quiet enough that Maddie won't overhear.

Lucy directs her full attention to me. "I didn't say I wouldn't want to. This just can't be a date because you don't want me to pay you back."

She didn't say that she *would* either, I note. "Look, I asked you to come, so it's on me." Lucy nods in acceptance. "Do you want to give this learning hockey thing one more try? You may be able to follow it easier here."

"You can try."

CHAPTER 9

Winston

I HELPED MADDIE study last night after we worked out together. She's training for a 5K in February that a club here at the school is hosting. I didn't know that Maddie loved to run that much and is trying to build herself up to a 10K and so on. I think it's a little early to train for that, but what do I know? When we decided to start working out together, she told me she started running after I left for college.

We've gotten to a good place I think as she tells Lucy about the upcoming run. The first intermission has passed and let me tell you, it's hilarious listening to Grant explain the game to Lucy. The girl gets frustrated quickly when she doesn't pick it up right away. Maddie seems to have made a new friend in Lucy, too, which is pretty cool. After

Lucy and Grant leave to go buy drinks, Maddie turns towards me.

"I think I just talked her into running the 5K with me," she smiles with excitement. "You should do it with us too."

"I don't know. That's pretty advance planning. Something else might come up." There's no way I want to do that with her. She is a little faster than I am, according to only one race between us, and I wouldn't be able to survive a 5K. Not because of the running, but because I would have to see her half-naked, February or not, with her hair up in a tight ponytail, swinging as she runs, and little sprigs falling to hang around her face by the time she's finished. I don't need to see her ass or her tits either.

Nope. Not happening.

"It's first thing in the morning, Winston. Just say you don't want to do it."

"I don't want to do it," I say.

"Fine. You can study with me tomorrow before your game then. I have a test soon, and I want to be prepared."

"I'll be there," I promise. I have no clue why she's not doing well in this class because she knows the material inside and out. She might have test anxiety. Maybe we'll work on that instead of actually studying. My eyes travel over her features as she faces the ice once more. One thing that I haven't been able to surpass is how gorgeous she is. Maddie still invades my dreams in the hottest ways. It's ridiculous.

"They are so adorable," she gushes, placing her hand on my thigh to get my attention. On the ice are a bunch of little kids, playing a quick game before the intermission is over. "I don't think you could have been that cute when you were younger."

I laugh as I move so Lucy and Grant can squeeze back over to their seats, handing us our bottles of drinks on the way. The second intermission starts and I lean towards Maddie.

"Are you picking up on Grant's explanations?"

She shakes her head without looking away from the action. "I'm not listening. I want to watch and absorb the awesomeness. I don't need or want to know anything else. Ooooh!" Maddie sits up straight as a fight breaks out down below on the ice. Her eyes are captivated by the few punches that get thrown in before the refs break them up and ship them off to the penalty box. "God, that was sort of, kind of, really hot." She turns to Lucy. "Don't you think?"

Lucy blushes, shakes her head, and mumbles a 'no'. I'm not so sure that I understand what Grant sees in her, which would aid his 'she's only a friend' line. I don't think boys and girls can be *just* friends. Wait, let me correct myself. They can be friends, but someone is wishing they weren't. Like myself right now, for example. My mind is occupied more with Maddie than the game.

Which is crazy and wrong and bad, but it's the truth, so no need to deny it to myself. From the corner of my eye, I watch Maddie watch the game. She moves to the edge of her seat, entranced by almost goals, or jumps up with a goal, no matter which team scored. And then, sometimes, she's leaning back in her seat, looking bored almost. During the third period, I decide to see if she's actually enjoying herself or not.

"Having fun?" I ask.

Maddie looks over at me. "Yeah, mostly. Not really a

sports-watching kind of girl." With a grin, she adds, "I definitely like seeing you play, though."

I shake my head. What am I supposed to say to that? The game ends quickly it seems and we're on our way back to campus to drop the girls off. Maddie and Lucy are making plans to hang out soon. Grant walks Lucy to her dorm while Maddie and I head towards hers.

"Thanks for tonight, Winston," she says.

"You're welcome. You still want me to come over tomorrow?" Maddie nods. "Okay, I'll be here after practice." My phone starts vibrating in my pocket, so I pull it out.

"Let me guess? It's your other half," she deadpans, almost annoyed with me.

I laugh. "Yeah, it's Dave."

"I swear, y'all talk more than girls. Better let you go. Heaven forbid he finds out I'm with you," she finishes as we reach the door. "Thanks again." Maddie stands on her tiptoes, but I lean down to help her out as she places a soft kiss on my cheek. And then she's walking away before I can comment on what she said.

Swiping my finger over the screen, Dave appears. "You sure are spending a lot of time outside."

"Leave me alone. Just got back from a game and I'm about to head home. Did you decide when you're coming up yet?"

"No, not yet. My woman says I've already committed a weekend to her, but I apparently forgot about it. I'm having to wait for her to quit being angry before I pick a weekend."

"Your woman?" I laugh. "You can't say her name or something?"

Dave shrugs. "She likes when I call her that."

I shake my head as I come up on Grant's truck, where he's already waiting. "I gotta go. Maybe you should call your woman."

"LOOK WHO FINALLY decided to show up," Maddie snaps as soon as I open the room to her dorm.

"Sorry. I'm here now," I try, feeling a little unsure of myself. I've never seen a pissed off Maddie. Practice ran super late because Vincent pissed off Coach.

"You couldn't have texted that you would be late?" She picks up her pillow at the head of the bed and then throws it down again in anger. Before I can answer, she keeps on ranting. "A text only takes five seconds, Winston. It doesn't matter anyway. I'm not in the mood to study or be around you today. Might as well leave."

What? She wants me to leave because I was late? Her tone pisses me off a little. "What the hell is going on with you? Are you PMSing or something?"

Maddie turns around slowly, the fury rolling off her in tsunami-sized waves. "Are you an idiot, Winston?" she yells. "You're seriously going to ask if I'm PMSing?!" She picks up a pillow and throws it at me, but I catch it easily.

"Well? Are you?"

Her shoulders sag. "Maybe."

I walk over and hand her the pillow. She clutches it to her chest and sits down on the bed. Following suit, I lean over to press a soft kiss to her temple because kisses make everything better, right? "Do you want me to go?"

"Yeah, I don't want to yell at you for no reason. Plus, I have to go to the store."

"I'll go. What do you need?" I ask, despite the sinking feeling in my stomach over what she's going to say.

She gives me an "are you serious?" look. "Don't worry, Winston. I can go."

Shaking my head at her, I insist, "Write down exactly what it is you need and I'll go get it." Reaching around her, I grab the sticky notepad and a pen from her nightstand. "Here."

Maddie doesn't argue as she writes down her preferred product. God, what has happened to me? I'm *offering* to go buy *tampons*. She didn't even have to ask me! She hands me the paper, and I look over her girly, loopy handwriting.

"Thanks, Winston," she says softly, kissing my cheek.

I give her a smile. "Yeah, yeah. I'll be back and when I do, you're studying, so get your ass in gear."

She rolls her eyes and pushes my shoulder playfully. On my way out, I notice her stack of Gobstoppers are low. The drug store is surprisingly scarce of people. I find the candy first and grab three boxes. That has to soften her up if she's still irritated when I return. I make my way to the correct aisle and look down at my sticky note and then back at the shelves upon shelves of feminine products.

Damn. Who knew there were so many brands and so many different kinds. I find the brand name first and then go down the line until I find the ones she wants. My hand reaches out and grabs it quickly. Now I can get the hell out of here.

"Winston?"

Fuck. I turn around to see Neil, a smile rising on his face as he spots the tampons and candy.

"What are you up to?" he asks, walking closer and I want to punch that grin off his face.

"I'm shopping, dumbass."

"Tampons? I didn't know you needed those."

"Are you done?" I'm in no mood to hear his crap. Shouldn't he be working or sleeping or something?

He smirks. "Why? Do you have somewhere you need to be?"

"Fuck you, Neil," I mutter, turning around and leaving his laughter behind. It's a girl at the cashier, which makes me feel a little better, especially when she makes a comment that I must be a great boyfriend. Her mouth parts in surprise when I tell her I'm only doing this for a friend.

There's an odd sense of satisfaction with my completed task as I return to Maddie's dorm. She's laying on her back on her bed. I set the bag down on the nightstand and sit next to her. The corners of her mouth lift slightly.

"I have a surprise for you."

"Really?" Maddie sits up, excited about what I might have for her.

"Mhm." I reach into the bag, grabbing a box of candy. When it makes some noise, a full-blown grin appears on her face.

"You certainly know how to make a girl happy," she says, taking it from me and ripping it open.

"Yeah, I guess so," I answer, not sure how to respond to her words. Maybe she doesn't realize she said it. After popping a few Gobstoppers into her mouth, she gets up with the bag and disappears into the bathroom. Her books are on her desk, so I grab them before laying on my stomach on the bed. "Where's your roommate?" I question when she returns. She's never here.

"I don't know. We aren't really friends." Maddie lays next to me and rests her head on my shoulder. Her eyes focus on the books. "I hate this class."

"Why? What are the tests like? I've been meaning to ask because you know this stuff, Maddie."

"Fill in the blank and essay. I can't ever remember the key terms once I get started, and without them, I can't answer much."

"Well, let's work on that."

While we work on test taking strategies, Maddie keeps bumping her foot into mine, her head still on my shoulder. Two hours pass with her next to me before I have to leave. We've got a game tonight.

"Just remember to relax and do what I've told ya. I gotta get going. We have away games this weekend, so you'll have to survive without me."

Maddie rolls her eyes. "I'm sure I'll do just fine. If not, send me some half naked pictures to get me through." She winks and I chuckle, shaking my head.

"OKAY, HERE'S THE deal. I don't have long before I have to be at the rink for tonight and then I'm booked all weekend. I'm so fucking behind on homework, so I brought my books. We're going to have to multitask," I tell Audra, taking a seat at her kitchen table, which is already filled with textbooks.

"That's fine. It's what I'm doing too." She frowns as

she gazes at me. "You look exhausted, Neil."

I give her a half smile. "Once I get into more of a routine, then it won't be so bad. How are you doing?"

Audra groans. "People are noticing now, and it's making me feel like a cow. I wish you would gain weight too. But I'm feeling pretty good and she keeps moving around." Audra places her hand on her stomach, smiling. "Do you want to feel?" she asks, lifting her head.

The more I'm over here, the better we get along. I think Audra is actually warming up to me. I mean, she just asked if I would like to touch her stomach. She was super surprised when I first asked, and now she's basically offering. That's progress. Nodding, I reach out, placing my hand where hers just was, but I don't feel anything. It's honestly a bit of a disappointment. Why does Audra get to experience this all the time and for me, it's all about luck? Being in the right place at the right time. She moves my hand a few times before I finally feel the movement.

"It never fails to be amazing," I whisper.

"I know." Audra takes a deep breath before adding, "We should get to work." We start on the mountain of homework and talk here and there throughout. "Have you told your parents yet?"

"No, I don't really talk to them on a regular basis, so I was going to wait until they called."

"Oh, do you have a good relationship with them?"

"Yeah, I guess," I answer without looking up. That's the truth. I mean, they are parents. We don't sit around and talk about all our life problems. If I need them, they are usually there. They don't hover, aren't stern, and we don't argue, but it's kind of hard to argue when you barely talk. They raised me and shipped me off to college. That's pretty much it. Actually, it's a bit more complicated than that, but my current relationship with my parents is more my fault than theirs.

Once something is broken and more and more time passes, it's hard to remember how to piece it back together. It's difficult to see what things were like before, so much so that you feel like you aren't missing out on anything. Or even worse, that things are better now. That's my relationship with my parents. That's my life in general. I was destroyed four years ago, utterly obliterated, and life has been fine. Just fine. A word that should be erased because it holds nothing but an empty truth. Audra and this baby present a light at the end of this dark tunnel I've been on for so long. I have no choice but to go towards it.

A few minutes pass in silence. "How old are you, anyway?"

"Twenty-three."

That makes me raise my head. "You're older than me?"

She giggles. "Yeah, is that a problem?"

"No, I just didn't realize that you were older. So, is this your last year?"

Audra nods. "I got a little behind, but yeah."

"What's your major?"

"Marketing. Yours?"

"Computer Science." I watch for the surprised reaction I know is coming. Her eyes widen, her eyebrows raise, and her mouth parts. Instead of waiting for a response, I add, "No more talking. I need to get more work done."

We work in silence for the most of the remaining time I'm there. Audra gets up a few times to find something to munch on.

"I getting a few days without you around?" Audra teases with a smile as I start packing my things up.

"Yep. Don't be too excited. I'll probably call to check in, make sure you're doing all right." My stomach is already in knots about having to leave. I can't help it. Bad things happen when I'm not around.

"You're a worrier, aren't you? Never would have guessed."

"Yeah, me either. You don't mind if I call while I'm gone?" I don't want to aggravate her when we seem to be doing so well.

"No, I don't mind, but you'll probably get the same answers each time." She smiles.

"That's okay."

Audra walks me to the door. "Oh, I can't remember the exact date now, but I do have an appointment coming up. It's only a checkup. I'll text you the date and if it doesn't work for you, let me know and I'll change it."

"Thanks. See you later, Audra."

"Bye, Neil." I'm halfway down the hallway when her voice calls, "Hey, Neil?" I turn to face her. "You should really go ahead and tell your parents. It's their grandchild, after all."

I nod, but don't make any promises.

CHAPTER 10

Grant

THE LOCKER ROOM is subdued with a loss hanging over our heads. I sit on the bench with my head in my hands, replaying some of my mistakes, so I can make sure it doesn't happen again.

"Hey, Grant, head up, man," Neil says, taking a seat next to me. He's already changed and showered. "It's not like we haven't lost before."

"Yeah, but it's not like I've ever played that badly either." Five. We lost five to zero. I've had a rough night, obviously, and I hate nights like these. It could easily be my worst game.

"We didn't help much, Grant. Shake it off, remember what a badass goalie you are, and maybe we can get a shutout or two this weekend." He grins, ready for the challenge. He's right. We were all terrible tonight.

"Thanks, Neil."

He slaps my shoulder, stands, and leaves. I pull off my shirt and upper pads as some of the other guys start to trickle out. Winston stepped out a few minutes ago, but has popped his head back in.

"Grant, Lucy's out here for you. She said hurry up."

Lucy's waiting for me? Curiosity gets the better of me, so I go ahead out to meet her before it gets any later. Sure enough, she's standing in the hallway, leaning against one of the walls with her camera hanging from her neck. She looks up when she hears me. Lucy looks over my body before focusing back on my face.

"What's up?"

"I need your help with a picture, but we need to do it before the Zamboni runs over the ice. Could you help me? It won't take but twenty minutes, promise."

"Yeah, give me a second." I turn and go down the hallway until I find the man I'm looking for. I politely ask him if he would give me twenty minutes before he resurfaces the ice. Then I return to Lucy and lead the way.

"Thanks," she smiles when she sees me.

"No problem."

When we reach the ice, I step onto it first and turn to take her hand, so she won't slip and fall. She did say she needed my help. I figure she needs me on the ice with her. She mentioned some shot near the net on the walk here. Lucy eyes me carefully as I hold my hand out.

"Grant." My name. That's it, but it's enough to stop me.

"What?"

"You're sweaty."

I run a hand over my short, wet hair, and look down at myself. My skin shines where the light reflects the layer of sweat over me. "Well, yeah. I just finished a game, Lucy."

She reaches out and runs her fingers down my arm, over the slick sweat. Her touch raises goosebumps along my skin. "Are you sure we won't get in trouble?" Those blue eyes come back up to me.

"If we keep standing here, talking, then I can't make that promise." No one will really care that we're here, but it's fun to see that flash of panic in her eyes. I wipe my hand over my pants and stick it back out, waiting.

"Couldn't you have at least worn a shirt?" she mumbles, taking my hand as I glide over the ice while she walks slowly over to my cage. I smile, but refrain from saying something. "I need to sit up here to get the angle I want, but I need help doing that." I nod to show her I'm listening. "And don't let go once I'm up there. I might tilt and fall over."

"You won't, but I'll hold onto your hips, just in case."

"And no funny business," she adds.

I laugh. "If you're sure that's what you want," I tease. Somehow, I'm always doing what she wants, and I honestly don't mind. I enjoy it, and I have thought about asking her out on an actual date, but she makes me nervous. So freaking nervous and I worry that if I set the pace, so to speak, I'd lose what we already have. What Lucy wants is what I'll give her. Too bad she doesn't know this yet.

Lucy snaps her head over to look at me, almost losing her balance. "I don't want to fall, Grant!" She clutches her camera tighter, choosing not to comment directly on what I said.

As we come to a stop with her standing in between me and the net, I grab her hips, one of her hands going to my shoulder for balance. I lift her up to sit on the net and murmur, "I'd never let you fall, Lucy."

"Thanks," she whispers.

The air is suddenly too heavy, so I clear my throat. "Is this where you want to be?"

"Hold tight," she orders despite what I told her. I squeeze her hips, ducking a little, as she lifts her camera to check. "Perfect."

"Do you want me to bend down so I'm out of the shot or move behind the net and hold you from there?"

"Just bend down. I might fall while you're moving back and forth."

I crouch a little bit, enough to be out of her shot, still holding her hips, but not too far down. It's an awkward position to be in as her camera clicks away. Maybe conversation will help. "Why this shot tonight?"

"I wanted your view, but a little higher. Think one day you could get the guys out here for a few with people on the ice?"

"I can try," I answer honestly. No telling how many favors I might have to do to get them out here.

"Neil, at least, if he will." Lucy leans over, her camera over my shoulder.

"What's so special about him?" Wasn't I her favorite to photograph? Why am I even asking that question?

At this, she leans back to look at me with a blank expression. "He's the captain." A blush takes over her cheeks before she even finishes. "He would be perfect for it." Well, then. "I've got enough, I think. Plus, that guy is looking impatient."

I look over my shoulder at the guy waiting to finish his job. Without a word, I set her back down on the ice, take her hand, and lead her back off. Her voice is so low that I almost think I'm hearing things.

"I think I like you sweaty."

"Do you want a picture?"

"No." We step off the ice, and I turn to face her. "Thank you, again. I'm sorry that y'all lost tonight."

"You're welcome, and it's no big deal. Losing is part of the game." I grin and add, "I should probably go finish changing, so I can shower and stop being so sweaty." I smile wider when Lucy gives me a small one in return with a blush.

"Please, go do that. I'll catch you later, Grant. I have pictures I need to edit."

My stomach grumbles. "Hey, do you want to grab something to eat with me?"

"I'm not really hungry, but if you don't mind running me by my dorm for my laptop, I'll go with and do my edits while you eat."

"Great. You can wait in here while I shower, if you want. I'm the only one left, so it'll be fine."

She follows me into the locker room and takes a seat on the bench near my locker. I remove my skates as she pulls out her phone to text someone. I almost want to tease her that she's probably texting Patrick to let him know, but I don't. A few minutes later, I'm heading to the showers for a quick wash.

When I return, fully dressed, Lucy has her head down, most likely flipping through some of the shots she took tonight.

"Ready?"

She looks up with a smile and stands. I grab a few of my things before we head out. Not much is said as we run by campus for her laptop and then drive to a fast food place. Lucy goes on to grab a table while I order. Her eyes are trained on her computer screen when I take a seat.

"Did you get some good shots?" I question.

"Yeah, I guess."

"You guess?" I raise my eyebrows at her.

Lucy sighs and talks while I eat. "I kind of feel bad that my photos are actually really good because y'all lost. It almost makes me want them to be terrible."

"That good, huh?" She turns her laptop around to show me how good they are. And I mean, they are fucking fantastic. "Wow, Lucy. What sport are you wanting do once you graduate?"

"I'm not sure anymore. I enjoy baseball, but I was set on football because of my brothers and I did like it more. But now..." She stops like she's thinking it through.

"You like hockey that much or you don't like any of them anymore and you want to try a new sport?"

Lucy looks up at me from her laptop. "I like hockey that much." A grin quickly appears on my face. Before I can add anything, Lucy continues, "There's something about it that football and baseball don't have. It's highly physical, but somehow almost graceful. I might not understand most of it, but I'm still drawn to it more than the others." I nod, understanding what she means. "What do you want to do after college, Grant?"

I clear my throat before answering, "I want to be a history teacher."

She doesn't even look surprised. "That makes sense. You were reading a historical fiction book that day in the library, right?"

"Yeah, I was. I've always loved history, so I think being a teacher would be a good fit for me."

"Hey, Luce," Jonathan says as he walks up to our table, a girl on his arm. He sends a subtle glare my way. "Grant." Hey, at least he acknowledges me before focusing on Lucy again. "Surprised to find you here."

"You're always surprised, Jon," she laughs. Lucy turns her attention to the girl. "Hey, how are you? I haven't seen you in a while."

"Pretty good," the girl answers. "We'll have to get together sometime for a girl's night out or something."

"Yeah, sure." Lucy nods.

"All right, well, I just wanted to come say hey and tell Grant to make sure you get back to campus safely."

God, I hate this guy. "I'll even tuck her into bed, if you want, Jonathan."

Just as I figured, that pisses him off. Lucy stands, hugs him, and kisses his cheek before he can respond. "I'll see you later, Jon. Love ya."

"Love ya too, Lucy," he replies before turning and walking away.

Lucy starts giggling once he's out the door. "That was funny, but you made him mad. I'm glad he left though."

"Why? I thought you loved your brothers?"

"Oh, I do, but he's ridiculous sometimes and I don't like his girlfriend."

I raise my eyebrows at her. "Really? Didn't y'all plan to hang out only a second ago?" Okay, I'm officially confused.

"Yeah, but it won't ever actually happen. That's my brother's girlfriend and unlike them, I try to be polite. He won't stop dating her because I don't like her and I wouldn't want him to either. So I smile and get along with them regardless."

Nodding in understanding, I ask, "What don't you like about her then?"

"My brother could do better," is all she says.

"Are you coming with the team this weekend?" A change of subject is needed, it seems, because Lucy doesn't look like she's going to say more.

"Yeah, I'll be there," she answers with a smile.

MY PARENTS ARE going to be at one of my games this weekend since Thanksgiving is in two weeks and I'm not coming home for dinner. This isn't new. I usually stay here for the holidays. Sometimes, I'll go to the Lanier's. Anyway, I've been thinking about what Audra said, but something is holding me back. It's not a conversation I want to have right now, but I still have to have dinner with them, which is why I'm walking into a restaurant. Maybe I should go ahead and tell them.

"Hey, son," my mother smiles when I find their table and take a seat.

"Hey, Mom, Dad," I lift my lips at them.

"We went ahead and ordered a salad for you," she says.

"Thanks." Not that I wanted a salad, but it'll work.

"That was one hell of a loss the other night," Dad

starts the conversation with a glare from my mom because he cussed. "I hope you've regrouped for tonight's game."

"Yeah, we have. It wasn't our night, but we're ready to come back and win."

"Neil," my mother rests her hand on my arm, "are you getting enough sleep?" She lifts her thumb to brush under my eye. "You look a little tired. You aren't overdoing it with hockey, are you?"

"No, Mom, I'm not. It's been a busy week, that's all."

She nods and lets it go. Surely, I don't look that bad. I slept the whole ride here. Mom is probably imagining things. She's where I get my worry from. And that makes me think about Audra. I manage small talk with my parents, the conversation staying on school and hockey and their jobs. They don't ask if I'm seeing anyone or what I'm doing in my spare time. School and hockey are all we talk about. That has been the limit of our conversations for a while now. Not like I can place all the blame on them because it's my fault too.

Memories swirl around while I try to stay focused. But it makes me anxious, especially when my dad says something about asking for the bill, so we can leave.

Clearing my throat, I figure this is it. "Actually, I need to inform you about something before we go."

They glance nervously at one another and Mom says, "You know you can tell us anything, Neil."

Yeah, okay. We'll see. I haven't forgotten what happened the last time they said that. "I've, um, not been the nicest guy lately, in terms of girls. There's been a lot of them to, uh, be a notch in the bedpost, I guess. Anyway, a girl showed up not too long ago and she's six months pregnant."

My mom looks like she's seen a ghost, her eyes wide, and her face pale. Dad almost looks pissed with his lips in a firm line, but otherwise, he's expressionless.

"You didn't find out immediately?" he asks. I shake my head. "Are you sure it's yours?"

"She says it is, and I believe her."

Dad shakes his head. "You need a paternity test, Neil. You don't need to take care of a kid that isn't yours. There doesn't need to be any doubts now or down the road. If she won't do that, then we can get a law-"

"She's willing," I interrupt, annoyed with his tone.

"What's her name? Maybe you should come home this year, Neil, and bring her so we can meet her," Mom finally speaks, though her words are seeped with uncomfortableness.

"Audra Garcia." I glance at my watch, purposely ignoring the rest of what my mom said. She doesn't really mean it anyway. "I'll talk to her about the test, Dad. I need to get back to the rink, though."

We quickly wrap things up with reluctance and relief from my parents, and once I'm back at the arena for pregame warm ups, I call Audra for the second time today.

"Oh, look, it's you again," Audra chuckles.

I roll my eyes at her. "How are you doing?"

"The exact same as the last time you called, but I've had a cramp or two in my legs since. I've actually taken Sunday off from work because I want to lay around and be lazy all day." She sighs and sounds a bit more serious. "I'm exhausted, Neil."

"Well, make sure you rest then. I'll be by sometime Sunday, okay?" I want to add that we need to talk, but it can wait until I actually get there.

"Yeah, that sounds fine."

Bo, Winston, and Grant are walking my way, so I wrap up my conversation. "I need to go. See you later, Audra." As soon as she says goodbye, I hang up.

"You're looking secretive, Neil," Winston laughs. "Got a girl we don't know about?"

"Nope. Y'all ready for the game?" I ask as we all begin heading to the locker room to change.

"Of course," Bo answers and the others nod.

We all catch sight of a black-haired girl by the locker room door. "Isn't that Lucy Kennedy?" I ask Grant.

"Yeah, she traveled with us because the paper still needs coverage. She rode over here with all of us. Where have you been?" he jokes.

"Lost in my head, I guess," I mumble.

Lucy smiles once we reach her. "Hey, guys. Hey, Grant." Looks like he gets his own special greeting.

We all reply back to her, but go on into the locker room. Except Grant, of course. He stays behind to talk to Lucy. As we change into our gear, all of our other teammates are already in here. Grant walks back in, muttering something under his breath before he starts to change.

"I need a favor," he finally says.

"What does Lucy want you to do now?" Winston laughs.

Grant throws his glove at him. "She doesn't ever ask for much," he retorts.

"At least she didn't ask you to go buy tampons," I chuckle, directing my gaze to Winston, remembering that I saw him in the store. My comment drags laughs from everyone as they start picking on Winston, who glares at me.

Once they calm down, Bo returns the conversation to

Grant. "What does she want?"

"Some shots with a couple of us before the game. Particularly, you, Neil, Winston, and Vincent. She said it'll take like two seconds."

"She can catch us on our way to the ice, but it better be quick. We don't want to piss Coach off. I'll let her know. I need to go find Coach anyway." He mentioned he wanted to speak with me, so I better do that now that I'm dressed.

Grant says thanks, and I step into the hallway to let Lucy know before going to find Coach. He's in a little office nearby, jotting down some notes.

"Hey, you wanted to speak with me?"

He smiles and says, "Yeah, have a seat for a moment." Once I do, he continues. "You know that I keep a close eye on all my players." I nod, wondering where he's going with this. "Instructors send me any red flags if they want me to be aware of something out of the ordinary. A few of your instructors have informed me that you've turned in a few assignments late and Bo said you're working a night job. This coming after you almost started a fight with Winston during practice, I wanted to see what's going on."

If I was standing up, I would be pacing. "I was out of line that day with Winston."

"I know," he interrupts. "I don't want any stalling, Neil. I want to be informed on my players, so let's hear it."

Sighing, I run a hand over my face. "I've gotten a girl pregnant, so things have been a bit stressful since I found out. I'm working, trying to get to know her better because I didn't really know her before, and I got a little behind, but I'm caught up now."

He nods in understanding. "How far along is she?"

"Six months now."

He nods again. "Well, make a schedule to manage your time better. You don't need to get behind on homework. Keep me updated, Neil."

"I will."

"Good. Go get everyone and meet me on the ice."

I do that, gathering the guys for Lucy's picture. She wanted us together and smiling and then quick individual shots. It took longer than two seconds, that's for sure. Thankfully, Coach doesn't say anything to us. With a deep breath, I step onto the ice, focusing solely on what it'll take to get a win.

CHAPTER 11

Winston

I GRUNT AS a guy slams me into the boards. Son of a bitch, these guys are killing me. My legs work on double time to push me forward to regain possession of the puck. There's two minutes left in the third and we're tied 1-1. I'm tired and not one to normally complain about hockey, but I'm ready for this damn game to be over. I steal the puck and pass it to Neil, who passes it to Vincent. He passes it to Bo, who ends up giving it back to Neil to slap it in!

Thank God.

We've got a lead.

Now, we need to hold onto it for a little bit longer. The puck travels down the ice towards Grant, who's ready and waiting. He's been killin' it tonight. This team we're playing against has been hounding him, testing his every ability, waiting for him to slip up. And he's only slipped once. We regain possession and get the puck away from him as the seconds countdown, leading to the buzzer.

I bump my stick against Grant's leg in congrats as we head back to the locker room. He especially seemed to need this win after the loss the other night. Although, he did seem fine once Neil talked to him. The room is buzzing from the win, but I'm too tired to be a part of it. Faintly, as I change, I remember what Maddie told me before I left, so I send her a quick text.

Me: How are you doing without me? Here's your chance for a half-naked pic! Lol

Her reply is almost instant.

Maddie: Going to go with no pic. I might orgasm on the spot. ;) Bahaha

I laugh, shaking my head with wonder at her. She's not sticking to our plan. Friends aren't supposed to say things like that.

**Me: True. I'm a damn good looking hockey player.
Maddie: Speaking of, y'all win?**

I reply that we did.

Maddie: You won & I got a B on my test! :D How are we going to celebrate? ;)

Could a winky face be deceiving? I want to punch

myself as soon as the thought passes my mind. This is the problem with texting. There is too much room for misinterpretation. Is it a harmless, little sign of flirting or are there dirty thoughts behind that wink? Or maybe Maddie is just a winky face addict. That is the second one she's sent me in this conversation.

Me: How do you want to celebrate?

There. Now she can tell me her intentions. While I wait for a reply, we load up onto the bus, heading to our hotel for the night. Grant, Neil, Bo, and I are all sharing a room. Bo seems to be in his own world, Grant has snuck over to Lucy's room for a bit, and Neil has stepped out to make a phone call.

"Who does he keep calling?" I ask. Normally, I wouldn't care, but Neil has been almost suspicious behaving, and it's making me curious.

Bo shrugs. "If he wanted us to know, he'd say something, you know that."

I guess. Neil doesn't hide anything, but he doesn't go out of his way to share it either. Funny how Bo included himself into that "us" when I'd bet my life that he already knows what's going on with Neil. Something is up. He's gone more than usual, makes secretive phone calls, and is working his ass off.

"He's not gotten himself into any trouble, has he?"

Bo finally looks at me from his channel surfing. "No. You're starting to sound like Grant with all your questions." He chuckles and resumes flipping through the channels.

Neil comes back in, his face tight, looking a bit concerned. Remembering Bo's comment, I don't ask any questions. Neither does he. Neil grabs a change of clothes and disappears into the bathroom. Grant walks in with a smile on his face.

"What the hell is wrong with you?" Bo jokes.

"Did Lucy show you her appreciation for fulfilling the favor?"

Grant cuts me a look that could kill. "Shut the hell up."

"Someone's touchy about their girl," Neil comments, coming out of the bathroom.

"She's not my girl," he defends himself, making us laugh.

Neil shrugs. "Could be worse. You could be like Winston."

"Will you stop with that?" I wish he had never seen me in the store that day.

As Neil goes to lay down, he surprises the hell out of all of us. "Fine. I give you props for buying tampons for a girl you aren't even dating. You should be proud of it actually."

He's stunned us with what he said. I don't think any of us knows what to say. He turns off the lamp, so we begin to change for bed as well. Maddie finally texts me back, and I read what she said.

Maddie: I've always wanted to have a campout in the backyard.

Seriously? I text her back and tell her to count on us doing that one day soon before I settle in for the night.

LAST THING I expect to find when we get home on Sunday is Maddie sitting on the front porch steps. She smiles when she sees us and the guys go in ahead of me. I sit next to her on the steps.

"Hey," she says.

"Hey. What are you doing here?"

"Depends." Maddie looks a little anxious as her knee starts bouncing like it did that night on the bench.

"On?"

"If you have plans today." When I shake my head, she blows out a steady stream of air like she was holding it in. "Then you're hanging out with me."

I grin. "You aren't going to ask if I want to? Did you miss me that much?"

Maddie glares at me, stuffing her hands into the kangaroo pocket of her hoodie. "Don't be an ass, Winston. I need a *Madea* day again. So are we going to freeze our asses off or watch some movies?"

Standing, I hold out my hand to her. She takes it, and I pull her up before leading her inside. I keep her hand in mine as we walk to my room, Neil and Bo heading out for their Sunday routine.

"What are y'all about to do?" Grant asks with nothing but genuine curiosity, leaning against the door to his room. That's how all his questions come across, with pure curiosity.

"Watch a *Madea* movie. Maybe you can call Lucy and we can all watch it together."

"Sure, that sounds like fun. I'll call her." He disappears into his room, and I face Maddie.

"Get the movies and I'll fix some popcorn."

She smiles. "Thank you, Winston." Maddie places her

hand on my shoulder for leverage and pushes herself up with her tiptoes to kiss my cheek. She quickly walks around me and into my room before I can react. I head into the kitchen to get started on that popcorn. Grant appears moments later, saying that Patrick is bringing Lucy over.

"What's going on between you two? Seriously."

"What's going on with you and Maddie?" he counters, grabbing a drink from the fridge.

"What are y'all talking about?"

We turn to find Maddie with her hand propped on her hip and the DVDs in her hand. I almost feel like I've been caught red-handed stealing a cookie from the cookie jar when my mother specifically told me I couldn't have one.

"Winston thinks there's something between Lucy and me. I was trying to piss him off," Grant explains.

Maddie seems to shrug it off, hopping onto the counter next to me. "Well, why haven't you made your move yet, Grant? What's holding you back?"

He moves to sit at the kitchen table. "Maybe I don't want to date Lucy." His eyes are on the table, and I say exactly what I'm thinking.

"I call bullshit. You're just chicken because of what she said at the game."

Grant shakes his head. "That's not it. Why are you ganging up on me, Maddie? Has Lucy said something to you?" There's a bit too much interest in his voice.

Maddie shrugs a shoulder. "I think she likes you and you should ask her out already."

He shakes his head again just as there's a knock on the door. I grab a bowl and the popcorn, almost forgotten in the microwave, and Maddie leans over to whisper in my ear conspiratorially while I try not to think about how close her lips are to my skin.

"Do you think he's really too scared to ask? Or do you think there's something going on we don't know about?"

"Not sure. Grant asks questions and rarely ever gets asked any." I turn the conversation back to her. "Do you get homesick often? Has this happened before? You know you'll be home soon, right?"

She rests her chin on my shoulder, it's digging into me a little when she talks. "I know. Maybe I wanted an excuse to hang out with you." Maddie hops down and goes to meet with Lucy and Grant in the living room. I hear her greet Lucy, "What?! No camera? I'm proud of you, Lucy."

I roll my eyes, finally entering the living room with a bowl of popcorn. Grant and Lucy are already sitting on the couch while Maddie pops in the DVD. I sit next to Lucy, giving her the popcorn so it's in the middle.

"Hey, Winston," she greets.

"Hey, Lucy," I reply. Maddie turns around and frowns. "What?"

"If I sit over here, I'll feel lonely and won't have access to the popcorn."

"Come sit with me then."

Maddie raises an eyebrow but walks over, taking a seat in my lap. I pull the lever on the side of the couch to make the foot come up. Maddie moves, so most of her upper body is on my right side.

"Happy?"

She nods as Grant presses play on the remote. Lucy looks a little uncomfortable, but doesn't say anything. As the movie starts, Maddie gets really comfy, which only distracts me. She'll reach for some popcorn and in between munching on that, she's got a hand at the top of my left thigh. As if sitting on my lap isn't enough distraction. Why did I even suggest this? I should have sat in the other chair by myself and let Maddie sit here. Her thumb keeps moving back and forth, driving me crazy.

I don't really want to draw attention to the fact that she's doing this and that I want her to stop, but if she doesn't, she might start feeling something beneath her. So when she goes for more popcorn, I place my own hand on my thigh to prevent her from putting hers there again. All I can seem to think about is what she said. That maybe she wanted to come hang out with me. Maddie consumes my thoughts until the damn movie is over.

"I'm hungry," she states. "Why don't we all go out to eat?"

Lucy glances at Grant, who smiles and says, "Can you survive without your camera for that long?"

She slaps his shoulder and he laughs. "That sounds like fun," Lucy tells Maddie.

"Great," I cut in, pushing the foot back down. "Maddie, up." I can't stand another moment of her in my lap. She was too cozy there, too touchy-feely, and enough is enough. When she stands up, I subtly take a deep breath of relief.

Grant offers to drive, so we head out to a restaurant across town. Everyone in fucking town must be here because we have to wait for a table and there's no sitting room left. We huddle in a corner, standing pretty close together. Maddie suddenly wraps her arms around my waist in a side hug, she tilts her head back to look at me. Absentmindedly, I put my hand on her lower back. I wish I could slide it lower into her back pocket, but I can't do that.

"Thanks for letting me hang out with you."

The way she says it makes it seem like she means because she really was homesick. But I want an answer, damn it. I lean down, thankful she lifts herself on her tiptoes, and my lips brush her cheek as I ask, "Because you were homesick? Or a different, better reason?"

She grins at me. "Both."

Maddie doesn't remove her arms until she and Lucy excuse themselves to the restroom.

Grant

"NOTHING GOING ON, huh?" I chuckle and shake my head at Winston.

"She's confusing the hell out of me, Grant. We're supposed to be friends." He rubs his hand on the back of his neck, and I notice that he really does look torn about it.

"Throw caution to the wind then. Ask her out," I suggest.

"Shouldn't I be telling you that?"

I shake my head again. "No, I'm pretty sure caution is needed."

"Caution for what?" Lucy asks curiously as they rejoin us.

"A situation with Neil," I lie.

We're saved from any further questions when we're finally called because our table is ready. Part of me is surprised as hell that Lucy is even here, but then again, we had fun this weekend. She sits next to me in the booth, close enough that she isn't on the outer edge, but far enough away that we won't bump elbows while eating. After the waitress takes our orders, I notice that unlike us, Maddie is sitting dangerously close to Winston. Hopefully, he'll take my advice because it sure seems like she wants him to.

"How's training going for the run?" Maddie asks Lucy with a big smile. "I'm so excited. Grant, you should do it with us! Winston's too much of a loser." She gently pokes him in the ribs.

I shrug her off as Lucy answers, "It's going good. How many people are they expecting?"

"Over a thousand have already signed up. It's supposed to be huge."

Lucy swallows hard and tries to cover it by taking a sip of water. Wanting to comfort her, I pat her thigh twice, but before I can remove it, she covers my hand with her own. Lucy hasn't been a touchy kind of person, so her action surprises me. She doesn't ask me about running with them, though.

"How long is a 5K anyway?" Winston questions.

"3.1 miles," Lucy says.

"Is it your first run?" he adds.

Lucy nods as our food arrives. She finally releases my hand, so we can eat. Our conversation breaks in two as Maddie and Lucy continue talking and Winston and I focus on more important things. Like food.

"How did your date go, Lucy?" Maddie asks, catching everyone's attention. She gives me a quick pointed glance, like this is evidence that I should make my move soon before someone else does.

I turn my head to look at Lucy, whose cheeks are

flaming red. "Date?" I repeat. She never mentioned it to me, but then why would she?

"Yeah, I set her up with someone last week," Maddie inputs. "I can't believe I forgot to ask you about it!"

Lucy looks around the table, realizes she has everyone's eyes on her, and stumbles over her words. "Um, I, uh, didn't go. Sorry, Maddie."

"How come?"

"Seriously, Maddie? He..." Lucy slides her eyes over at me briefly before shaking her head. "He just freaked me out."

Maddie looks confused, like that's not possible, but I know firsthand that it doesn't take much to freak Lucy out. And that guy must have done a number if she didn't bother going out with him. Honestly, that makes me feel pretty good about myself because I've said the not-so-right thing to Lucy before and she still hangs out with me. Conversation seems stilted after that and soon we're going back to the house.

"I can take you back to campus, Lucy," I offer as I park. I need to go to the library anyway, so it won't be out of my way.

"Thanks." She looks into the backseat. "I'll text you later, okay?" she tells Maddie. I see Maddie nod in my rearview and then she and Winston are getting out and heading inside. When we're on the road again, Lucy says, "Maddie's something else, isn't she?"

I laugh. "What makes you say that?"

"She's very outgoing, I guess. I mean, right after we went to the game, she wanted to set me up with that guy and..." Lucy shivers like she's cold.

"That bad?" I question curiously.

"I'm probably overreacting, but he was a little on the creepy side to me when we were texting. I feel bad though."

"Why?"

"I canceled last minute," she answers as I park near her building.

"Don't feel bad, Lucy." I reach over to squeeze her knee, earning myself a smile.

"Thanks. I'll catch you later, I guess."

I wait until she disappears into the building before I leave for the library. I'm still not so sure about asking Lucy out myself, and I would like to relax for a bit after this weekend. After finding my favorite, secluded table, I take a seat and pull out my latest read. Not even an hour passes with me hunched over the table, reading, before I start hearing that subtle clicking noise.

Lucy.

That sneaky girl. A smile quirks up the corners of my mouth, and I try not to let her know that I've noticed she's here, but it's followed by a sigh to my left.

"You heard me." She sounds so upset that I chuckle.

I turn to find her exactly where I saw her the last time. "Did I ruin it?"

"Yeah, sort of," she says as she walks over to the table. "You ruined the shot I wanted, but you still gave me a good one."

She only has her camera with her, so I ask, "Do you ever come here to study? Or just to find people to photograph secretly?"

"Do *you* ever come here to study?" she fires back, pulling my book from my hands to read the back.

"Sometimes, just not today." I take my book back.

"Well, I'll let you go back to reading and I'll go back to secretly photographing people. Later, Grant."

I laugh as she stands and walks away. Forget Maddie. Lucy's something else, that's for sure.

NEIL

"WHAT ARE YOU doing for Thanksgiving this year, boys?" Mrs. Lanier asks as we wrap up another Sunday dinner.

"Please come eat with us, Neil. Please, please, please," Alice begs. "Bo can come too, right, Mom?"

Mrs. Lanier laughs. "Of course."

"I'm going to see my parents, actually. Thanks for the invite, though," Bo tells Alice.

"Neil? *Please*," Alice tries one more time. "You could invite Audra! When is the baby coming anyway? When can I meet her and the baby? Have you picked a name yet?"

"Calm down," I laugh. "One question at a time. The baby will be here in February and we don't have a name yet. I don't know about Thanksgiving, Alice."

She frowns. "You'll be here for my birthday, won't you?"

"Of course! I wouldn't miss it for the world," I tell her.

She smiles, hugs me, and then looks to her mom. "Can I go play now?"

"Sure, sweetie."

Once she's out of the room, Mr. Lanier asks if I've told my parents yet. I sigh. "Yeah, I told them this weekend. I don't think they are exactly thrilled, and they want a paternity test. She said she would understand if I wanted one, but..." I trail off, not finishing my sentence. I'm a bit nervous about bringing it up to Audra, despite what she said.

"I'm sure it'll be fine," Mrs. Lanier reassures me.

I repeat her words in my head as I play with Alice as promised, as I take Bo back to the house, and as I drive to Audra's. Those words become my mantra until I knock twice on her door.

"Come in," I hear Audra yell from the other side of the door. When I walk inside, her mother is in the kitchen cooking, and she's laying on the couch with her feet propped up.

"Feet bothering you?" I question, lifting them so I can sit down, placing them in my lap.

"Yeah. Ma decided to fix dinner for me. How'd your weekend go? You know, when you weren't calling me?"

I smile, beginning to rub her feet. "It was great, but I'm tired. Does this feel good?" I question, referring to the work my hands are doing.

"I think I love you," she moans, causing me to laugh.

"That has to be the hormones talking," I say as I continue to massage her feet.

Her eyes are closed from the pleasure and she doesn't miss a beat when she hums her agreement. "You're probably right because I've been really horny lately too. But I'll definitely accept the foot massage."

My hands stop moving at her words, and I stare at her. Audra has completely thrown me. I can't believe she would say something like that, especially since she's caught the attention of her mother as well. Her eyes pop open, her head lifts, and she raises an eyebrow.

"Finding it hard to chide a pregnant woman, aren't you?" she asks us, glancing back and forth. "God, I love being pregnant. People won't say anything to some of the stuff that comes out of my mouth. It's like I'm an old lady and they don't think they can say anything because I might burst into tears, which is totally plausible, by the way."

"Yeah, well, don't plan on getting knocked up again at any point in the next five years, Audra," her mother orders.

"No worries, Ma. Keep rubbing, Neil."

Chuckling, I follow orders. Her mother finishes cooking, bringing a plate to Audra minutes later.

"I have to go, Audra." She leans down to kiss her forehead. "Call if you need me."

"Thanks, Ma. Really, thanks."

"You're welcome. Maybe next time, we can get to know each other better, Neil."

"That sounds great, Mrs. Garcia," I reply.

She and Audra exchange goodbyes before she leaves. Audra pulls her feet from my lap to sit up, so she can eat. It looks like some sort of creamy soup.

"Feel free to fix yourself a bowl, Neil," she offers.

I decline, having just eaten. Maybe this will be a good time to bring up the test. For a moment, I watch her purse her lips to cool down her spoonful of soup. Part of me is extremely relieved because Audra isn't too bad to be around. She's been easy to get along with and hanging out with her has almost been enjoyable. Shaking my head and clearing my throat, I decide to get it over with.

"I saw my parents over the weekend."

"Really? Did you tell them about the baby?"

"Yeah. They are insisting on a paternity test." I watch her carefully for any ounce of a bad reaction. She shouldn't give me one, but who knows.

Audra nods in agreement. "Okay, cool. At least if we do it now and you know, then you can't ever bring it up when we get into an argument or use it as an excuse to leave me high and dry with a baby."

And there goes how good I felt about things. Not like I can blame her for saying shit like that. On the other hand, just because I'm a guy who has fucked around a lot, doesn't mean I'm a terrible person with no morals.

Or maybe it does.

What the fuck do I know?

I clench my jaw to refrain from saying something I'll regret because it'll probably make her cry. That's the last thing I want to do. But my mind won't stop thinking. The girls all know that there's nothing between me and them and that my intentions are only to have sex. Nothing more, nothing less. That has to count for something, right? That I'm honest and upfront? Or does none of that matter because I'm still a shitty guy who will sleep with pretty much any girl? Not that I've had the time to get laid lately...

Maybe it's not even about that. Maybe it's because I

told her to give the baby up for adoption that day. Audra may have that locked in her mind, and she's really worried that I'll leave her "high and dry" at the first opportunity. Either way, I'm pissed. If I was going to do that, I would have already.

"Sorry, Neil. That was wrong of me to say, wasn't it?" Audra looks genuinely remorseful, but I don't give two shits. I'm not here to impress her. I'm here because I need to know my kid's mom so we'll be able to raise her together.

"It doesn't matter. How about we keep our talk limited to things concerning the baby and not what kind of people we are?"

"Yeah, okay," she mutters.

We're silent as she finishes her bowl. She sets it on the table and leans back, getting comfortable. I don't think I can open my mouth yet, so I keep quiet. Audra seems to know this because she stays quiet too. When I finally feel ready, I turn to look and find Audra asleep.

Ugh, great.

Audra's killing me! She needs to stop falling asleep on me. Her hand moves to her belly, and I wonder if the baby is moving. Gingerly, I place my hand near hers and feel a kick. Moving a little closer, I lean down to whisper.

"Hey, baby girl." I glance at Audra, but she hasn't stirred. "How are you doing? Moving around a lot these days, huh? Your momma might want you to nap too." There's more movement under my hand, and I'm amazed. Part of me feels crazy for talking to her belly, but I can't seem to stop either. "In case you didn't know, I'm your daddy," I continue, talking softly. "Don't listen to all this nonsense your momma is saying either. I wouldn't leave her or you, baby girl. She doesn't know yet that I'm a decent guy. Don't worry. I'll prove it."

With a lot of care not to disturb Audra, I kiss her stomach before leaning back into my seat. I actually feel a little better. Maybe I am going crazy. About thirty minutes pass and she still hasn't woken up. I grab the notepad and pen on the end table and write a note that I left. Quietly, I go to the door, turn the knob, and I'm so close to stepping through the threshold when I hear Audra's voice.

"Neil?"

Turning, I face her, closing the door almost all the way. She's sitting up, watching me. "You were sleeping, so I was going to head home before I have to go into work."

"Oh, sorry about falling asleep on you."

"It's fine. Later." I turn once again, but she stops me.

"Neil?"

"Yeah?" I look at her to see that she's standing now and moving towards me, but she stops about halfway.

"I just wanted to apologize again about what I said."

I give her a little smile. "It's okay, Audra. Promise. I should go, though."

"Right. Bye."

One final time, I turn to leave, opening the door all the way. On the other side stands some chick, who smiles when she sees me.

"Well, hello hottie. Would you like-"

"Don't even!" Audra almost shouts, rushing to stand in front of me, holding her arm out behind her like she wants me to stay back. "He's off limits, Mimi, so don't even say it."

The girl, Mimi, looks me over again. "He's too hot to

be off limits, Audra. Who is he anyway?"

"Neil," I offer. Mimi's eyes widen, and she's connected the dots of how I know Audra. I put my hands on Audra's shoulders and twirl her to face me. "I'll see you tomorrow. Call me if you need anything." She nods. I kiss her temple before stepping around the girls to leave finally, not exactly knowing what to think about this Mimi, Audra's reaction to whatever she was going to say, and the kiss I gave her.

MY EYES ARE trying their hardest to shut as I buckle up. I've just finished working for the night and it's tempting to sleep in my car instead of driving home. The loud ringing of my phone snaps me out of it for now. When I pull it out of my pocket and see Audra's name, panic sweeps through me. What has happened? Why is she calling me so late?

Gulping, I answer, "Audra? Is everything okay?"

"Yeah, everything's fine. I haven't been able to sleep and I'd really hate to bother my parents, so-"

"So you called to bother me?" I chuckle.

Audra laughs softly. "Pretty much. Could you come over? Are you still at work?"

"Just got off, but I can come over if you want me to." Not sure how that will help, but okay.

"Thanks, Neil." She pauses, hesitating before adding, "Would it be too much trouble to stop by the store?"

"No," I answer, cranking my car. Looks like I won't be getting home any time soon. "What do you want?"

"Pretzels."

"Pretzels?" I question as I back out and start heading towards the nearest 24-hour grocery store.

"And cheese sticks. And maybe some chocolate pudding too."

Shaking my head at her, I laugh. "Pretzels, cheese sticks, and chocolate pudding? Anything else?"

"No, I think that's it. Are you sure you don't mind?"

"Not at all. Almost to the store now, so I should be there in twenty or thirty minutes. Text me if you think of anything else, though I can't promise you'll get it. I won't go back to the store after I've left."

"Okay. Thanks, Neil."

"Welcome." I hang up, having the urge to bang my head against my steering wheel. I need sleep. Not to run around, buying things to satisfy Audra's wacky cravings. With a deep breath, I push the negative thoughts away. Those aren't going to do me any good anyway. As fast as I can, I grab what Audra wants, ignore the curious look from the cashier, and go to her place.

It takes her a moment to answer, almost giving me enough time to rest my head on the doorframe. Even a few seconds of sleep would be good. Audra looks relieved when she opens the door and sees me. I hand her the bag as I'm invited in. She rubs her lower back on her way to the kitchen. I go sit on the couch, and she appears moments later with a spoon.

"Sit here," I tell her, patting my thighs twice.

"Why?"

"Just do it."

"I might break your legs." She looks really serious, and I laugh.

"You aren't that big. Sit."

Audra does, placing the bag on the coffee table in front of her, and she leans forward to pull out her item of choice. She goes for the pudding first.

"Do you trust me?" I ask. She shrugs. I rest my fingers on her shoulder and begin to massage. A low moan escapes her lips, causing me to smile. She doesn't say anything as I work my thumbs down her back along her spine. When I get to her lower back, the moan is louder. I swallow hard when I realize the sounds she's making are turning me on.

"God, I forgot how good you were with your hands. First my feet and now this, mmm," she finishes in an appreciative hum.

"Be quiet and eat your food," I mutter.

I keep massaging while she moves on to the pretzels and a cheese stick. My yawning is getting out of control, but Audra hasn't noticed yet. My hands slow as all my energy starts to leave me. I've been up for almost twenty-four hours. Sleep, that's what I need. My eyes droop close, but they peer open when Audra looks over her shoulder at me.

"Oh! God, I'm so sorry. Look at you. You're exhausted and I'm keeping you awake."

Barely. "I'm going to sleep right here, okay? Not a good idea to drive." All my thoughts are revolved around three words: Go to sleep.

Audra stands, nodding, and my body moves almost on its own accord. I lay down, stuffing the throw pillow under my head. My eyes close as a cover is placed over me.

"Do you have a morning class?" I hear.

Not sure if I answer or not before I'm asleep.

Winston

"NEIL DIDN'T COME home?" Bo questions, his brows furrowing.

"Doesn't look like it," I answer, grabbing a bowl for some cereal.

"He's not answering," he comments. I look over my shoulder to see his phone pressed to his ear.

"Should we be worried?" I question with confusion. It's not like Neil hasn't stayed out all night before. He hasn't since he's been working, but hey, maybe he found some chick to bang after work.

"I don't know," Bo replies and I can hear the worry in his voice. "He does get off really late and he would have been up for almost an entire day by the time he got off. He might have fallen asleep while driving..."

"I'm touched you're so worried," Neil voices as he rounds the corner into the kitchen.

"You look like hell," I say, taking a seat at the table to eat. His hair is all over the place and he's still in his rumpled work uniform. He even has bags under his eyes.

Neil groans and sinks into a chair. "Fuck, it's going to be a long day and a long week."

"Where were you?" Bo asks.

Neil quickly looks at me, almost so quickly that I could have missed it if I wasn't already looking at him. "Crashed at a friend's place that's close to work. It was late, and I was too tired to stay awake long enough to drive here."

Bo nods in understanding. "Go shower and be thankful we have the day off from hockey."

Neil folds his arms on the table and rests his forehead on them. "Let me rest here for a minute first."

Again, I wonder why the hell he has a job. He's going to burn himself out, either in school or hockey. We need him in tip top shape and the job is hindering him. I don't know Neil's business, so I can't say anything.

After I finish eating, I go to my room to start on my task for today. I don't have a lot of time before class, but I plan to take advantage of our day off and stop by between classes to get everything ready. Once Maddie went home last night, the plan started to form. Tonight, I'm going to ask her out. I'm going to fix things between us and start anew. At least, I hope so.

My stomach tightens at the thought. For the millionth time, I wonder if I should or should not. This will open a whole new can of worms full of potentially rotten ones. She's Dave's sister. If Maddie said yes and we start dating again, how am I going to tell my best friend? If things go bad, I could lose that friendship. We've been friends for too long. I'm not supposed to find her attractive or even want to ask her out. Pretty sure I'm supposed to view her as my own little sister, but that's never been the case, and certainly isn't now. Not to mention that I have to make up for not defending her all those years ago. We never talked about that, not really, and that's something else we're going to have to do.

Torn barely touches how I feel about it. Yesterday, it seemed as if all Maddie did was find ways to touch me and then Grant had to tell me I should throw caution to the wind. There's a lot on the line if I make this move, though.

My friendship with Dave, my best friend since I was five.

My current friendship with Maddie.

If I lose either of those things, I don't just lose them, I lose their family as well. And I'm as close to them as I am my own parents. With so much at risk, I can guarantee that I'm not going to do anything that could possibly mess things up again. That is, if Maddie says yes.

Grant

"LUCY?" THERE'S A girl who looks just like her laying in the grass, and if it wasn't for her heaving chest, I'd think she was dead. The girl groans in acknowledgement, so I walk over and find that it is indeed Lucy. Her face is flushed, and she's still breathing hard. I start laughing, earning myself a glare, but I can't help it. She looks funny to me. Kneeling, I ask, "Everything okay?"

"I'm dying," she breathes.

"Want mouth to mouth?" It slips out of my mouth without much thought. Lucy groans, but I notice her eyeing the bottle of water in my hand. "Here, let me save you."

I move over to her shoulders, set the bottle down, and lift her shoulders so she's leaning against my chest with part of her back on my bent leg. Lucy rolls her head back onto my shoulder. I reach for the water, remove the cap, and hold it up. "Drink this," I say softly.

Lucy picks up her head and drinks like she's been

thirsty her entire life. She quickly gulps down all my water without pause. When she's done, I remove the bottle from her lips and set it down next to us.

"Thank you. Would it be too much to ask you to carry me to my dorm? I don't think my legs work." She's looking at me now, her face so close. Too close. Lucy looks down and suddenly realizes her skin is slick with sweat. She must have really worked herself to be sweating. "Oh, I'm sweaty, Grant." She tries to pull away, but I keep her where she is.

"I don't mind." Without thinking, I plant a soft kiss on the crook of her neck, tasting the saltiness on my lips. "You like when I'm sweaty. Who's to say I don't like you the same way?"

She laughs. "Not all the time. Sometimes, you really smell." Lucy wrinkles that cute little nose of hers.

"Whatever. What are you doing anyway?" I ask.

"Trying to train for that stupid 5K run, duh. I don't think I'll make it. Maddie's going to be disappointed"

"I'm surprised you haven't asked her or your brothers to help you."

Her laugh is short and harsh. "I didn't ask them because I wanted to do something on my own." She pauses before adding, "Plus, they are mean trainers. Maddie is too, because I did run with her once." She rests her head back on my shoulder.

"So if I offered to help, you'd turn me down?" Lucy is always dragging me into helping her somehow. I never know that I even want to help until the words are already out of my mouth. And I have no freaking clue why I want to do this with her because running isn't my favorite thing to do.

"I'm probably too slow and you'll end up waiting on me."

I laugh. "I'm a slow runner too. We wouldn't have to be fast, Lucy. We only need to be able to finish."

"Well, well, well. What do we have here?" Patrick and Jonathan walk over to us.

Lucy immediately sits up, but she's still leaning against me a little. I wonder if she really is that worn out. Jonathan squints his eyes slightly in a glare. He rubs me the wrong way, and I think I do the same thing to him. Patrick, I can handle. Jonathan, I just want to tell him to go the fuck away. They both cross their arms over their chests and stare down at us when they finally reach us.

"She was dying, and I saved her," I explain.

Their faces blanch, their eyes immediately scanning over her, looking for something. Lucy elbows me in the gut, but I don't understand why.

"He's joking. I went for a run and I'm so not a runner."

"You okay, Luce?" Jonathan asks. There is more to his words, some heavier meaning, but I'm not sure what.

Her shoulders sag as she nods. "Yeah, I'm fine. You two?"

The conversation has shifted to a topic that I'm not aware of. The brothers nod.

"Do you mind if I hang out with Grant tonight instead?" Instead? Instead of what? Why is she asking them for permission? She hasn't even mentioned hanging out to me. I hate when they talk about something only they know about, purposely leaving me out in the cold unknowing. All it does is leave me confused and slightly worried. There is always too much weight to their carefully chosen words.

The brothers glance at me. "Corey won't be happy, Lucy," Patrick sighs.

"Well, he didn't talk to me at all last week, so I don't care."

Jonathan frowns. "But we're always together. I'm sure he has a good reason."

"I don't want to." Her voice is quiet, and her head is down when she says it. I'm surprised they even heard her, but her reply pisses them off and worries them at the same time. What the hell is going on?

"Luce-" Jonathan starts, but Patrick holds up his hand to stop him.

"If she doesn't want to, she doesn't want to, Jon. Leave it alone." He may be younger, but his authoritative, final tone shuts Jonathan up. Patrick bends, reaches out to lift her chin so she'll look at him. "Are you sure?" Lucy nods. "Corey will want to see you no matter what, you know that."

"Tell him to meet me at 8 then. I might still be with Grant, though."

"What are-" Jonathan starts.

"Shut up," Patrick scolds over his shoulder. Jon throws his hands up, curses under his breath, and walks away. Patrick gives a sweet smile to Lucy. "I'll handle them, don't worry. Do whatever you feel you need to do, okay?"

Lucy nods and reaches over to hug him tightly, which presses her breasts on either side of my knee. I probably shouldn't notice, but I do. "I always knew you were my favorite."

Patrick chuckles. "They may be older, but I'm the

wisest when it comes to you. I love you, Luce." He kisses her temple.

"I love you too," she whispers, her voice strained.

Then he stands, waves goodbye, and walks over to a pacing Jonathan. I'm so lost, and I wait to see if she's going to explain. She doesn't.

"So can I hang out with you tonight?" There's a hint of laughter in her tone as she looks at me with hopeful eyes.

I have to ask. There's no ignoring it anymore. I want to know what they were talking about. "Lucy, what-"

The hope disappears and is replaced with pleading as she interrupts me. "Please, don't."

Two words. Two words said with so much desperation that I know immediately that I'll do whatever she wants me to tonight. That's all it takes. Still, I stare at for her a moment.

"What do you want to do?" I finally say.

"I want to be around you and not them, so anything else doesn't really matter. Around *only* you," she corrects. Her words mean something, something big. I'm just not sure what. It feels like she's giving me a gift of sorts, but too many pieces are missing for me to put together what exactly. "Where do you go when you don't want anyone to bother you?"

"The library, but *someone*," I give her a pointed look, "always finds me." I grin and Lucy rewards me with a smile. "Where do you go?"

She dismisses my question easily. "My brothers know all those places. Today, I don't want them to be able to find me until I'm ready."

Ready for what? I want to ask so badly, but she's

asked me not to do so. "There's a sports bar across town and a game will start in about an hour. Want to go there?"

Lucy rests her head against my shoulder, her eyes closed. "No people, remember?"

"No people at all? Even strangers?"

"Especially not strangers," she whispers.

"Neil and Bo will be out for a while. Winston is hoarding Maddie in his room, but we can still go to my place."

"Perfect. I need to shower first though." She looks down at herself and seems to remember that she was running.

"Grab your things and shower there. Then you can ride with me."

"Thanks."

CHAPTER 13

NEIL

"I'M SO SORRY to do this to you, Neil," Audra starts when I answer the phone.

"What are you talking about?" I interrupt, parking at a fast food restaurant for lunch.

"My appointment was rescheduled for this afternoon because the doctor has to make a trip out of town. I tried to get it on a different day when I knew you could come, but I wasn't able to do that. I know you wanted to go. I'm sorry." She sounds near tears, and I hate hearing that.

"What time is the appointment?"

"At one thirty." Shit, she's calling it close. "I know it's last minute, but I got busy at work this morning and couldn't call."

"I only had two morning classes and we don't have practice today, so I can come. Have you had lunch yet?"

"No, I was about to head to my parents' place."

"I'll meet you there, okay?"

After she agrees, I head that way. Today, I'll get to see baby girl, and we'll also have to do the paternity test. At least I feel more rested than I did this morning. I may have dozed during the little break between classes. Tonight when I go to Audra's, we're definitely going to have to work on homework again.

Audra's sitting at the same table as last time, but unlike then, her mother is sitting with her. Audra is facing the front and smiles when she sees me. That's new, or at least, it feels like it. I kiss her temple again before sitting down next to her. I can't help it. She's carrying my baby girl, and she was worried I would be upset that I wouldn't be able to go with her to the appointment. I want her to feel good about things, so a little, innocent kiss there should help with that.

"Hey, Audra. Hey, Mrs. Garcia. Are you eating with us today?" I ask.

"Yes, I am. Audra said you've been very sweet with her." What? When have I been sweet? I've only been like normal and nice. Maybe there's not a difference between nice and sweet. Upon seeing my confusion, she adds, "She told me about last night. I told her she could have called me, that I wouldn't mind and besides, it sounds like you have quite the load on your shoulders. You play hockey, correct?"

"Yes, ma'am. It's really not that much and I didn't mind going to the store for her."

Mrs. Garcia smiles at me. "I don't think we've ever watched a game before. How long have you been playing?"

"Since I was old enough. We have a game Thursday night, if y'all want to come." It's risky inviting them because what if Audra wants to see me afterwards? None of the guys, except Bo and Coach, know about her or the baby.

The waitress brings us a pizza and Audra starts to devour a slice.

"Would you like to go, Audra?"

"Um," she wipes her mouth with a napkin and finishes chewing the bite she took, "I've seen a game before, that's how I eventually ended up meeting Neil." She puts a hand on the top of her stomach. "But if you want to go, then we can. I haven't been to one this season."

Mrs. Garcia smiles. She's obviously looking forward to this. In between eating, she continues to ask questions. "Where are your parents? Do they live around here? What do they do?"

"They live a few hours from here and they own a realty company. We used to live around here, but they moved once I started college. I stay with a couple of teammates in a house they used to rent out." I figured it's best to go ahead and give her all the information before she could ask.

"What are y'all looking to do once the baby comes as far as living arrangements?"

"We haven't talked about that yet, Ma," Audra inputs.

"Then what have you been doing?" She narrows her eyes at me first and then Audra, like we're doing something very wrong.

"We've been trying to get along. I didn't exactly know him before and we didn't start off great. I'm pregnant, Ma. It's not like we're partying or going at it like rabbits." I really don't feel comfortable, sitting here while Audra talks to her mom about sex. Audra takes a sip of water, clears her throat, and adds, "We need to get going. I'll call you later."

She stands, and I follow suit all the way to the doctor's office. While we're waiting, she apologizes for her mother.

"It's okay. Are we changing our living arrangements? Where are you going to put the crib and all the baby stuff? Would you even want to live together? I guess it would be very helpful for those late night wake up calls."

"Wouldn't you want to stay at your place so girls could come and go as you please?" She doesn't say it to offend me, which is a good change of pace. Audra absentmindedly rubs her belly.

"I'm sure if I wanted to sleep with someone, I'd go to her place now. I don't pay rent at my place and it's bigger, so..."

She laughs. "I doubt your friends would like not only a girl in the house, but a baby too. Can we talk about this later, Neil?"

"They could move out, Audra," I tell her, refusing to stop talking about this. I'm here because I'm supposed to help her take care of our baby. How can I do that if she won't even talk about how we're going to do just that?

"You aren't kicking them out. We don't even have to live together! Stop trying to push me into something, Neil. Stop trying to control the situation. You aren't in control, I am. So just stop, okay? Fucking stop already." She's talking too loud and is getting too aggravated.

"Okay, okay," I soothe, wondering why she reacted so severely. I wasn't trying to be in control. All I wanted to do was start talking about this. Maybe she's in the middle of a mood swing or something. "I'm sorry," I add in a soft tone for good measure, noting that she's still rubbing her stomach, looking highly uncomfortable. When she doesn't say anything, I repeat, "I'm sorry, Audra. I didn't mean to upset you."

Her shoulders sag just a little. "It's fine." Her words are slightly clipped, so I drop the topic altogether.

Thankfully, the doctor calls us back. I stay silent throughout her visit, not wanting to further upset her. When he does the ultrasound, I perk up a little. I definitely do not want to miss this. Once my baby girl is on the screen, Audra reaches for my hand and holds it. I don't think I'm breathing. How can I? It's breathtaking. I'm not even sure I pay attention after that. All I know is that as we leave, I have a picture of the sonogram in my hand. It feels like things are sealed now, more real, and as I gulp, I realize that I'm a little excited.

Terrified and worried, but most definitely eager to meet my baby girl. Even if Audra does seem distant as we part for the day.

Winston

I LOOK OVER my room, seeing what Maddie is seeing. My bed has been moved a little closer to the couch. Using my bedposts, the couch, and a lot of duct tape, I've formed a fort with blankets. It's too cold to actually camp outside, so this will have to work. I even have my iPod playing the sounds of crickets chirping and frogs croaking. The lights are off, but there are nightlights lit around the room to put off dim lighting. Plus, I found a bunch of Christmas lights and taped them to my ceiling.

"What's all this?" Maddie asks with confusion.

"We're celebrating my wins and your B. You said you wanted to campout and this is the best I could do without going outside."

She doesn't turn around or say anything. Instead, she moves forward to crawl into the makeshift fort.

"Be careful," I order.

There is a plate of hot and fresh s'mores in there on top of two sleeping bags. I follow in after her on my hands and knees, wishing my bedposts were taller. Maddie has already stuffed her mouth with a s'more. She grins when she sees me, chocolate all over her mouth.

"You are seriously the best, Winston."

I smile and take a s'more too. "I may have a hidden motive."

"Oh?" She raises an eyebrow as she wipes the corner of her mouth with her thumb before sucking off what it just wiped away.

Clearing my throat, I nod, deciding to go ahead and ask. "Would you like to go on a date with me?"

"A date? You're serious?" she questions skeptically.

"Thanks for your enthusiasm. Yes, I'm serious, Maddie!" Maybe this was a bad idea.

"What happened to your 'can't we be friends' and 'you're Dave's sister' crap?" She's surprised more than anything.

"Being friends with you is harder than I ever thought possible."

A slow smile takes over her lips. "You still want to kiss me, don't you?"

She doesn't even know the half of it. Before I can answer, my phone vibrates in my pocket. I pull it out to see a video call from Dave. He hasn't talked to me lately because we've both been busy. He just had to choose the night that I'm with Maddie to call?

"Don't make a sound," I tell her, flashing my eyes up at her. Swiping my finger across the screen, Dave appears. "Hey, what's up?"

"Where the hell are you?"

"I'm kind of in the middle of something."

"Something important?" he asks.

"Everything I do is important."

He laughs and a glance at Maddie shows me she's pissed.

"I'm sure. But fine. Call me later. I need your advice on something."

"Okay," I say before ending the call. Maddie watches me without saying anything. "What?"

"No. You wanted to be friends, Winston. That's what we are. You couldn't even let him know that I'm here now and you think you'll have the balls to tell him if we start dating? My answer is no. I can't believe you." She shakes her head and starts to climb back out, but I grab her hand.

"Maddie," I start, but she interrupts me.

"No, Winston! No. I refuse to go back to hiding a relationship, and it's not like I haven't forgotten what happened either. You knew I hated him calling me that. You didn't stand up for me, not to him, not to that other jerk either. You told me to leave! We had sex the day before and then you told me to go home!

"You haven't asked how or why I lost that weight, Winston. Aren't you the least bit curious? Don't you want to know that after being humiliated by my brother, his friends, and you, that I decided I was sick of it? I couldn't tell anyone why I was upset. I couldn't tell anyone you hurt me or that we were over. I had to deal with that all by myself! And it's all your fault! So I started running and going to the gym to lose weight and to stop thinking about *you*!"

Her voice softens. "Are you seriously so terrified of telling him? Are you that much of a coward? You said you loved me, but you couldn't even fight for me, Winston. Why would I want to go through that all over again? Why would you want to put me through that? You just proved that nothing's changed, Winston."

"Come here." Placing the rest of my s'more back on the plate, I hold my hand out for her. She eyes my hand like it's a shark about to bite her before taking it. I pull her into my lap so she's straddling me. "I'm sorry, Maddie. I'm so sorry. I've hated myself for doing that to you and you're making things confusing now. I said friends, but we're slowly slipping back into what we were. I don't know what to do to make up for what happened because I can't change it. He's been my best friend since I was five, Maddie. It's like I was being made to choose between the two of you and-"

"And you chose him," she interrupts, her eyes watery. "You loved me, but you chose him, Winston." The tears spill over before she rests her forehead against my shoulder, crying freely now.

"I didn't want to," I whisper. "I don't know why I did. And you know that I loved every inch of you. Dave was stupid. You didn't have to change because of him." I turn my head, my nose hitting her hair as I inhale my new favorite smell. "I've missed you so much."

"It feels nice to be missed. If only it mattered."

I lean my head against the couch behind me. Either way, I won't win. Maddie shifts against me, and I know she's sitting up now.

"I sort of get it, Winston, I do, but then again, I don't. You don't want to lose Dave as a friend, but you're willing to lose the person you're supposedly in love with? That doesn't make sense to me."

At this, I lift my head to look at her. "You don't think I love you?"

She shakes her head. "You may have, but it wasn't enough then. That's all I meant." After a pause, she adds, "Why on earth should I give you a second chance?" She places her hands on either side of my neck and rests her forehead against mine. "I want to. God, I want to, but it feels like it would be stupid of me to trust you again. And I meant what I said. I won't hide us. We're either in this all the way or not at all, Winston."

I place a soft kiss to her forehead, and before I can speak, she does.

"You know, I used to think that you kissed me on my forehead because I was short and that was closer to you than my lips."

Chuckling, I kiss her forehead again. "You're partly right."

"So what are you going to do?" she whispers, watching me carefully, a wall already built in case I don't give her the answer she wants.

"Dave's supposed to come up for one of my games. I could tell him then." I can't believe I'm doing this, but I can't let her slip away again. We were damn near perfect together.

"But you want to keep it hush-hush until then? Winston-"

"Only because I want to tell him in person, Maddie."

"You really think he'll be upset? It almost feels like you're overreacting," she tells me.

"I know him better than you do. He won't be happy, but I can convince him that he should be."

She nods, seeming to accept it. With a small smile, she says, "You still haven't answered my question."

"What question?"

She slightly puckers her lips. Oh, yes. Do I still want to kiss her? I lean forward until my lips are mere millimeters from hers.

"What was your question again?" I steal her breath when my lips become a feather-light touch against hers. She blinks a few times, and I barely graze my mouth along her jaw and down her neck. "Your question, Maddie," I remind her.

The sound of doors opening and closing sound down the hall before we hear the shower running.

"Who's here?" she whispers.

"Probably Grant," I answer. Maddie is surprised when I flick my tongue over her skin, kiss it, and then pull away. She swallows hard, and I smile. This is going to be a lot of fun. "You never answered my question either."

"I think we have the same answer."

"We do?"

She nods. "Yes. Both answers are yes." Maddie plucks the beanie off my head, tosses it aside, and then wraps her arms around my neck. "You're positive about this?" All it takes is a nod of my head, and she presses her mouth to mine.

It's hurried and urgent and better than any of my dreams. My hand runs down her back before cupping her ass. She wiggles closer to me, kissing along my jaw before pulling my earlobe into her mouth and gently biting. God, she's going to drive me insane. When her hands go to my side and grab the hem of my shirt, I stop her.

"Maddie, we need to slow down."

"One more." She clutches my sides and kisses me hard one more time, like she said. "I've been thinking about that for a long time."

"Me too." I kiss her forehead before grabbing her hips and lifting her out of my lap. "We need to get back to camping. Time for a scary story, don't you think?" I question, grabbing a flashlight to hold under my chin.

Chapter 14

Grant

WE WERE QUIET for a long time. While she was getting a change of clothes, while we walked to my car, while we drove to my house. I only talked upon our arrival to tell her where things are in the bathroom. I use the down time to think and analyze what's happened. Sure, we've become friends of sorts. Lucy's as comfortable around me as she is around her brothers. We have stolen moments where something changes or happens between us, but we haven't really acknowledged it.

Today means something though. It's a day where she's usually with her brothers and has always been. Their reaction to her saying no made that obvious. This day means something to all of them, and they were none too happy that she was spending it with me instead of them.

The fact that her oldest brother is going to make sure he sees her makes me think that whatever it means, Lucy is at the center of it.

Which brings me back to the next obvious question. One that I may be able to ask. Why did she choose me? Why me over her brothers or her other friends? Is it because I'm the only one in the dark about the mysterious situation? Lucy plops down next to me on the couch, dragging me from my mind. Her hair is wet and in very loose curls around her shoulders.

"Has the game started yet?" she asks, watching the TV for clues, but it's on a commercial.

"It's about to." Lucy scoots closer to me and presses herself into my side, resting her head on my shoulder again while holding my hand in hers. It's an intimate gesture for her. It's just enough to give me the nerve to ask. "Can I ask just one question?"

"I might not answer."

"Why me, Lucy? Why not them?" Straight and to the point.

Lucy sits upright to look at me. She's going to answer, and I'm going to listen to every sound that leaves her mouth. "I'm not sure I can explain it, Grant. My brothers have always made me feel safe, but you make me feel a different kind of safe and that's what I wanted tonight. Not their safety. Yours."

The announcers appear on the TV and Lucy returns to how she was sitting before. That's all I'm going to get. It feels like I got too much though. I make her feel safe? Why does she need to feel safe? There's always so many questions surrounding Lucy. Who she really is under the surface, and sometimes, I think all she lets me see is the surface.

That's not entirely true. Lucy gives me more all the time. It's just in small pieces, and I never know what to make of it or how to put it all together.

"I've never met Corey before."

Lucy frowns. She must have thought we were done talking. I don't even know why I said that. It's not like I want to meet the guy. "He's the worst of the three when it comes to me. Jon bothers you, doesn't he?" I nod. "Then you definitely won't like Corey. Can we watch this? No talking."

We're back to the silence with the exception of the game on TV. She keeps squeezing my hand in hers every couple seconds. It's almost like she's making sure that I'm still here. She's been doing it on and off for about twenty minutes now. When I squeeze her hand back, it catches her off guard, and she looks up at me, a small smile playing on her lips.

"Thank you," she whispers.

"For what?"

She lays her head on my shoulder again. "This."

We're quiet again until midway through the second period. "Still don't know what's going on?" I ask with a hint of laughter.

"Number 25 is about to score. That's what I know."

I'm about to ask her what makes her think that, but I'm interrupted because he scores. Son of a bitch. How did she know that?

"I could tell based on how he's playing. I've learned a lot by taking pictures, even if I'm looking through the lens."

To say I'm impressed is an understatement. Lucy

calls a few more goals before there's a knock on the door.

"That's probably Corey." She stops short of getting up. "Unless you're expecting someone?"

I shake my head and get up to answer the door for her. Standing on the other side is an older version of the other two brothers. "You must be Corey. She's in here."

His mouth is in a firm line as he steps past me to go find Lucy. Well, hello to you too. I hear him say hello to her, but when I reenter the room, Lucy looks like a pouting, angry child.

"What are you doing, Luce?" he asks her cautiously, but there's a lace of suspicion in his voice.

"What does it look like I'm doing?" she snaps. Woah. Never seen this side of her. Maybe this brother brings it out of her.

"That's not what I meant." His voice is low and threatening. Corey sends a glare at me. I'm obviously not wanted here. It's then that I notice he's sitting on my coffee table in front of Lucy with his hands on her knees. Who is he to come here and sit on my coffee table like he owns the place? Okay, it's not mine, but that's not the point.

"Do you want me to give you two some privacy?" My question is directed to Lucy, but Corey answers.

"Yes."

"No," Lucy inputs angrily. "You saw me, Corey. I'm fine. Go home."

"I'm sorry I haven't called you, Luce, but you can't, not today."

She huffs. "I'm pissed at that, but that's not what this is about." Did she say pissed? It fits her mood, but it's too vulgar of a word for Lucy's pretty mouth.

Corey is fuming, but there's something else underneath the surface that's bothering him. I'm clueless because Lucy won't tell me anything, and they are being vague.

"Let me take you back to campus, at least." He wants her away from me. Whether it's because she's with me and not them or if it's so they can talk or both, I don't know.

Lucy sighs. Her voice is full of heartache when she says, "No, Corey."

"Seriously?" he asks incredulously.

I don't know what's going on, but he needs to stop. She doesn't want to go, and he doesn't need to make her feel guilty about whatever it is. "It's time for you to go." Both heads snap to look at me with surprise, but Lucy also looks thankful while Corey still looks pissed. "I'll make sure she gets back safely when she's ready to go."

"Who the fuck are you anyway?" He stands and so does Lucy.

"Corey," Lucy warns. "Patrick understands, I don't get why you and Jon don't."

"Because it's bullshit, Luce. After everything-"

"Leave," she interrupts. Her lower lips is quivering slightly, and I wonder if he sees how much he's upsetting her.

"Damn it. I'm sorry." Corey reaches for her, but she steps towards me and away from him. Now, he looks betrayed. "Luce." It's one word, a plead, an apology, a surprise, but ultimately disbelief.

"Patrick is our barrier until further notice."

What? I don't know what it means, but Corey sure does. His eyes are wide, but what she said seems to hit him hard finally. Corey nods, steps forward to kiss her forehead, whispers he loves her, and without another word, he leaves. The moment the door closes, Lucy falls back onto the couch and buries her face in her hands. She doesn't make a sound, but her shoulders shake. The bastard made her cry. And I'm still completely in the dark over what.

I gently sit down next to her, desperately wanting to comfort her. Lucy leans over and lays with her head in my lap, the tears streaming silently down her face. That's the scariest thing about it. Who doesn't make a single sound when they cry? Not a gasp, a whine, a sob, nothing. She grabs my knee and squeezes. I rest my hand on her hip and let my other play with her hair. What I really want to do is go beat the shit out of her brother.

"What can I do to make it better?" I whisper. I don't want to speak too loudly because she might break. Hell, she might already be broken. I don't know. I'm freaked out that she's not making any noise. Not even a sniffle. Lucy shakes her head in reply. The front door opens, and Neil cracks a joke at Bo. "Come on."

She stands and as I start to lead her down the hallway to my bedroom, Neil catches sight of us.

"Grant! What-"

"Good night," I cut him off.

"What the fuck?" I hear him say in confusion.

Ignoring him, I open the door to my room, pulling Lucy inside. We sit on the bed and she leans into me, the tears never missing a beat. With every passing minute that silence emits from her, the more worried I become. After thirty minutes, five words leave her mouth, and I couldn't be more thankful.

"Can I stay here tonight?"

"Yes, of course." Whatever she wants, I'll give it to

her. I don't like seeing her so upset, and I want my happy Lucy back.

She sits up to look at me, reaching up to wipe the tears away, but I beat her to it. "No, don't say it because I was crying. Grant, don't let me stay because you feel bad for me and want to make me feel better. Do it because...because..." Her voice trails off like she doesn't even know what she wants anymore.

"Stay, Lucy. I don't want you anywhere else but here with me." She gives me a small smile, and I know that's what she wanted to hear. "I'll be right back, okay?" Lucy nods, so I reluctantly leave her to go talk to the guys. I'm more than ready to go to bed. Dealing with three Kennedy brothers in one day is exhausting, but I need to do this first.

"What the hell, man?" Neil asks, but he's only curious. "Was that Lucy?"

"Yeah. Sorry about a while ago. She's having a rough day."

"Everything okay?" Bo questions.

"Fuck if I know. We're going to lay low in my room. Don't be asses, all right?" Neil smirks, like I'm joking. "I'm serious, Neil. Don't even think about it. I've had to see all three fucking brothers tonight, and Lucy is not having a good day. Make the wrong move, and I-"

"Okay, okay. Damn, go to bed, Grant."

Satisfied, I leave them to return to Lucy. She's already under the covers, asleep. Her face is peaceful, but my favorite thing is that the corners of her mouth are up, like she's dreaming about something that's making her happy. That's my Lucy. She stirs, and I realize I've been staring too long. Time to change and then crawl into bed next to her.

Usually, I'm pretty good at defining relationships and what they are. With Lucy, I'm completely lost. We have an intimacy that we share without sleeping together. We'll hold hands here and there, but I haven't even kissed her. Not on the lips, at least. We haven't been on a date. There is something between us. I just don't know how to label it.

As I lay next to her without being able to see her face because her back is to me, I decide we don't need to be defined. Whatever it is, I like. I don't want to analyze it and try to make it fit on the shelf with textbooks when it's obviously a storybook. I don't need to perfect what this is because it's fine the way it is.

I can't help but feel a little helpless though. Something about this day surrounds the four siblings, and I don't know what. It's not even about satisfying my curiosity. It's about having Lucy know that that part of their life is safe with me too. My mind begins to wonder about what it could be. Did something happen to Lucy when she was younger to make them as protective over her as they are? Was today the anniversary?

I start coming up with outrageous horror stories. Each of them makes me sick to my stomach to think that something bad could ever happen to my sweet Lucy. The house goes quiet as everyone turns in for the night, but I'm still awake, still thinking. Lucy rolls over and snuggles against me. Her body makes me relax with sleep moments away.

AN ELBOW HITS me in the gut, waking me with pain. What the hell? Lucy is thrashing next to me, her arms flailing, her face contorted in fear as silent tears fall down her face. I go to reach for her arms, but she manages to clock me right in the jaw.

"Lucy!" I grab her wrists, but she's fighting against me with all her might. "Lucy!" I half-yell again.

Her eyes flash open. Her chest is heaving, and the fucking tears are gliding silently down her cheeks. She looks terrified. By now, I'm hovering over her, pinning her wrists down on either side of her head. Her breaths quicken sharply. Her eyes are still glazed like she's not aware she's awake yet.

"It's okay. You're awake, Lucy. You're okay. You're with me." I repeat those four sentences again, but she's still breathing too fast, about to hyperventilate at any second. Her eyes start jumping around the room and ever so slightly, her wrists begin to tug against mine. "Lucy," I start, loosening my grip, "You're with me and everything is okay. Say it."

Her voice is pure terror and shaky, but she whispers, "I'm with you and everything is okay."

"Again."

"I'm with you and everything is okay."

"One more time."

"I'm with you and everything is okay." She's breathing normally again, looking more alert, but she hasn't stopped crying yet. "Can you let me go?"

I release her wrists and lay down next to her. Lucy immediately turns and presses against me, wrapping her arms tightly around me. Now that things are calm, my jaw starts to ache. It doesn't matter, though. I hold her as tightly as she's holding me, kissing the top of her head and leaving my lips there. I want to ask her what the fuck that was, if she's okay, but I don't. I wait for her to speak instead. And she eventually does.

"I need Patrick," is all she says.

Keeping her close to me, I reach over her for her cell and search for his number. Once I find it, I call him. It rings four times before he answers, and he sounds panicked but awake even though it's three in the morning.

"Luce? Is everything okay? Lucy?"

"She needs you," I repeat her words to him. I don't even know what else I'm supposed to say.

"Where?" His voice becomes different when he realizes that he isn't talking to his sister.

"My place."

"What the fuck happened, Grant?" I can hear him shifting around and someone in the background talking to him.

"She only wants you," I add, ignoring his question. She didn't say she needed her brothers. She said Patrick.

"Jon, stay here. I gotta go get Luce," he says. Jon says something back, and Patrick snaps at him. "Yeah, well, I told y'all to leave her the fuck alone!" To me, he adds, "I'm on my way. Is she crying?"

"Yeah."

He curses and then the call disconnects.

"He's on his way," I whisper into her hair as I feel my t-shirt become wet. Lucy doesn't respond except to wiggle closer to me. We lay like that until I hear a distant banging, and I know that Patrick is here. "I'll be right back."

With so much reluctance, I leave her to let Patrick inside. He repeats his earlier question the moment I open the door.

"After Corey stopped by, she wanted to stay with me. She was crying and I didn't want her to go back to campus anyway after that. We fell asleep, but I woke up to her thrashing around, hitting me and crying. Once I got her to calm down, she said she needed you."

He nods, like this has happened before. "Where is she?"

I lead him to my room, but hang back by the door as he goes over to her. Patrick sits on the edge of the bed and whispers her name. Lucy rolls over, sits up, and he pulls her into his lap as if she's a child, hugging her and comforting her like only a big brother can. He continues to talk to her softly, bringing her away from whatever ledge she was on. I almost feel like I'm intruding.

I almost hate him. Only because I want to know what is going on, and I want to be the one making her feel better, especially when part of this is their damn fault.

"Where are her things?" Patrick directs his question to me. How did he even know she had anything? Wordlessly, I go grab her bag by my closet and her cell off the nightstand. He nods a thanks for getting them. "Lucy, are you ready to go now?" I watch her shake her head. "Do you want to stay?" She shakes her head against his shoulder again. Patrick gives her a few more minutes, whispering into her ear, while running his hand up and down her back.

Without any pushing, Lucy stands, turns to face me, and gives me a breath-stealing hug. Patrick takes the bag and cell phone from my hand, so I can hug her back.

"Patrick is taking me with him," she says into my chest. "I'm sorry and thank you."

It's then that I don't want her to go. She can't leave me, not like this. Not when I'm so lost about what's wrong. Lucy looks up at me.

"He'll take care of me." Of course he will. Out of the three Kennedy brothers, I know Patrick will think of her first without a doubt. But then she stabs me in the heart. "Will you give me a few days before you call?"

I glance at Patrick and his look dares me to tell her no. "Call me whenever you're ready, Lucy." Ready? Ready for what? There's too much left in the unknown and now, I can't even talk to her for a few days.

Lucy places a kiss on my cheek. It's simple and quick and before I can even acknowledge it, she turns to Patrick. He takes her hand, leading her away from me. I wait until they are gone to lock the door again.

CHAPTER 15

Winston

SOMETHING POKES ME hard in the stomach, waking me up, and I hear a voice whisper, "Winston!"

"What?" I grunt, pulling Maddie's already close body closer without opening my eyes.

"Did you hear that?"

"No, I was trying to sleep on this piece of shit floor." I finally open my eyes to see her glaring at me.

"I think someone's here."

"Three other people live in this house, Maddie. I'm sure someone is here."

She pokes me hard in the stomach again. "Don't be a smart ass." Maddie starts to roll away from me, but I hold her tightly in place.

"I'm sure it's no one. Let's go back to sleep."

"Will you go check to be sure?"

I give her an 'are you serious' look. Clearly, it's a yes. Withholding a sigh, I crawl out of the fort and leave my room. Grant is looking rough as he walks this way towards his room.

"Everything okay?"

He looks up at my question, almost startled. "Hey, Winston. Yeah, everything is fine. Sorry if I woke you."

"It's okay."

Grant retreats into his room, and I do the same. Maddie has destroyed my fort and is underneath a pile of covers on my bed.

"What are you doing?" I ask.

"You complained about the floor, so..."

Oh. I climb in beside her, and she snuggles against me. "You heard Grant moving around," I explain.

"Thanks for checking and for tonight. It was a lot of fun," she whispers.

And it was. After my lame scary story, we ate more s'mores. It was easy to hang out with her because I already know her really well. We kissed a lot and played a few board games. Maddie hates to lose, just like I remembered. After I won the first time, I let her win the rest.

"So, we're really doing this?" her soft voice breaks the silence. I thought she had fallen back to sleep, but I guess not. She has her forehead pressed against my chest, her arms bent between us, much like the first time I woke up to find her in my bed.

"Yep. I'll be that give-it-all guy for you. Promise."

She snuggles closer, and I'm happy she's here and with me again. Dave is going to blow up when he finds out I am dating his little sister. At least I have a little more time to figure out a way to tell him.

"WINSTON, WINSTON," A soft voice sings my name over and over. When I open my eyes, I realize I'm laying on my back and Maddie's laying on top of me. Her arms are folded over my chest and she's resting her chin on her forearms, smiling at me. "Good morning. I know it's early, but I have to get going in a few minutes. There's no way I can leave without a kiss though."

"Oh yeah?" I ask as I bring my knees up, making her legs fall between them. I hook a finger under her chin to pull her closer to me. With a grin, I lift my head to kiss her, but kiss her forehead instead of her lips. "There you go."

Maddie frowns and I laugh. "Oh, come on, Winston. Be a man and really kiss me." Her eyes widen a little, and she adds, "Or are you the kind of guy who wants the woman to be in charge?" She laughs like that's the funniest thing she's heard all day. But then her laughter dies out and like the first time I kissed her, she demands it. "Come on, hockey player. Kiss me." Her voice is low, almost sultry.

Equally low, I reply, "Where? Here?" I kiss her cheek and then roll us over, so I'm on top of her. "Here?" I question, kissing her jaw. "Maybe here?" Dipping my head, I kiss a swell of cleavage peeking out from her tank top. My hands are at her hips and glide her shirt up just above her belly button. "Here?" I breathe over her skin before kissing her hip. I bring myself back up to her face, my lips just above hers. "Or here?"

Maddie's breathing is shallow now and just enough air escapes for her to answer, "Everywhere."

I smirk. "We don't have that much time." Her eyes flutter when my lips brush against hers. "So is this spot okay for now?"

"Mhm."

My mouth presses to hers, Maddie's immediately opens up. Her tongue slips into my mouth first, and I feel her fingertips on my sides. That one little touch for whatever divine reason drives me crazy, especially when she digs her fingers into my skin. Once those legs of hers wrap around my waist, I know it's time to stop the kiss. I pull away, notice her slightly swollen lips that are wearing a smile and her flushed cheeks and kiss her forehead, whispering, "You're gorgeous, you know."

Maddie grins. "I know." I chuckle and she adds, "So where are we going on this date you want to take me on?"

"Don't you have to leave?"

She glances at my alarm clock. "Yeah, but-"

"Either way, I'm not telling you yet." Okay, so maybe I don't know where I'm taking her. I didn't exactly get past asking her out. And by the sparkle of excitement in her eyes, I know it better be a damn good date.

"Okay then. You're going to have to get off of me, so I can leave though."

I move aside and she gets up and starts grabbing her things so she can leave. I watch her, seeing her comfort, her confidence, and her beauty move around my room. Now, I have to figure out where I'm taking her. Surely I can think of something from our childhood that she might like to do. People grow out of things like that, though. Why am I overthinking this? I've been on plenty of dates before, especially with Maddie. I don't need to think this hard about it.

Maddie comes back to the bed, leans forward, and gives me a quick peck. "I'll see you later, Winston."

I PACE IN the living room much like I did the day Audra told me she was pregnant. I've been wearing a path in the carpet for over two hours now. Ever since I came home from class, this is where I've been. My phone is clutched in my hand while I wait for Audra to call. I hope she calls before my game. I won't be able to focus otherwise. It's been a few days, but today is when we find out the results of the paternity test. I believed her when she told me baby girl was mine. So why am I full of uncertainty now?

It's all because there is one huge what if looming.

What if there was someone else and baby girl isn't mine? Audra did freak out a little at her doctor's appointment when I was trying to get her to talk about things, so maybe I should be a little doubtful. I can't believe I'm freaking out about this. But I am because what if she's not mine? There will be no more quiet, secretive talks to a baby, my daughter. That one thought makes my stomach roll with anxiety and nerves more than anything else. She has to be mine.

"You okay?" Grant asks as he walks into the living room and sits on the couch.

I nod my head in a lie. Once Audra calls and confirms that she's mine, then I'll be okay. Until then, I'm fucked. Grant watches me pace, probably debating saying something more knowing him. Winston walks in and repeats Grant's question, sitting next to him.

"I don't need a fucking audience," I mutter as Bo enters the room, taking a seat on the couch as well.

"Guessing you don't know yet?" he questions with curious glances from the other two.

"Does it look like I know?" I glare. Just then, my phone rings and I answer it before the first ring can even finish. "Hello?"

"I told you so," Audra's voice smugly says.

With a deep sigh of relief, I stop pacing and run a hand over my face. "Thank you," I whisper in gratitude. She's still my baby girl.

"Did you think she wasn't yours? That I was lying?" There's a tinge of annoyance in her voice.

"No, but I was worried anyway. Just in case." I glance at my peanut gallery. Bo has a small smile, and the others look confused.

"Worried? That she wasn't yours?"

"Yeah, I want this." The guys still don't know, so I'm having to censor my responses.

Audra is quiet before she asks, "Are you coming over, Neil?"

"I wasn't planning on it because I have a game, but I can afterwards before work."

"No, that's okay. You should get some rest in first. I'll just see you tomorrow and you can bring dinner." She sounds a little letdown to me. Or maybe that's wishful thinking.

"Are you sure?" For some reason, I want her to want me to come over. I want to go. Maybe I'm in withdrawal or something because I haven't seen her nor spoken to her since the doctor's appointment. I must have really upset her with my comments. Who knows. I've pulled the sonogram out of my wallet so many times that it's already slightly wrinkled. The urge to pull it out right now surprises me, but I don't. Not with the guys watching me.

"Are you sure you won't mind?" she asks. Before I can answer, she barely audible says, "I've kind of missed you, Neil."

It takes everything I have to swallow. I don't know if I should comment on that or not, but decide to sort of say something. "I know what you mean, and I'm positive I won't mind. Are you coming tonight?" She did tell her mom that they would go to one game.

"Oh, no. Ma can't make it tonight, but we'll be there for your next one." After a pause, she adds, "Thanks, Neil."

"You're welcome." I hang up and face the expectant peanut gallery. "What the fuck are y'all looking at?"

Grant laughs. "There's the Neil we know and love."

Winston nods. "Yeah, we were worried about you for a second."

Shaking my head, I don't bother answering them as I leave the room, texting my parents the results. Bo follows me into my bedroom though. It's tempting to throw his ass out because I don't want to hear whatever he is about to say.

"You like her, don't you?"

"I care for her because of, well, you know," I finish, glancing to see that he left my door open.

"You sure that's all there is to it? You haven't really said much about this and with your past with-"

"I'm not going there," I interrupt, sitting on the edge

of my bed.

"Does she know?"

"Why would I tell her?" Seriously. Why in the hell would I tell Audra anything about that? The past is the past. I don't need to dig it up to inform her of something that has nothing to do with her.

"I don't know, Neil, because it's a part of who you are! You are about to spend the rest of your life around this woman. I'm not saying you should do it for her, but maybe you should for you. Neil, you haven't been the guy I knew in high school since we came here for college. But that's who you become every time you talk about Audra. I'm just saying that maybe she isn't so bad for you."

"What the fuck do you know, Bo?" He's pissing me off with his advice and all this talk about the past. Things are fine as they are.

"They're coming to the game, aren't they?"

"Not this one, but the next one."

"Maybe it's time to tell the guys then."

I shake my head. Not going to do that. Not yet. Bo stands two feet away in front of me with his arms folded over his chest. I reach into my back pocket, pull out my wallet, and find the sonogram. I hand it to him wordlessly. His demeanor softens immediately. Quietly, I explain how I'm seeing things right now, "That's my baby girl, Bo. She and Audra are my focus. No one else matters."

He nods in understanding. "All I'm saying is that one day, you're going to want the Lanier's to meet her. Might not think so right now, but you're too close to them not to want to share that baby with them. One day, you're going to have to explain Sundays to Audra."

I hadn't thought of that.

Grant

THREE OF THE longest days of my life passes. That's how long it takes for me to hear from Lucy. I'm so relieved that I see her rather than get a phone call or text first. I'm walking across the courtyard, heading towards the library for a bit before the game, when I look up from my phone to see her walking straight towards me. Before I can say hello, she wraps her arms around my waist in the same breath-stealing hug as the last time I saw her. Lucy presses her forehead into my chest, squeezing tightly as I return her hug.

"I've missed you," she whispers.

"You have?" God, it's good to hear her voice and have her here with me. I tug her closer.

"Yes." Lucy pulls away, but it's only enough that she can look up at me. She isn't smiling and that's not how I wanted to see her. "Didn't you miss me?" she asks as if she would be upset if I didn't.

"Yes, I did," I reply honestly. Her lips lift in a smile. "I've been worried too."

"You didn't need to, things are fine." Things are not fine. I'm tired of being in the dark. Before I can tell her so, she changes the subject. "Can I stay with you tonight? I want to be around you, if you want me there."

"I have a game." Her shoulders sag before I can even finish. "Pack your things, so you can leave with me afterwards, okay?" I wouldn't tell her no, and I'm surprised that she hasn't caught on yet that I have never told her no.

Lucy lifts her arms around my neck and nearly suffocates me. "Thank you, Grant. Thank you so much."

When she pulls away, I kiss her cheek. "We're going to talk. It doesn't have to be everything, but something, okay?" She seems to think about it, so I try to explain why I need this from her. "Lucy," I begin, pushing a strand of hair behind her ear. "You and your brothers were being weird all afternoon. They were upset that you were with me and not them because of something important. You cried and didn't once make a sound. Then I wake up to you hitting me in your sleep, crying, and completely panicked.

"Once Patrick got there, you left me. I was clueless and scared to death with worry about you. No one offered to tell me what was going on and you left, telling me not to call you. You even got someone to go take pictures for you. Something was wrong and you dropped off the face of the earth, walking away from me. We have to talk."

I hate that by the time I finish, she looks guilty. "I'm sorry, Grant. I didn't even think about that." She leans her forehead against my chest again as her arms go back around my waist. My fingers of my right hand dance up her back to her soft hair. Lucy sighs heavily. "I'll tell you everything, but you have to promise me two things."

Then I feel guilty. "I'm sorry. Unless you really want to, don't tell me. I shouldn't try to force you to tell me because I don't like not knowing."

"No, I want to tell you. You need to promise me though."

"Okay."

"You have to go with me somewhere and it has to be in two days."

"Is that it?" I could do that.

"Yes." After a moment, she hastily adds, "Wait. Let me stay with you until then. I don't want to stay in my dorm. I want to stay with you." A long puff of air leaves her mouth. "My brothers are going to be so mad with me." Lucy looks up at me. "Can I?"

"Yeah, of course." Before I can ask why her brothers are going to be mad, she rests her forehead against my chest again.

"I wish you didn't have a game. I don't want you to go anywhere. I've missed you and...I need you," she whispers.

A weight lifts off my chest. I'm so fucking happy she's back. "I'm not going anywhere, Lucy," I reassure her.

"You're going where I can't touch you." She squeezes me as evidence.

"Oh, so you need to touch me? Mm. Why didn't you say so?" I tease, just wanting her to smile. I suggestively run my hands down her back to her ass.

Even better, she laughs and shoves me away playfully. "Grant, don't go typical guy on me. That's one thing I like about you."

I tilt my head. "You like that I don't hit on you?" Not sure how I feel about that.

"Well, I mean, that's what makes you you."

"That's not what I asked." She needs to answer because I want to hear her say it.

Lucy crosses her arms over her chest defensively. "We're friends, Grant."

I pull her back to me, wondering if she truly thinks that's *all* we are. "I'm teasing, Lucy. Don't go anywhere. I just got you back." She wraps her arms around me again, and I feel her leaning into me as much as possible. "And your brothers won't be mad. I don't know why they would be, but they won't be, okay? As long as you have Patrick on your side, you won't need to worry about the other two."

"He's going to be mad too. The other day, he understood. He won't understand me telling you and taking you where we're going. They aren't going to like that I'm spending the time with you over them either. Once, they could get over. Twice? Not so much."

Sighing, I hook a finger under her chin to make her look at me. As I stare into her eyes, I wonder if I'm right in what I'm asking her to do. "You always leave me with too many questions."

Lucy gives me a small smile. "You can ask one right now, if you want."

"Why won't they understand you telling me? Are you sure that you want to? Don't let me sway you, Lucy. I don't want to do that."

"That's more than one question, Grant," she teases. "I'll answer both." She looks solemn again. "I do want to tell you, but they won't understand because we don't tell other people. We don't really talk about it with each other, but we're always together. I'm going against both of those things by doing this with you. It's what I want, though."

CHAPTER 16

NEIL

THAT GIDDY, HAPPY go-lucky mood is dead tonight. We lost, but it was a tough, well-fought game. It's better to go down fighting than to be on the ice like there isn't a hockey game in progress. So I'm not happy, but I'm not angry either. Only sore from a couple of hard hits and my mood is pretty mellow, really. I'm hoping Audra will still be in a good mood. I knock on the door and brace myself, just in case.

She opens the door with a subtle smile. Her long, dark brown hair is up in a ponytail and she's wearing sweatpants and a shirt that engulfs her figure. Yeah, she's pregnant, but there's still a body in there. And besides, I like seeing her belly.

"Hey, Neil," Audra greets, surprising the hell out of me when she steps forward to hug me.

"Hey, Audra. Is everything okay?"

"Yeah," she sniffs, not sounding okay at all. I lean back and cup her cheeks to see her eyes are a little puffy.

"C'mon," I say gently, taking her hand and tugging her inside. We go to the living room, and I see a couple of Kleenexes lying on the table. I pull her down next to me on the couch and turn towards her. "What's wrong?"

"You're late." That's all she says as if that explains everything. I am late because I forgot my work clothes at the house and had to go back to get them. So I'm only like thirty minutes late. Audra glances at me, sees my confusion, and starts rubbing her stomach, something I've learned she does when she's upset. "I tried to call you, but you didn't answer. I started to worry because I didn't know if you had gotten into an accident or got really hurt in the game or something and you suddenly died and then I wouldn't have any help and our daughter wouldn't have a dad." Her voice cracks on that last word before she bursts into tears.

I pull her into a hug and try to soothe her. "I changed my phone to silent before the game and I did text you to let you know, but it must not have gone through for some reason. I'm sorry I worried you, Audra," I whisper into her hair.

"I'm pregnant, you should never have your phone on silent," she scolds through a hiccup.

"Won't happen again," I promise, wishing she would go ahead and stop crying. Hate, hate, hate seeing pregnant women cry, especially Audra. She pulls back, wiping her tears away, but I tug her to me again. "You look tired. Do you want to go lay down?"

"No, I'm fine. How was the game?"

"We lost, so it's good that you didn't go." I chuckle. "Here, rest your head right here and lay down. You'll make me feel better." I grab the pillow from next to me and place it on my lap. Audra rolls her eyes at me, but lays down anyway. "How was your day?"

"Aside from my breakdown just now, pretty good. Yours?"

"The same."

We're quiet for a few minutes before she speaks again. "When did you decide that you really wanted her?"

I clear my throat to buy a little time, but I decide to be honest. "I don't know when exactly, Audra. It was just obvious today."

"We'll need to start childbirth classes soon."

"Okay."

"I'm going shopping this weekend too, if you want to go."

"Okay. That sounds like fun."

Audra laughs and rolls onto her back so she can look at me. "Really?"

"Of course." Okay, I don't like the idea of shopping itself, but I haven't bought anything for baby girl yet, and I do want to do that. "Saturday, right?"

"Yes." She reaches up, grabs my chin between her thumb and forefinger and turns my head left and right a couple of times.

"What are you doing?" I laugh.

"Between you and me, she's going to be a beautiful."

I put my hand on her stomach and nod. "Yes, she will be." Seeing Audra like this, I realize that there's something else I want. We need to talk more about how things will work after the baby comes. But there's something else. I don't know if I should bring it up or not. Hopefully, I won't upset her. This is all Bo's fucking fault anyway. I'll blame him if I do.

"Audra, could I talk to you about something?"

"Of course."

"I would like for us to at least try to be in a relationship, if that's something you might want."

She tries to hide her surprise, but she doesn't do a good job. "You want us to be in a relationship?" Audra asks skeptically. "For the baby, right?"

I shake my head. "No, for us. I don't want only a parent-type relationship with you. It wouldn't be so terrible to see if there was something romantically between us, don't you think?" I want to roll my eyes at myself. That sounds so ridiculous, but I don't have the perfect words to explain what I mean.

Audra is quiet for so dreadfully long. She watches me, obviously thinking about it. "I don't always say nice things to you," she starts.

"I know," I interrupt, preparing myself for her to say something not-nice again.

"And you still want to date me?" Her voice is soft, and I feel like there's something else she's worried about.

"Yep. Without a doubt." I might not be good with words, but I have no problem being honest.

Audra slides her hands around her stomach and then rests them on her thighs. "I look like a whale. Are you just remembering what I looked like before when you look at me? Because I'm not getting that body back anytime soon. How are you even attracted to me right now?" She frowns like that is a seriously troubling question.

"You don't feel attractive, Audra?"

She shakes her head. "Not really."

Audra's beautiful. Always has been. I don't like that she's not feeling pretty. "Stand up. Do you have a full length mirror and some lipstick?" She nods, looking confused. "Take me to it." Reluctantly, she does. After she grabs the lipstick, I place it on the foot of her bed. I'll use that later. Her room is tidy, but small. I position her in front of the mirror and she's right. Our baby will be beautiful. We look really good together.

My fingers curl under her shirt and Audra tenses. "I'm going to take this off," I tell her in a low voice.

"Neil, no."

"You're beautiful and you know it because you said our baby would be beautiful too. I want to show you that you're beautiful like this too. Please?"

She stares at me through the mirror for a moment before nodding. I take her shirt off and throw it behind me without looking. Audra giggles, but sucks in a sharp breath when I rest my hands on her bare hips.

"Pants too," I urge.

Her eyes widen. "Neil, definitely not." She shakes her head. "I haven't shaved lately. Too much work, so it's not happening."

"If it makes you feel better, I won't even touch your legs."

Audra stares at me through the mirror before she unhappily removes her pants. She's tense, standing in front of me, our eyes still on the mirror. Audra looks tempting and lovely. Her bra is plain nude, but her underwear is a pair of black boy shorts. I kind of like them. I want to loosen her up a bit, so I grin. My hands slide up, turning into fists, and my knuckles brush the sides of her breasts.

"These," I point at her breasts from the side, "are knockouts, huge and ridiculous." They are larger than when I originally met her, and they are a great starting point to make her laugh. Audra gives me a small laugh and rolls her eyes. "I can guarantee you that these are grabbing a guy's attention way before this does." I move my hands to her stomach.

I reach for the lipstick, uncap it, and move to the mirror. "Do you mind?" Once she shakes her head, I step out of the way and draw over where her breasts are in the mirror. Two circles side by side, and then I step in front of it, so she can't see it. Just above them, I write in all caps, 'KNOCKOUTS!' Then I write 'huge' in the left and 'ridiculous' in the right. When I move back to Audra, she laughs.

With my hands on her hips again, I let her look in the mirror for a moment before I make my next move. Slowly, I slide my hands down her sides as I lower my body. My hands are close enough that if I'm not careful, I'll touch her legs. I hover my hands over her thighs. First, down the back of them, then the sides, the front, and the sides again. I never touch them, and my eyes remain on hers the entire time.

"These legs are still fantastic. They lead the eyes all the way down," my hands move to her calfs and back up, "and then up again."

"They are thunder thighs," she says quietly as if she doesn't want to mess up what I'm doing, but couldn't resist saying so. Her thighs aren't sleek, slender, or small. There's meat on those bones, and there's enough to make a man want to spread his fingers out, grab onto them, and wrap them babies around his waist. These legs, completely normal and sexy, add to her curves.

"And they work wonders because of it. Trust me."

I move to the mirror and outline her legs. Just like last time, I move in front so she can't see. I decide she needs one more funny truth before we get serious. So this time, I write 'Thunder thighs make Neil go crazy'. When I step back, Audra smiles. I step behind her again and recount what we have so far.

"Okay, so we have 'huge and ridiculous knockouts' and those gorgeous 'thunder thighs' of yours."

Audra almost sounds shy when she asks, "What's next?"

With my hands now on her arms, I glide them up to her shoulders. My fingers grab a handful of her hair. "Love your hair." I place my hands on her neck with my fingers stretched out so I'm not holding her neck. I rub my thumbs up and down the back of her neck. "And your neck." I drag a finger from her chin, up her jaw, to her ear. I trail her nose, lips, and eyebrows. "And your face. Everything about it is kind, sweet, a bit bad ass. It's beautiful."

I outline her face and write in a column 'kind, sweet, bad ass, beautiful face'. Behind her again, I saved the best for last. With open palms, I rub her belly and turn my head towards her ear.

"My favorite," I whisper. "This shows what your body is capable of. It's a reminder that our daughter is in there, being protected by her mom while she grows until she's ready to meet us. This is a pretty, round stomach that is carrying a life. What's more beautiful than that?"

She gulps as I leave her to go outline her stomach in the mirror. All I write inside it is 'our daughter'. When I turn around to face her, she has tears in her eyes. Thankfully, they don't fall over.

"Thank you," she says softly. "You put it all into perspective and made me appreciate the changes." Audra turns and starts to redress.

"We didn't even talk about your ass," I comment, dragging my eyes down her backside. Audra starts laughing and it's such a good sound to hear. I hope my daughter has that laugh. "So?"

"So what?" she asks, slipping her shirt back on to be fully dressed again as she faces me.

"Are you going to go on a date with me? Do you want to, I mean?" The urge to pace creeps into my system, but I resist.

"Yes, I do. Where are you going to take me?"

I smile. "I'll think of something."

She raises an eyebrow. "You asked me out without having an actual date in mind?"

"Yep."

And then, my gut tightens with nerves. My what if's have changed. I no longer think that my baby girl will feel like a simple obligation. She's my daughter and I'm her father. I'm excited to meet her. What if something happens and I don't meet her? What if I fall in love with Audra and I mess up? What if I do something so stupid, Audra tries to keep baby girl away from me? I don't think she would, but more bad things seem to happen when you're in love. Anything is possible.

That's the scariest thing of all.

I'm just getting ahead of myself because of past experiences.

"Neil?"

I blink. Audra's standing in front of me now.

"Are you okay?" she asks, placing a hand on my arm.

"Yeah," I answer. She doesn't look like she believes me. "Why don't we go lay down before I have to go?" I want to talk to baby girl, so I'm really hoping she'll fall asleep.

"Okay, sure." We go into the living room, and I lay down first, pressed against the back of the couch. Audra looks unsure for a moment before she comes to lay in front of me. I rest my hand on her side before sliding it forward to the front of her stomach. "Neil?"

"Yeah, Audra?"

"I don't know what you were thinking a minute ago, but by the look on your face, it wasn't good and it's worrying me. Please don't start freaking out or being distant or anything. I mean, don't change, okay? I need you to stay who you have been with me lately. I don't want you to go anywhere." She puts her hand over mine, interlocking our fingers.

I swallow hard. "I'm not going to leave, Audra. Promise."

Her voice is low, but I definitely hear her. "Good because I like having you here."

No words come for a response. It only takes about five minutes before she's sound asleep. Unfortunately, not many words appear for baby girl either. I gently rub her belly as I utter into Audra's shoulder, "I love you, baby girl. That's all I got tonight."

CHAPTER 17

Winston

I'VE BEEN OBSESSING over this date, over what to do, for what feels like days. And my best idea feels like it might be a bust. Maybe because it's such an ordinary date and I'm so nervous, but I think it'll go fine. I mean, it's Maddie. Unless she is expecting so much more from me, which she totally deserves, then we'll be fine. I'm just overthinking everything. Maddie is already outside her dorm when I pull into the parking lot.

Damn.

She's dressed in charcoal skinny jeans and a mint-colored top. A big smile is already on her face as she makes her way over to where I am. I get out and meet her at the front of my car.

"Hey, Winston."

"Hey, all ready?" I lean down to kiss her forehead.

"No, I'm standing out here because I need to run back inside and fix my makeup real quick." She slips her hand into mine as I laugh and lead her to the other side, opening the door for her.

When I get in, I say, "You look great." My hand is on the gearshift between us, about to slide it into reverse, but Maddie places her hand over mine. I look over at her. She leans towards me and points to her lips. Grinning, I close the space between us and kiss her softly. A gentle meeting of our lips, a simple hello.

"Where are we going?" she asks, sitting back properly in her seat as I finally back out.

"Movies." I glance at her to see if there's any disappointment, but she's still smiling. See? No need to worry. This is Maddie. We're friends at our core, and Maddie will speak up if something isn't working well. Only difference is that this time, I'm treating her like my future Queen instead of like a back alley hooker I don't want anyone to know I'm seeing. That was a bad analogy because Maddie was far from hooker, but I think it somewhat works.

"Did you already pick out what we're watching?"

I nod. "That new comedy with Adam Sandler."

"Ooh, I've been wanting to see that."

Point for Winston. "Did you have a good day?"

A quick glance shows an eye roll. "No. Let's not talk about that, though."

"Why? What happened?"

"Roommate troubles, but it doesn't matter. How was your day?"

I look to see if I should question her further, but she seems fine. "It was good."

She nods. I can tell she is smiling, even though my eyes are on the road. "I see you left your beanie at home. I can't say that it didn't cross my mind that you would be wearing it tonight."

Laughing, I say, "What is up with you and what I wear on my head? You're the only one who ever says anything about it."

"I don't know. I guess I thought you would grow out of it or something. I like it, just teasing you."

Absentmindedly, I run my fingers through my hair. After parking the car, I get out and open the door for her. She wraps an arm around my waist, so I do the same, finally sticking my hand into her back pocket. We don't say much as I buy our tickets and we head inside. Maddie loves popcorn, so I get us a tub. We find seats at the very top and munch on popcorn through the previews.

"We should come see that once it releases," Maddie leans over and whispers.

The lights dim and everyone falls silent as it starts. It seems surreal that I'm here with her. I'm probably about to jinx myself, but I feel like a bomb is going to drop on us too soon. Like things won't stay good for long. An impending doom, if you will. Maddie glances at me with a smile. She reaches for a popcorn and holds it up to my mouth. Once I part my lips, she pops it in there, grinning like she accomplished a hard task. Her focus shifts to the movie, so I do the same.

Once it ends, we leave the theater, holding hands.

"I need something sweet after that popcorn," Maddie says.

"Then you're going to want something salty after that," I laugh, knowing good and well that's how she is.

She smiles. "Yeah, but after that, I'll be fine."

"Okay. There's a frozen yogurt place not too far from here. We'll go there and then go through the drive-thru for some fries."

Her smile widens as I open the door for her. "You know me so well."

I just have a good memory. After we get our frozen yogurt, topped with our favorite toppings, we sit down at a tall table inside. "I can't believe you want something cold when it's freezing outside."

Maddie shrugs. "I think this winter is going to be brutal. It's not even Thanksgiving yet and they're calling for snow this weekend. Are you going home to see your parents?"

Going home to see my parents would usually mean seeing Dave. Their parents moved last year, so I won't have to worry about that. Maddie would kill me if she knew I was thinking this. Clearing my throat, I nod. "It'll be good to see them, but will probably be the same as every year." Thanksgivings are pretty normal with my family. There won't be any drama to talk about. "I bet you're ready to go home."

She gives me a sly grin. "Yeah, I am. You know, I'm feeling a little homesick now that you mention it. Don't you want me to stay with you tonight? To make me feel better, of course."

I laugh. "Have you been faking it?"

"No, I haven't. It's weird living with someone, especially when you don't get along with them. It makes me want my own room back. Tonight, I'm lying, but not the other times."

My gaze rests on the spoon sliding out of her mouth

before rising to meet her eyes. "You can stay with me tonight if you want."

She frowns. "If I want? Gee, thanks for making me feel welcomed."

Rolling my eyes, I lean over to whisper in her ear. "Stay with me. We have a lot of lost time to make up for."

When I pull away, she's grinning. "That's more like it."

Grant

I'M REALLY SURPRISED we're in my room right now. Maddie is here with Winston. They just got back from their first date, and Bo and Neil both aren't here. I thought that since Maddie is here, Lucy would want to hang out with them, but she waved to them and dragged me to my room.

"Want me all to yourself?" I grin.

She rolls her eyes as she climbs into my bed, a sight that I'm loving a bit more every time I see her do it. "You aren't going to let what I said earlier go, are you?"

"No," I answer, getting in next to her. Faintly, I think of us as an elderly couple and start laughing. We're seriously climbing in bed, and it's not even midnight yet. Lucy gives me a curious look, but I shake my head, sobering up. Laying on my side with my head propped in my hand, Lucy doesn't bother waiting until she's nestled against me. There's no way I can stop myself from asking, "Are we just friends, Lucy?" That has been bugging the hell out of me since she said it.

Lucy tilts her head back to look at me. She blinks, but doesn't hide her face in my chest again. "Honestly, I don't really know what we are. We're us." She shrugs her shoulder like that is an acceptable, satisfying answer. It is, but it isn't.

I cup her cheek, noting her small smile, and stare into those blue circular beauties that are to die for. My gaze drops to her lips, so close to my thumb. This moment feels like it's now or never. The only choice is now. My thumb lightly moves over her bottom lip twice when they move.

"Are you waiting for permission?" Lucy says quietly with a teasing tone as she tries not to smile.

"Do I need it?"

She shakes her head. I've been wanting to kiss her for so long, I don't waste a second before I press my lips to her mouth. My tongue runs lightly over her lower lip as she parts them, and I move it inside her mouth. Mmm. Just like I imagined. Sweet, delicate, and addicting. Rolling to lay on top of her, Lucy's hands run over my short hair before resting at the based of my neck. I kiss her as if my life depends on it.

My hands travel down her sides, wanting desperately to explore further. I kiss the corner of her mouth and then kiss my way along her jaw, down her neck, and across her collarbone. My lips move along the edge of her shirt to kiss the bit of cleavage showing. When I flick my tongue over the swell, she inhales sharply.

I want to go to so many more places, but I curl my fingers around her hips and come back up to that pretty mouth of hers. Right now, Lucy, her lips, her tongue, and her body are like water. I've been dying of thirst for weeks, months, years, a lifetime it seems. She moves one of her legs, causing it to come between mine as she kisses me fiercely, consuming me.

When she pulls away, I feel like I took a small nibble on a decadent dessert, and I want more. Her chest is pressed into mine while we breathe heavily. I kiss her one more time to leave her even more breathless as she exhales my name. I close my eyes and rest my forehead against hers, waiting to see what will follow.

"We need to stop for a second."

Oh. Have I misunderstood something?

Lucy waits until I open my eyes to add, "You overwhelm me. I needed a breather. I feel like I always need a breather around you."

"What do you mean?" I ask with confusion, going back to lay on my side.

She turns towards me, her cheeks flush. "It's not like I haven't had crushes or boyfriends or a makeout session with a boy before. It's not like I haven't ever flirted before or anything like that. But that first time I met you, it was as if I was struck dumb and was completely innocent or something. That's why I was so nervous. Because you're the only person who has ever overwhelmed me."

"How?"

"I don't know. Just *you*. It's crazy." Lucy reaches out to rub my head with a smile. "Your hair is freaking soft. I didn't know that."

I grin. "The shorter it is, the softer it seems to be, but this is as short as I'll go."

"Mmm," she hums in appreciation, moving closer to me.

"Why do you think-"

Lucy lifts a finger to my lips to silence me. "I've been waiting a long time to kiss you, Grant. So it would be really great if we could kiss now and talk later, okay?"

What's a better answer than a kiss? Lots and lots off kisses. It takes a lot of restraint not to kiss her anywhere other than where I already have. She does, however, let me explore a little more of her. I glance up, my fingers around the bottom of her shirt, and she nods. We're apparently going tit for tat because she pulls my shirt off too.

Placing a kiss on her shoulder as I hover over her, I mumble, "Do you wish I was sweaty?"

She giggles. "Maybe a little."

My chuckle is cut short when I feel the tips of her fingers and her nails on my lower stomach, slowly drag over the skin there.

"Grant?"

"Yeah?" I lift my head to look at her.

"Are you going to kiss me or just breathe on my shoulder?" she laughs softly.

"Sorry." My eyes find her hands, her knuckles now brushing a little lower before coming back up. "You distracted me for a second."

Lucy grins, apparently proud of that fact. Before I can kiss her, she lifts up to meet me and kisses me, getting me lost in her again. My hands trace her upper body as I kiss every piece of skin available to me. Her sigh when I kiss the skin in the middle of her chest, just above her cleavage, nearly does me in. I want more. I want everything. Lucy's not ready for that though. At least, I don't think so.

Once we're all kissed out, we lay on our sides, facing one another. Lucy lightly trails a finger over my lips.

"I wish I could take a picture of you like this."

"You don't have your camera?" I question skeptically with a smile.

Lucy laughs and nods. "Yes, I do, but it won't be the same if I go get it and come back."

"Go get it. I want to take one of you."

She looks so surprised, as if no one has ever wanted to take her picture. Wordlessly, she slips out of bed and begins to walk over to her things. However, there's something between her shoulder blades that catches my eye and surprises the hell out of me.

"You have a tattoo?"

"Yeah," she answers without looking back at me. I sit up and when she returns to the bed, I make her sit with her back facing me, so I can look at it. It's a camera with film coming out of it's side and falling below to twist, turn, and loop into the shape of a heart. "Let me guess. You didn't think I would have one?"

"No, but I didn't necessarily think you wouldn't have one either."

"Here," she says, turning to lay back down as she hands me the camera.

I lay on my side, propped up by my elbow, and turn it on. Lifting it to my face, I look through the lens at her. Before I take one, Lucy holds up her hand and leans down to pick up her shirt from the floor. She puts it back on and lays down again. Then I start clicking away. After the fourth shot, she holds out her hand.

"You're making me nervous."

"How so?" Because I'm taking pictures of her?

"You have my camera. I don't ever let anyone hold it, so you're making me nervous. Not that I don't trust you, but give it back before I get paranoid."

I laugh, handing it back over. "Sounds like you already are."

Lucy sets it on the nightstand and cuddles up to me. She's quiet for a few minutes, her fingers constantly moving around the small area of my back where her hands are. "I'm a little scared about telling you. Things might change between us or even worse, you'll treat me like Jon and Corey. Like I'm fragile when I'm not."

"I know you aren't, Lucy, but you can back out if you're worried about it."

"No, I'm not going to do that. I just wanted to tell you I was scared. I...I haven't talked about it in a long time, so be patient with me, okay?"

"Of course."

Her phone rings and she sighs before getting up and going to grab it from her purse. "Hey, Patrick," she answers, coming back to me. I listen to her side of the conversation. "I'm with Grant. Yes. No. I'm sure." She laughs. "I love you too. Bye."

"Checking in?"

"Yeah. Let's go to sleep?"

I pull her closer and kiss her softly. "Whatever you want."

Those blue eyes peek from underneath long, black lashes. "Thank you, Grant."

AUDRA HAS CLASS tonight, so I'm meeting her at her

place for lunch before she goes into work for a couple of hours. I text her that I'm on my way, and she responds that she wants a quick back massage before I leave. I can't help but smile. Ever since I left her house the other night, I've had a good feeling about things. We start childbirth classes next week, plus a doctor's appointment again. Our date is Sunday afternoon with a three game weekend starting Thursday. I want to ask her about moving in, but I'm not sure. Not to mention that means kicking my friends out. This baby will be here before the school year ends, so I don't know if they'll be able to find another place or not. Especially when they aren't paying rent now. I can think about it later. Maybe ask Bo his opinion.

"Audra?" I call as I walk into her apartment with the bag of food.

"Down here," she answers.

I follow the sound of her voice after placing the bag on the kitchen table, which leads me to the hallway leading to her room. My eyes almost pop out of my head as I see her balancing on a stepladder as she reaches for something in the top of the closet.

"What the fuck are you doing, Audra?" I shout, rushing to her and grabbing a gentle hold on her hips. "Get down! Are you fucking crazy?! You could fall!" The images of the horror play in my mind as she steps down back onto the floor. "I told you I was on my way. Why the hell couldn't you have waited? God damn it!" I run a hand in my hair and begin to pace now that she's safely on the ground and off the death trap of a stepladder.

"Neil, I was fine."

"No, you weren't! You could have lost your balance, Audra! You can't do shit like that! I can't-" I turn to face her and stop myself before I can yell at her further. Her eyes are watery. Shit, I've upset her and probably scared her. I reach out to take her hands, pulling her into my arms, wrapping her in a hug. "I'm sorry. I'm so sorry," I whisper over and over to her as her shoulders shake while she begins to cry.

"You can't what?" her voice croaks into my chest, asking the one question I wish I didn't have to answer. Maybe if I'm silent long enough, she'll magically forget it. "You can't what, Neil?" she asks again.

I sigh. "There's something I should tell you. You might hate me afterwards."

Audra lifts her head, granting me the opportunity to wipe away her tears. "Why?"

"C'mon, let's go sit down."

She follows me into the living room, and we have a seat on the couch. Audra turns towards me, so she can listen to every word. For a moment, I wonder if I could get out of this somehow, but then Bo's words about the Lanier's pass through my mind again. I was going to have to tell her eventually. With a deep breath, I tell her what no one at the university knows, with Bo as the sole exception.

"In high school, I was dating this girl, Candace. She meant everything to me, especially once I found out that she was carrying my baby. We were in our senior year and we were careless. Not once did I question being there for them both. I wanted to be. I loved her." I take a shaky breath.

Audra holds my hand and quietly asks, "What happened?"

"Her parents and little sister left for the weekend and she wasn't feeling well, so she didn't go to my game." My throat tightens and I remove my hand from hers, leaning forward with my elbows on my knees to rest my face in my hands. God, I don't want to go through this. I don't want to say it. I don't want to tell her. Audra starts rubbing my back for comfort.

"There was something on the top shelf in a closet that was at the top of the stairs that she wanted." I swallow what feels like a huge lump in my throat. "She was short to start with, but she needed a stepladder to reach that far up. When she fell, she was so close to the stairs that she tumbled all the way down, and...she was dead before the game even started that night. I didn't get there until after my game was over."

I squeeze my eyes closed as images of her on the floor resurface in my mind. She hit her head a few times on the way down, which killed her before she could get any help. Once she died, so did our baby. The panic I felt overwhelmed me at seeing her like that was just as strong as what's still surging through my veins at seeing Audra on that stepladder. I take another deep breath, so I can keep going.

"I didn't know she was lying at the bottom of the staircase dying while I was at my game. Calling her parents was one of the worst phone calls I've ever had to make." I swallow hard and continue, "Afterwards, I had a really hard time dealing with it. Almost quit hockey and my relationship with my parents was really rocky, still is. That's why I panicked when I saw you. I can't lose you too, Audra. I can't."

Finally, I turn to look at her. The tears are back in her eyes, so I pull her to me. My chest feels a little lighter now than it did a while ago. She doesn't say anything for a bit, and neither do I. I have no words left right now.

"That's why you're so good at helping me," she whispers. "Because you been through it before. I'm so sorry."

"Don't do anything risky ever again," I plea softly.

"I won't."

"Thank you." I kiss the top of her head, ready to be away from this topic already. "Hungry? What did you want in the closet?"

"My quilt. It's a little chilly at night in my room, and I keep forgetting to get it down. And yes, I am. What did you bring?"

I get her quilt for her and then we go into the kitchen. I start pulling out our dinner, burgers.

"Mmmm," Audra hums. "Just what I was wanting too."

I smile, feeling accomplished. "What do you want to drink?"

"Iced water, please," she answers, taking a seat.

I fix it for her and ask her to stand. She does and gives me a look when I take her seat and pat my lap. "I'll let you know if my legs fall asleep," I grin. "C'mon. You want a back rub, don't you?"

"Yeah," she says, taking a seat on my lap. "But aren't you going to eat?"

"I can eat on the drive back."

"Are you sure? You shouldn't eat and drive."

"Pretty sure you mean text and drive, but I'm positive." I don't bother starting at the top like last time. I dig my thumbs into her lower back, immediately earning a groan.

"Both are dangerous, but I don't care if you eat while you drive. Don't stop," she ends with a moan.

"Might want to quit making all the noise, so *you* can eat."

"Right. Go a little lower."

Between the burger and my hands, Audra makes a grunt-like moan or a long "mmm." I can't stop grinning. It's ridiculous how good and accomplished I feel by doing this for her. It's also crazy that it turns me on. My hands aren't stopping, so let's hope Audra doesn't notice.

"Neil?" she questions after a few minutes.

Something about her voice makes me look up from the work I'm doing. Her burger is halfway to her mouth and her bottom shifts in my lap, like she's trying to get comfortable. Suddenly, she stands and faces me, her eyes about to bulge from the sockets.

"What is that?!" she exclaims.

"What?" Her gaze drops to my black jogging pants and I laugh. "Nothing you haven't felt before, Audra." Her eyes get even wider. "Sit back down." I take her hand, pull her back to me, and make her sit.

She seems cautious as she begins to eat again. No sounds come from her now. After a few minutes, she says softly, "I'm sorry about what happened with Candace. I can't stop thinking about it. You finding her and then having to tell her parents." Audra shakes her head. "I wish it didn't happen and that it wasn't you that had to be the one to do those things."

My hands freeze. Part of me hoped that once I told her, that would be that and we wouldn't have to talk about it anymore. I rest my forehead between her shoulder blades with my eyes closed.

My voice is gruff as I try to stay in the present. "They know about you."

"Who?"

"Her family." Clearing my throat, I explain, "Bo and I visit them every Sunday. They don't live too far from here. That Sunday after you showed up, Bo told them what happened, how I treated you. Her father is the one who helped me get the job. They reminded me of the type of person I was before. So, here we are. Every week when I go see them, they ask how you're doing and her little sister wants to know when she can meet the baby. She's so excited."

Audra turns sideways in my lap and wraps her arms around my shoulders. I bury my face in the crook of her neck. Her fingers dig into the hair at the base of my neck. "How old is she? Her little sister?"

"She's six. Turns seven this weekend. I have to go to her birthday party." As an afterthought, I add, "I still need to get her a present."

"You could get one Saturday when we go shopping. Unless her party is then?"

"No, it's Sunday." I pull away from her neck, my stomach a ball of nerves as wonder if I should ask this. Bo was right, damn it. I hate when he's right. "Do you want to go with me?"

I wasn't expecting a frown, but her lips do indeed dip. "Are you sure they would want me to be there?"

"They would love to meet you, Audra. If you don't want to go-"

"No, I'll go if you want me to," she interrupts. One hand goes to her belly, a tell-tell sign that she's nervous about this. Me too, Audra. Me too.

"It'll be fun," I promise. "What's more fun than a bunch of six and seven year olds at a birthday party?" She nods but doesn't say anything. I kiss her temple, wishing I didn't have to leave yet, but I do. "I need to go. So do you. Don't forget that I won't see you Friday, but call if you need anything, okay?"

"Okay. Ma said we were going to your game Saturday, by the way."

Once I nod, she stands. I grab my burger, kiss her temple one more time, and then leave. I'm not really hungry anymore, so I go ahead and call Bo. As soon as he answers, I go right into it.

"I told her everything. She's coming to Alice's birthday party and she and her mom are coming to the game Saturday. What in the hell has my life become?" I'm a breath away from freaking out.

Bo laughs. "I'm glad you told her and that things seem to be going well. Alice is going to go nuts. Does this mean I get to have Sunday off?"

"Seriously? That's what you're focused on? Audra is going to meet the Lanier's!"

"Calm down, Neil. It'll be fine."

I hope so. I can't handle anything else. "There's another thing."

"What is it?" he asks.

"She lives in a one bedroom apartment. My place is bigger and I'll be more helpful if we live together, but there are issues with me asking her. She got ill the first time and then there's all you guys. I mean, y'all can stay if you want, but I doubt y'all are going to want to always be careful about waking a baby or having to listen to her cry."

"Don't worry about us, Neil. As long as you give us plenty of time, we're good. As for Audra, maybe wait a little longer to bring it up to her. You don't want to overwhelm her."

No. No, I don't.

Instead of going home, I go to the rink. I want to get away for a while.

CHAPTER 18

Grant

DREAD FILLS MY stomach as Lucy leads me through the cemetery. We drove two and a half hours to get here, and Lucy has barely mumbled a word the entire time. She stops in front of one large headstone and then turns to face me.

"Sit," she orders. I take a seat on the long wooden bench. "I have a few conditions that I need you to do for me." I nod. "Open your legs, so I can sit." I do and Lucy presses her back against my chest. My hands immediately go to her hips, but she takes them and pulls my arms around her. "Hold me tight." I squeeze her closer to me, so she knows that I will. "Absolutely no talking once I'm done. None, Grant."

"Okay," I agree.

Lucy holds her hands out to the headstone in front of us, and I finally read the names. Marvin Kennedy and Jennifer Kennedy. Son, Daughter, Father, Mother, Husband, and Wife are each written on the respective sides.

"They are my parents," she says quietly. The date of their deaths is the same and Lucy had to have been six, I believe, when they died. The date was the other day when her brothers made a fuss because she wanted to be with me. That must be why. She chose me over them on the day their parents died. Now that it's about to happen, I'm not so sure I want to hear her story. "Today is the anniversary of their funeral. What I'm about to tell you will answer any questions you've ever had about me.

"My brothers went to spend the night at my grandparents. I stayed home with my parents because I was sick. I was asleep in their room because I always slept with them when I didn't feel good, but I was awakened by yelling and screaming from the other room. Something wasn't right about it. My mom sounded like she was crying and there were voices I didn't recognize. My dad was pleading, begging for something. It scared me, so I grabbed my favorite stuffed animal and hid in the closet.

"I started crying, but when I heard footsteps coming towards the room, I was terrified. My parents were yelling something and I didn't want to be loud, so I somehow managed to be completely quiet. I think my dad said something to piss the person off because he turned around and walked away."

Lucy stops talking as her breathing has sped up a little. I rest my chin on her shoulder and pull her closer to remind her that I'm still here. Tears begin to fall. I want to tell her to forget it. That she doesn't have to tell me anymore.

"Then I heard lots of commotion and gunshots. People were walking around really fast and someone came into their room. The closet door swung open and a guy saw me. I remember that he looked really surprised and a little worried. He put his finger to his lips to show me to stay quiet. Then he closed the door and I heard him running down the hall, talking. After about five minutes, I think, tires squealed as they were leaving.

"The house was so quiet, so, so quiet," she whispers, lost in her memories. "I wanted to go find my parents, but I was too scared to leave my hiding spot. So I stayed there all night, wondering if the people were coming back, and what happened, and why my parents hadn't come to get me yet," she finishes, her voice catching.

"Next thing I remember were my brothers screaming and a lot of crying. Patrick kept yelling, 'I know where she is! Let me find her!' Finally, he swung the door open, found me, hugged me, and then they were all there, surrounding me. They kept hugging me as my grandparents took us outside. Cops were everywhere. I don't really remember much after that.

"My parents were murdered for some gang initiation. That's why they robbed and killed my parents." She pauses for a few minutes. "I stopped talking for a while after that, but when I started again the only person I would talk to was Patrick. I didn't really know what was going on except my parents weren't there anymore. Patrick was like my barrier. Whenever I got overwhelmed or just couldn't keep talking to people, he would do all the listening and talking for me to make people leave me alone. I haven't done that in a long time, which is why Corey reacted like he did the other night. That's why my brothers are the way they are. They haven't left me since that night."

I'm glad she told me I couldn't talk because I have no idea what to say. Tugging her even closer, I rest my chin on her shoulder. She places her hands over mine and squeezes. So much make sense now. I wish I could make her feel better. She probably doesn't want me to move my arms, so I kiss her shoulder. Lucy relaxes into me, the tears still falling. I hate those tears so damn much.

"Luce?"

Our heads turn at the sound of Corey's voice. Patrick and Jonathan are standing on either side of him a few feet away. She quickly wipes away the evidence of her crying. The brothers silently walk over, each taking turns kissing her forehead. Then Patrick sits to my right while Jon and Corey sit to my left. Not a word is muttered as we stare at the headstone. Lucy seems to be fighting for control, but suddenly she leans forward and the only reason I know she's crying is by her shaking shoulders. She buries her face in her hands.

I run one of my hands up and down her back while leaving the other around her waist. After a few minutes, she's still crying, her breathing too rapid. I grab her hips, push her to stand, and turn her around before pulling her back in my lap, so she's straddling me. Lucy immediately throws her arms around my neck as droplets of tears fall onto my shoulder. I hug her to me as tight as possible.

She told me not to talk, but I can't bear to see her like this anymore. Turning my head, I let my lips brush over her ear and whisper as quietly as possible.

"Hey, do you remember what I told you?" Lucy nods. "Say it."

She is barely audible, but I hear her voice crack as she says, "I'm with you and everything is okay."

"Again."

"I'm with you and everything is okay."

"One more time for me."

Lucy says it again, takes a deep breath, and sits up with a tiny smile. She gives me a quick, soft kiss on the lips before turning towards Patrick.

"You okay, Luce?"

"Yeah, I'm okay." She looks at Jon and Corey. "Are you mad?"

The brothers glance at me, and I wish they would tell her yes, so I could finally beat the shit out of them. They shake their heads though, and she turns back to Patrick.

"Are you?"

"No, Luce, of course not. Believe it or not, I trust your judgment. If you want Grant here, then I want him here for you."

Lucy leans over to hug him, whispering something to him. Then she stands and returns to how she was sitting before, in between my legs, and I tuck her against my chest once more. "I think I'm going to stay with Grant for a few more days," she announces quietly. "If he'll let me, of course."

"You know you can," I interrupt before she can continue.

Lucy smiles, intertwines our hands in appreciation, and faces the headstone once again. We're quiet for a few minutes before Jonathan interrupts it, pulling something from his pocket, which I just notice is full of something.

"Look what we found." He pulls out a small Minnie Mouse stuffed animal.

Lucy gasps as she snatches it from his hand. She seems at loss for words as she stares at it, turning it over to inspect it. I rest my chin on her shoulder, realizing this must have been the favorite stuffed animal.

"Minnie Mouse, huh?" I chuckle. It fits perfectly.

She wrinkles her nose at me. "Yes, what's funny about that?" She clutches the animal to her chest.

"It's so you, that's all. Soft voice, big smile, and entirely too nice and sweet."

Lucy rolls her eyes at me, but there's a hint of a smile upon her lips. "Thank you, Grant," she says, and I have a feeling it isn't only for what I said.

"You're welcome."

She stands and faces all of us still on the bench. "I think we're ready to go." Lucy reaches her hand out for mine, so I take it and stand with her. "Same place as always tomorrow?"

"Yep," Patrick answers as they nod and stand.

He hugs her first, then Jon, and then Corey. Lucy keeps her hand in mine the entire time. Because of this, I can hear each whispered "I love you" and Corey's, "Are you sure, Luce?"

"Yes, I'm fine, and he'll take care of me if I need him to."

I'm not going to lie. A shit ton of pride swelled in my chest when she said that. You're damn right I'll take care of her. Better than they have these past few days. Their hug ends and we begin the walk back to our vehicles. I open the door for Lucy while she says one more goodbye to her brothers, and then we're on our way back to the house.

Winston

FOR SOME REASON, I almost expected our first time having sex again to be a little awkward, but it wasn't. Maddie is so much more sure of herself. It makes sense because the last time was her first time, and she's slept with someone since then. We've been pretty addicted to one another since. She sleeps over here so we can do a lot more than sleep, which explains her naked presence in my bed this morning.

I woke up to her straddling me, her fingertips on my sides above her knees. That's a silly thing to notice with the distraction of her tits against my chest. Her body is pressed against me in some places and a few inches apart in others, her hair tickling my face as it falls forward.

"You can't keep spending the night, Maddie. I'm sure Neil doesn't want-" I attempt to come up with some logical reason as to why she may need to stay in her dorm, like I actually want her to do that.

She rightfully cuts me off with a kiss. "Neil is never here. He won't care."

"Your parents are paying for you to live in a dorm." My phone vibrates on the nightstand, and I know it's Dave. Damn it. I never realized how often we actually talked until I had something to hide from him.

"Don't answer it. I'll love you forever." Maddie starts kissing down my jaw. "What my parents don't know won't kill them. I'm usually only here at night, so no big deal."

My eyes have been eyeing my phone anyway, and my

hand flings out to grab it before it vibrated itself right off and onto the floor. Somehow, I manage to connect the FaceTime call with Dave.

"Bad time?" he asks. My phone is facing the floor, so he sees Maddie's bra, I'm sure.

Maddie glares as she sits up, and I move the phone, so he can see me. Only my stupid thumb hits the button at the top of the screen, and it swivels so Dave sees Maddie's naked self.

"What the hell?!" he yells as I frantically try to switch the screen back to me and Maddie's eyes widen as she covers up, realizing what has happened. "What the fuck are you doing with my sister, Winston? I'm going to kill you! What the fuck?!"

I sit up, lean against the headboard, and glance at Maddie, who is removing herself from my lap. "I didn't mean for you to find out like this."

"I hope not! God, Winston! I saw my sister without a shirt or a fucking bra! You're sleeping with my sister?" He shakes his head, the fury rolling off of him. "What the hell were you thinking? What the hell was *she* thinking?"

"I'm dating her," I correct. "And don't make out like I'm bad for her, Dave."

"You're my best friend! You aren't supposed to fuck my sister!"

Maddie has been getting dressed, and she opens her mouth, but I lift my finger to her lips. She doesn't need to say anything to fuel his fire. She frowns.

"It's not like that, Dave." I run a hand through my hair.

"When were you planning on telling me this?"

"When you came for my game."

"I wish you had, so I could hit you. How would this even come about?" He shakes his head like it's impossible. I don't want to tell him about our past, but I may not have a choice. Before I can reply, he goes, "Where's Maddie? Is she decent now?"

I hand her the phone.

"Hey, Dave," she gives him a half smile.

"Explain this to me, Maddie. He was only helping you study, or he was supposed to be doing that."

"He did. Um," she glances at me, "you asked how it started." I reluctantly nod. "Remember when I kept getting in trouble for sneaking out in high school? Before y'all left for college?"

"Yeah. You were with some jackass who took your virginity and broke your heart."

Her eyes widen. "Who told you that? I never said anything to you."

"No, but you told Christina after she badgered you for weeks about what was wrong." Christina was Dave's ex-girlfriend from high school. They broke it off over the summer and Maddie was close to her. Really close apparently. "Wait. Are you telling me that was Winston?! She said you were heartbroken. What the hell are you doing back with him? I can't believe this shit."

"You acted like you suffered so much because you kept it a secret. But you did talk to someone. You lied to me," I say to her. I can't believe it. Yeah, it's probably not something to be that upset about, but she made a big deal over having to deal with it all by herself.

"Have your couples quarrel later," Dave snaps.

"No." I take the phone from her and end the call. "What the hell, Maddie?"

"Winston." She leans forward to touch my arm, but I get out of bed, slipping a pair of sweatpants on. "I don't even remember telling her! We went to a party and I remember her asking me about it. She kept refilling my drink, so I guess I told her at some point. I wouldn't have said what I did if I thought I actually told her. Come back over here," she finishes softly, holding her hand out for me to take.

I allow her to pull me back onto the bed, sitting on the edge beside her. I'm not so sure how I feel about all of this, so I stay quiet for now and let her do the talking. My phone is vibrating again with another call from Dave.

"Don't answer it. You can call him back later."

"You don't remember telling her?" I ask. "I don't care if you told someone, Maddie, but there's no need to lie about it now."

Her hazel eyes gaze at me sadly. "You know I wouldn't lie to you." We're silent as we process what just happened. Dave knows because he saw his sister half-naked sitting on top of me. He also knows part of what happened in high school with us. "What are you thinking?"

"I'm thinking that was a shit way for him to find out." Maddie's phone starts ringing. "Go talk to him. Doesn't look like he'll stop until you do."

"Are you sure?"

I nod and she leaves my side to go answer. I don't really want to hear it, so I grab some clean clothes and head for the shower. Honestly, it feels like things could be worse. Maybe Maddie can calm him down and talk some sense into him. I doubt he wants to listen to me. When I finish, she's still on the phone with him.

As I walk into the room, she says, "Okay. Hold on." Maddie holds the phone out to me. "He wants to talk to you. I'm going to take a shower."

I take the phone from her and press it against my ear. "Yeah?"

"I've known you practically my entire life. I know everything you've ever done, good and bad. Why the fuck should I be okay with this, especially knowing what you did to her?"

"What did she tell you?"

"Seriously, Winston? That's what you want to know? You're supposed to be my best friend, not my baby sister's boyfriend. If you hurt her, how could we still be friends? If things don't end well, I'm going to have to choose sides. Do you realize what you're risking by doing this?"

He's starting to really piss me off. "Of course I know! Why do you think Maddie ended things with us the first time, Dave? That was because of you! I wanted to keep my best friend and my girl. When I didn't tell you fast enough and didn't stand up for her to you, I lost her. Don't you fucking tell me I don't know what's on the line. That's the exact reason why I know I'll do everything I need to to make it work. Either learn to deal with it or don't, but I'm not going to lose her again."

Dave's quiet for what seems like a long time. Maddie reenters my room, frowns when she sees I'm still on the phone, and sits next to me on my bed.

"Well?" I ask, tired of waiting.

He sighs. "I gotta go. Tell Maddie I'll talk to her later."

Without saying anything further, I hang up. "He'll talk to you later."

"That's it?"

"That's it."

"He'll come around, Winston. Once he sees how we are together, he'll look disgusted, tell us not to kiss around him, and things will be back to normal." She kisses the corner of my mouth because I haven't turned to look at her yet.

"Yeah, I'm sure you're right. Let's hit the gym. It's going to be a long day."

I'M CONVINCED THAT Maddie is addicted to exercising. She seems to do it even more now that we're dating. Sometimes, she'll run beforehand or it'll be her second, sometimes third, workout of the day. It's insane. When she only eats a protein bar for "breakfast," I want to say something about how she should eat more, but I don't. I'm sure she'll eat more later. The only reason I'm really noticing is because of a nagging thought in the back of my mind about how what her brother said that night made her start exercising so much in the first place.

We usually chit chat a little, but today, we exchange few words. Dave was right. He knows about all the shit I've done over the years. The stupid, the not-so-respectful, but also the good and the thoughtful. There's a very good chance that he doesn't want to deal with this because of the simple fact of who I'm dating. I hope not because we've been friends for too long. Knowing Dave, he's probably more pissed about how long he was kept in the dark about it. Smart move, Winston.

"Are we going to keep not talking or what?" Maddie's voice sounds from next to me.

I put down my weights and face that small body with hands propped on her hips. "Figured we were just thinking this go round."

She shakes her head, stepping closer to pull the fabric of my shirt at my waist into her hands, absentmindedly rubbing it between her fingers. "I was waiting for you to freak out. You're much calmer than I expected."

"You wanted me to give you my everything, so that's what I'm doing. Am I a little concerned about it? Sure, but if you're okay, then I'm okay. Like you said, he'll come around."

"And if he doesn't? You're going to be fine with that?" She tilts her head to look up at me.

I lean down to kiss her forehead. "I could be fine with it for you."

NEIL

"NEIL, I THINK you went overboard," Audra says as we look at all our purchases from todays shopping trip. The week has flown by between school, games, and work. I never knew that I could actually enjoy shopping. Well, I somewhat did. Audra ooh'd and ahh'd over every little thing we saw. That part was fun to watch.

"I didn't go overboard," I laugh. Okay, maybe I did, but can you really ever have too many baby clothes? I didn't buy the entire store, so it's fine. Next time, we'll buy the other practical things she'll need. "Come sit." I sit on the couch and pat the space next to me. When she does, I pat my lap. She doesn't even make a remark, which tells me she either really likes me doing this, or she really wants it. Maybe both.

I rub her feet and her calves over her jeans, earning an

appreciative moan. "Y'all still coming tonight?"

"Yep. Ma's excited, which surprises me. I don't know why, but I think she likes you."

"Hey!"

Audra smiles. "I didn't mean it like that. I just mean she hasn't really been around you enough to have a valid opinion of you." Her hand goes to her stomach. "Do you still want me to go tomorrow?"

"If you're willing."

"I am." She swallows hard. "Are you nervous? I'm nervous."

"Yeah, a little." My honesty surprises her. "I'm not worried about how they are going to treat you or react because they are the best people I know. I'm more worried about myself and how you're going to feel. It has to be a little scary that you're meeting her family."

She nods. "What about you? Why are you worried about yourself?"

With a deep breath, I answer, "Before I told you, I haven't talked about her since the funeral. It's..." I gulp, my throat tightening. "It's hard, Audra. My past and my present are clashing."

She pulls her legs out of my lap, moves closer to me, and takes my hand. "Thanks for being open and honest with me, Neil. I really appreciate it."

I smile at her, really wanting to get away from this topic. "Can I do something for you?"

Audra looks at me skeptically. "What?"

"Is that a yes?"

"You aren't going to tell me?"

"No, but I promise it'll be worth it."

Reluctantly, she nods. I stand, and she follows me to

the her bathroom. Wordlessly, she follows my orders when I ask her to take off her pants and get her legs good and wet. When she finishes, she puts the toilet seat down and sits. I grab her razor and shaving cream, sit on the edge of the tub, and pull a leg onto my lap.

"Really? You're going to do this?" she asks surprised.

"Yeah. You said it was too much work, and I figured it would make you feel better, so..."

"Okay."

I lather up the shaving cream, rubbing it over the top and sides of her leg, and then lean back to rinse my hand under the spigot. I'll have to get the back of her legs later. Carefully, I begin to shave her legs. When I glance up at her, she's looking at me a bit strangely.

"What?"

"I just...I never thought you would be this type of guy."

I grin. "It's amazing what you learn when you actually get to know a person."

She sighs and frowns, making me stop what I'm doing to look up at her. "Don't make me feel bad, Neil. I feel like I always say the wrong thing to you anyway."

"You're saying what you think. There's nothing wrong with that, Audra."

That seems to satisfy her, so I go back to shaving her legs. It takes a while because of how we're doing it, but when I'm done, Audra surprises me by giving me a soft kiss on the lips.

"Thank you."

"You're welcome. I need to go. I'll see you later."

When I leave, I realize something. There's an odd feeling inside me, and I'm not sure about it. It feels good, but it doesn't at the same time. I feel...content. Happy. I hate that it almost feels wrong and foreign. My mind is lost in this for the rest of the evening. I should be happy, should be happy about being happy. All this talk about Candace is why it doesn't seem right, I believe. I'm waiting for something to go wrong, and I know I won't be able to handle it if it does.

Her death broke me. Bo wasn't kidding when he said I haven't been the same person since. How could I be? She was everything to me and then one day, she was gone. She didn't exist anymore. Our baby didn't exist anymore. It didn't seem real, much less possible. I struggled through the rest of hockey season, debating wanting to quit and never touch the ice again and trying to hold on to the only thing I had left.

And now Audra is here, carrying our baby, and being excited about it doesn't fit. It feels like it shouldn't. I don't know what to do. Maybe I should talk to Bo about it. Though, his advice always ends up pissing me off in the end, whether he's right or not. I try to push these thoughts away when I mess up a pass to Winston during our game, but I can't help it. Audra and her mom are here. How the hell am I supposed to focus on hockey when I'm wondering if she's still tired from our shopping trip? Wondering if baby girl is moving around in her belly right now?

"Neil," Bo cuts through my thoughts. "Focus," he grits.

"Fuck off."

With a deep breath, I do focus. I can't be a reason we lose this game. Not with who is in the crowd. I push myself, push my teammates, and try not to worry about anything else. We come away with a 2-1 win. Back in the locker room, my phone beeps with a text. Like I promised, it's never on silent. There's a text from Audra.

Audra: Tired. We're going ahead home.

I text her back: **okay.**

At least I won't have to tell the guys yet. I ignore questions from the guys about my play tonight. It wasn't awesome, but it was enough. I go to the house, take a nap, and then go to work for a few hours. I can't shake this bad feeling. It's probably nerves about tomorrow. My phone beeps with another text as I'm leaving.

Audra: Will you come over?
Me: Need to run home first, then I'll be on my way.
Audra: Thanks.

I wonder why she wants me to come over. This is a key reason why we should live together. Then there wouldn't be any of this back and forth mess. I'm not sure how to bring it up to her or the guys, despite what Bo told me. When I get to the house, Winston is awake, sitting on the couch watching TV. I mutter a hello and go about my business. Once I have my things to spend the night, I head for the door.

"You're seeing someone, aren't you?"

I freeze, slowly turning to see Winston watching me carefully. "What?"

"You have a girlfriend, don't you?" There's a small smile on his lips.

"Something like that," I answer before leaving him

behind.

I'm grateful I don't feel too tired because I definitely need to pay attention while driving. It did snow this weekend, so it's cold as fuck and the roads are icy. I'm almost grateful she texted me because seeing Audra does relieve a bit of my uneasiness. She smiles when she opens the door, stepping aside so I can come in.

"What are you doing up?" I ask.

"I'm having trouble sleeping. Thanks for coming." Audra closes the door and faces me. That's when I see it. The tired eyes, the slow blinks like she's trying to stay awake, and the overall need for sleep on her face.

"Come on," I say, taking her hand to lead her to her bedroom. "Go ahead and lay down," I tell her gently. She moves to her bed, not once objecting which really tells me how tired she is. I don't know why she's not sleeping though. I go to the bathroom, change, and get ready for bed. When I come out, she's sitting up in bed with the blanket up to her waist. I ignore the normal-ness of this, of us, as I slide in next to her. "What's wrong, Audra?"

"Nothing." She goes to lay down on her side, facing away from me. After a moment, I turn off the lamp and lay on my back. Her arm reaches out behind her, and her hand hits my stomach. "Come over here," she softly orders. I do, cuddling up behind her and slipping my hand between my stomach and her back to knead my thumb into the muscles there. "Is something wrong, Neil? I feel like something isn't right with you and it's making me worry."

I rest my forehead on her shoulder blade, not liking how easily she can read me. "I thought I was the worrier between us."

"Neil," she starts, trying to turn around to face me,

but I keep her in place.

"I'm fine. Let's get some sleep. We have a big day tomorrow."

Audra's quiet for a few seconds before she gives in. "Okay."

Thankful, I kiss her shoulder, close my eyes, and sleep comes soon enough.

"NEIL! YOU CAME!" Alice yells as she runs up to me.

I release Audra's hand to catch her in my arms. "Of course I did. I told you I would be here. I have someone for you to meet," I tell her as she wraps her arms around my neck.

Alice finally looks over at Audra, her grin getting bigger. "Is that her?" Alice whispers loudly to me.

Laughing, I nod. "Alice, this is Audra. Audra, this is Alice, the birthday girl. She's six today."

"Neil! I'm seven!" Alice pouts about my intentional mistake.

I kiss her cheek. "Oh, yeah. I remember now. Sorry I got it wrong."

"It's okay. Are you going to come play with me and my friends?" She looks at me with big, hopeful eyes.

"Yeah, let me go find your parents first, okay?" I set her back down and she runs off, happy with my answer. With a glance at Audra, I take her hand and lead her through the house to the kitchen. Mrs. Lanier is the only one in there. Mr. Lanier must be in the other room with the kids. "Hey," I say to announce our presence.

Mrs. Lanier turns from the counter to look at us with a wide smile. "Neil, I'm glad you're here. Alice was driving me crazy every five minutes, wanting to know where you were." She walks over to give me a hug before turning to give Audra one as well. "You must be Audra. It's so nice to meet you. We're glad you came today."

"Thank you for letting me come with Neil. It's nice to meet you too, Mrs. Lanier," Audra replies.

"Of course. You're welcomed any time. And please call me Sandra. I don't know why Neil won't, but you certainly can." She looks down at Audra's stomach. "How's the little one doing? Neil said you were having a girl."

"She's fine. Moving around a bit."

"Is she moving now?" We turn at the sound of Alice's voice.

"Aren't you supposed to be playing?" Mrs. Lanier asks.

"I was coming to get Neil. Is she?" She looks to Audra, who nods. "Can I feel? Please, please, please!"

Mrs. Lanier opens her mouth to chastise Alice, but Audra says, "Sure. Hurry before she stops."

Alice doesn't need anymore convincing before she rushes over. Audra takes her hand and places it on her stomach. I can tell the moment Alice feels it because her face transforms into pure wonder.

"Woah. That was cool." And just like that, her attention is back on me. "Are you coming to play with us?"

"Yeah, I'm coming. Can Audra play too?"

Alice nods, so we follow her into the other room where four other girls and Mr. Lanier are having a tea party. I hold back my laugh at seeing him sitting at the small table. After introducing him and Audra, Mr. Lanier excuses himself with my presence to go help Mrs. Lanier finish setting out the food. There's only one seat left. Mr. Lanier offers to get another, but I tell him it's no big deal as I pull Audra to sit on my lap.

This isn't my first tea party, so I know what Alice likes for me to do. One of which is to be really proper and speak in a terrible British accent. Audra and the girls can't stop giggling at me, which makes me want to be even more ridiculous. Whatever weird mood I was in yesterday dissipates with the laughter around me.

"Where's the bathroom?" Audra whispers in my ear.

"Down that hallway, second door on the right." I lift her hips as she goes to stand to keep her steady. She disappears down the hallway behind me and I lean in, gathering all the girls attention. "What do you think? Is she a keeper?" I ask in my fake accent.

The girls glance at one another before Alice speaks. "She's really nice and plays with us, so yes." The rest of the girls echo the answer and nod their heads. "Does she have a name yet?" Alice's eyes light up. "Oh! Can I name her?"

"I don't know. What names have you come up with?" I don't want to shoot her down outright, and she might actually have some good ideas.

Alice's shoulders sag. "I haven't thought of any yet. Do I get to play with the baby when she finally gets here?"

"Want to know a secret?" I ask instead. Alice nods her head vigorously. All the girls lean forward when I do. "You can be her aunt Alice if you want."

"Really?"

I sit up in my seat again. "Yep. You could be her first friend. It's a serious job, though. Are you sure you can do it?"

"I can! Promise, Neil, I can do it."

"Okay then. You're on the job."

Alice grins, but her mom peeks from around the corner behind her. "Anyone ready for cake?"

The girls jump up and start running for the kitchen as Audra appears next to me. I stand at seeing an unfamiliar look on her face.

"What's wrong?"

She shakes her head. "Nothing." That's when I notice a small smile. "You're kind of amazing, that's all. It's really sweet that she'll be aunt Alice to our daughter, Neil."

"You heard?" She's smiling, so that must mean she isn't upset about it. Audra nods. "I told you she was excited." I take her hand and start leading her to the kitchen. "C'mon. We're missing the cake."

The rest of Alice's party goes really well. Audra seems to be enjoying herself and Candace's family seems to love her. On the ride back to Audra's, she looks over at me.

"Can we stay in tonight? Watch a movie and relax? Unless you really want to go somewhere? I figured you might be tired after the games and work and all."

I glance at her. "You don't want to go out?"

"Not today. Plus, I have homework to do too."

"Okay, that sounds fine. Maybe we can take a nap first?" I didn't really sleep well last night, and I think it's Audra's bed. That may be why she's not sleeping well now that she's pregnant. I had a hard time, and I'm not, so maybe her body needs something better. It's simply not comfortable.

Audra nods in agreement. We get to her place and go to the couch instead of the bed. She sits down first at one end of the couch while I go grab a pillow from her room.

She props her feet onto the coffee table, but by the time I get back, Audra has her eyes closed. When she doesn't stir, I assume she's sleeping.

She's been quiet for a few minutes now. Perfect. I move to rest my head in her lap, facing her ever-growing belly. This has become my favorite part of my day. Gently, so I don't wake her up, I place my hand on her stomach, hoping to feel movement.

"Hey, baby girl," I whisper to my daughter. "It's Daddy. I hope you haven't given your momma too much trouble today." There's no way to suppress my grin when I feel a kick near my hand. I move it, hoping she'll do it again and that I'm in the right spot. "Looks like you're going to have an aunt Alice. She's pretty cool and I think you'll like her." My mind turns to hockey and I know I would want her to be on the ice one day too. "It's been a long week with hockey. I can't wait to take you skating to see what you can do on the ice. Think you'd want to do that, baby girl? Maybe you could play like me." This time, my hand is in the right place and I feel her move. I chuckle softly.

"She is not going to be a hockey player." Audra looks down at me. "You're already trying to get her hurt, Neil?" She's trying to hide a teasing smile.

"She would be tough. Have you been listening to me?" I almost want to frown, but I don't.

Audra runs her fingers through my hair. "I've been listening since the first time I woke up and heard you talking to her a while ago. Now, I pretend to fall asleep, but you're crazy if you think I'm going to let her play."

I smile. "You're crazy if you think I wouldn't make her a good player and tough enough to handle it. She wants to play. You felt her."

"No promises, Neil. Keep talking to her if you want." She plays with my hair, watching me. "I love listening to you."

"Sorry, I don't know if I can now that you're awake." It's the truth. Part of the reason I love this is because it's only my baby girl and me.

Audra frowns. "Really?"

"Yeah."

"I'm sorry." Her eyes start to shine, and I sit up in confusion. "I didn't mean to take that away from you, Neil." A tear falls and she quickly wipes it away.

"Hey, don't be sorry. I haven't even tried. I'm sure it'll be no big deal. Don't cry, Audra."

"But you were talking to our daughter and now you're always going to be wondering if I'm listening," she mumbles, trying to hold in her tears. "She loves when you talk to her, Neil. She moves every time you do and I've ruined it."

I wrap her in my arms. "You haven't ruined anything, Audra. See?" I lean away so I can bend towards her stomach, letting my lips move across the fabric of her shirt. "Hey, baby girl. Show your momma that it's okay. We can still talk, can't we?" I glance at Audra. "She move?" She smiles and nods. "See, everything is okay."

Laying back with my head in her lap, she runs her fingers through my hair again. "She doesn't move that much when I talk to her. I can already tell that she's going to be a daddy's girl."

Unexpected pride rises in me at her words. "You think so?"

"Don't look so smug, Neil," Audra laughs.

My smile falls away. "I hope I can be worthy enough

for her," I murmur, closing my eyes, so I don't have to see her reaction.

Audra's reply is just as quiet, "You already are."

I let her words sink in and hope like hell she's right. After a few minutes, I speak again, remembering Alice's question. "She needs a name. Don't you, baby girl? You need something besides baby girl, I think." I look up at Audra. "What are you thinking? Maybe I can test a few names out and if she kicks after one, then we know that's what she wants."

She laughs. "She kicks almost every time you open your mouth. We aren't letting her choose her own name, Neil. Who knows what we'll end up with."

I press my lips to her stomach. "Fine. Have it your way, but you let me know if she starts to go crazy in there." Audra chuckles. "What names do you like?"

She shrugs, the corners of her mouth dipping slightly. "I haven't really thought about it. I'm going to be terrible, aren't I? I haven't even thought of names for our baby yet."

"You are not going to be terrible, Audra. If either of us is going to fail, then it'll be me." That doesn't really make her happy, so I keep going. "Do you want us to pick a name all on our own or do you want to name her after someone?"

Audra thinks about it. "I don't want to name her after anyone. Do you? Like Candace?"

For a moment, I stop breathing. She's asking if I want to name our baby after Candace? I glance between her and her stomach before shaking my head. "No," I answer softly. "I can't do that. I don't want to." My eyes squeeze close, easily overwhelmed from her name.

"I didn't know and thought I should ask. I'm sorry for

upsetting you."

"It's okay," I say without opening my eyes. "I loved her and still miss her like crazy sometimes, and I...I don't want to link that to our baby girl. That sounds terrible, doesn't it? It's like I think it would be a disgrace or something, but that's not it, I swear."

Audra's hand moves in my hair. "You don't have to explain it to me, Neil. I think I get it. Tell me what names you like."

"Hmm," I hum. "What name do you want, baby girl? Victoria? Bailey? Olivia?" I put my hand over her stomach. "No? I don't think those fit either. Pearl? Mabel? Grace? Eva? Cora? Nellie? Ethel?"

Audra starts giggling. "Are we choosing names from another century now?"

"Does that mean you don't like any of them?" I pout my lips, making her laugh some more.

"Grace maybe," she yawns.

"Let's lay down for that nap."

CHAPTER 20

Grant

THANKSGIVING CAME AND went with everyone but Neil going home for the holidays. He's been more absent than he was before. I don't know where he is, but he doesn't stay here often. As far as Lucy, things have been pretty normal between us since she told me. I've been running with her for the upcoming 5K. December has brought even colder weather, too much snow, but plenty of opportunities for Lucy to press herself into me, so she can warm up. I'm pretty sure I love winter even more now.

Her brothers have still been touch and go, but I don't expect that to ever change much. Today, we're meeting them for lunch. All three. Yay, right?

"Don't look so enthused, Grant," Lucy laughs from the passenger seat.

I reach over to take her hand, resting our interlocked fingers on the console in between our seats. "I don't look excited?"

"Not really."

With a smile, I glance at her. "Don't worry. I'm perfectly okay being around the crazy Kennedy brothers for a meal."

"They're only a little crazy," she laughs. "Oh, we're going to be late. Corey hates when people are late."

"I know," I grin.

"Grant! You're terrible," she chuckles as I pull into the parking lot. "At least we aren't too late."

I park, get out, and open the door for her, reclaiming her hand once again. We cross the lot carefully, Lucy is already leaning into me because of the bitter cold. Once we step onto the sidewalk, we see all three brothers standing near the entrance, waiting for us.

"And you thought I didn't look excited," I whisper to her upon seeing the varying degrees of frowns.

She giggles, but doesn't get to say anything before we're standing in front of them. They mutter hellos to me and give hugs to Lucy before ushering us inside. We're seated at a round table, and I get lucky enough to sit between Lucy and Jonathan, my favorite.

"Are you doing well in your classes?" Corey asks her.

"Yeah, and finals shouldn't be too terribly hard. Are *you* doing well in *your* classes?" she teases.

"I'm doing fine," he says with a roll of his eyes. He went on to graduate school, mostly because he can't play football anymore. This is the first time I've ever seen him be anything other than pissed, so it's a nice change. "You better be checking on those bozos, not me."

At this, Lucy turns towards them. "Well?"

"We're good too, Luce," Patrick laughs.

"Great."

"How has football season been?" I ask, honestly wanting to have some input at some point of this conversation. Corey frowns and looks away while Patrick and Jonathan look at me like I've grown two heads.

"You don't know how the team has been doing?" Jonathan questions as if I should.

"Do you know how my team has been playing?" I don't follow football and I doubt they do for hockey, but Patrick laughs.

"Yes, we do. Luce tells us all the time about how the games go, and we have no choice but to listen to her yap about you and anyone else who impressed her."

Lucy's cheeks flush red, making my grin widen. Before I can comment, Jonathan adds, "I can't believe she doesn't talk to you about us like she does to us about you. Not to mention, we have to see all the pictures."

"How long have you been taking pictures?" I ask her.

She frowns and I almost wish I hadn't asked. "I don't really know why I love it so much or where it came from. I remember wanting to take lots of pictures of them at one of their games and I begged Grandma until she gave me the camera. There weren't many good images, but I loved doing it and haven't stopped since."

The conversation halts as our waitress drops off our drinks and then takes our order. Once she walks away, Corey clears his throat.

"Mom. She got you started. The, um, year before, she gave you a little camera for your birthday and she taught you how to use it. I remember because any time you lost it, you thought we hid it somewhere and Dad would make us search for it until we found it wherever you left it."

"Oh," Lucy says sadly. "I don't remember that."

"It's okay, Luce," Patrick tells her, taking her hand since he's on the other side of her. "We all have things we don't remember."

"Yeah, you're right. We're going to Grandma and Grandpa's house for Christmas, right?" Lucy sneaks her hand under the table to hold mine, a simple, but important action. We haven't done a lot, which is cool. Lucy is like a slow and steady type of girl. She doesn't want to rush into things or do something if she's unsure. She wants to feel like she's ready first or like she has a good sense of direction about things, which makes sense to me. Even if it didn't, I still wouldn't mind.

"Actually, my girlfriend wants me to meet her parents," Jonathan answers. "So I won't be going home."

A moment of disappointment passes Lucy's face before it's gone and she's looking at Patrick and Corey. "Y'all are going, right? Grandma won't be happy if it's just me."

"Yeah, we're going, Luce," Corey reassures her. Our waitress drops off our food, and we begin to eat. "You're a goalie, right?" Corey asks, returning the conversation to me.

I nod. "I played a couple of other positions when I was younger, but I was better as a goalie and I loved being in the net, so it worked out."

"He's really good too, Corey. You all should go with me to the game tonight," she says hopefully.

"I can't. I already planned to go out with-"

"Your girlfriend," Lucy finishes for Jonathan. "If you're spending Christmas with her, then I think you could cancel to spend some time with your little sister. She would understand, I'm sure."

"Like you ditching us for Grant last month?" His words are clipped, so I'm guessing he's still not happy about that.

Lucy seems stunned and upset. "I...you said you weren't mad."

Jonathan sighs. "I wasn't. I'm not. Sorry, Luce, I love you, I do, but we're not going to spend every holiday together for the rest of our lives. You should get used to that now. I'd do anything for you, you know that, but is it really a big deal if I rather to be with my girlfriend instead of going to a stupid hockey game?"

"No, I guess not," she mumbles.

"I need to head back to school, so I won't be able to either. Sorry," Corey offers.

"I'll go with you, Luce," Patrick tells her. "If it's decent," he jokes with a wink at his sister, "then we'll talk them into going to another."

Lucy agrees and the rest of our meal is spent with the guys learning a little more about me. On the way to the library to study for a bit, Lucy is awfully quiet. Patrick's words from what seems like a lifetime ago run through my mind again.

'Lucy's silence speaks loudly, and it's rarely a good thing.'

I give her a little bit more time to see if she'll say anything. We manage to make it into the library and to my favorite table without her muttering a word. I grab the leg of her chair and pull her closer to me.

"Hey," I whisper. "What's the matter, Lucy?"

She slides those bright blue eyes over at me, peeking

underneath long, black lashes because she has her head angled down a little. "I realized how right Jon is. We won't always be together. They could go off, get married, and move God knows where, and we'll only get together once a year if we're lucky. I don't..." she pauses, takes a deep breath, and continues, "I don't know what I'm going to do without my brothers around all the time. Corey's already absent a lot from being in grad school and he's only an hour away."

"You don't know that they'll move far away, but even if they do, it'll be okay. Just think about it like this. They'll be starting their careers and families, and you will be too. Even if they aren't nearby, you're their little sister and trust me, they aren't going to disappear on you." My words don't seem to soothe her as much as I want.

"Yeah, I guess you're right, Grant. I went into worry-mode for a second there. Thanks for bringing me out of it." She leans over to kiss me softly.

I used to think there was something delicate about Lucy, but I know now that there isn't. What can be mistaken for delicacy is more like reserved strength. She's not fragile. She's super strong. Her brothers must have taught her that. I only say that because Patrick seems the same way sometimes. Lucy's love for her family has no ends, and it's charming how happy she is when they are around. They may be overprotective at times, but she doesn't need them to be. She's independent with a quiet strength and presence. There's something about that combination that's overwhelmingly breathtaking.

She tilts her head, still close to me, as she runs a hand over my head from the front to back until her fingers are resting on the back of my neck. She loves to do that because she can feel how soft my hair is. "Why are you looking at me like that?" she asks quietly.

"Like what?"

"Either like you had a revelation or like you were so lost in your thoughts and you've just realized where you are."

"Remember how you told me that I overwhelm you?" She nods, unsure of where this is going. "I realized you do the same thing to me."

The corners of her mouth quirk up. "It's something else, isn't it? It's like suffering from pure bliss, only it's the best way to suffer."

Winston

I HAVEN'T HEARD from Dave since he found out. It's odd not talking to him, but I don't have a lot of time to think about it between hockey, Maddie, and studying for finals. The only reason why I'm thinking about it today is because this is the weekend he was supposed to come up to see me play and hang out.

"Winston! Get your head out of your ass and focus!" Neil yells familiar words.

Oops. I missed a pass. I run after it and Coach starts putting us through some drills. Part of me wishes Maddie would be here tonight, but she's going out with some of her friends, so I didn't ask. She doesn't really care for the sport anyway. She never has and I wouldn't expect her to become suddenly interested in it.

We have about fifteen minutes until we hit the ice for the game when my parents call me. They've been away on a second-honeymoon type trip to celebrate their anniversary.

"Hey, I don't have much time," I answer.

"That's okay, sweetie. We wanted to let you know that we're back home. Have you been doing well? We've missed you," Mom says.

"Yeah, things have been fine. Enjoy your trip?"

"Oh, yes. It was wonderful."

"Good. Let me call you after the game, okay?" I tell her, not really wanting to talk to her at the moment. She's going to make me feel like spilling my guts, and I don't want to do that yet.

We hang up in the knick of time. Once I get on the ice, I feel a little lighter. This is where, no matter what's happening, life makes sense. At least, in this moment, it does. I know what I'm supposed to do in this moment. I'm a defenseman. My job is to do my best to keep the other team from getting the chance to score. We're off our game though. The hits are hard, in their favor, as are the shots. The only reason we're still in this 2-0 game by the third period is because of Grant. The score could be so much worse. We don't do much in the third to get the puck into the net nor protect our own and we lose 4-0.

I hate games like these. I really hate the feeling afterwards when we know we could have done better, but we didn't follow through. When I exit the locker room, Maddie is there with Lucy, who is waiting on Grant, I'm sure. My frown already marking my face deepens when I see Maddie. She looks smaller. How is that even possible? Surely, she hasn't lost weight. That can't be healthy for her height and overall size.

She grins when she sees me. "Smile, Winston. You get to be with me tonight," she says once I'm next to her as she wraps her arms around my waist.

"That's the only good thing about today, that's for sure."

"We'll see you later, Lucy," Maddie tells her before dragging me down the hallway.

"Did you come to the game?" I ask once we're in my car.

"No, I just got here. Lucy told me y'all lost. Sorry."

"It happens." I debate mentioning her weight. Maybe it's her clothes that make her seem smaller. My mouth stays closed until we reach the house and are in my room. As soon as the door is closed, Maddie has her hands all over me, and we're undressing.

Sex after a loss always makes things better.

Until Maddie is laying next to me, and I notice that she still looks thinner. Clearing my throat, I decide to say something.

"Have you lost weight?"

She shrugs like she doesn't know. "Maybe. I've been running more. Do I look like I have?" Maddie smiles as if that would be a good thing.

"Yeah. Maybe you should eat more and run less. You don't need to lose weight."

This time, she frowns. "I'm not going back to Fatty Maddie, Winston."

I lay on my back and stare at the ceiling. Fucking Dave. "You weren't ever fat, Maddie. Dave was a dick to call you that and you shouldn't have believed him so much. You were fine the way you were. It's not healthy for you to lose weight when you're already so little. I'm surprised you have weight to lose."

"I was a little heavy, to say the least," she protests.

"I don't care how much you weighed or how it might have looked because you're short. You were *healthy*, Maddie. That's what mattered. Did you ever eat lunch after we worked out the other day?" I've noticed that she'll grab something small, like a granola bar, for breakfast, but I always thought she would eat a big lunch, especially because that's what she said. I've tried to get her to eat breakfast with me, but she won't.

"No, I wasn't hungry."

I roll onto my side to face her. "Are you still self-conscious about your weight, Maddie?" I question as gently as possible.

She rolls her eyes. "No."

"You're lying," I state simply. Maddie always absentmindedly pulls her lips into a subtle purse when she lies. Guess what her lips did right before she answered me? I pull her closer to me, holding her head in my hands. "I don't give a fuck that he teased you. You're gorgeous, Maddie. You were back in high school and you are now. But if you aren't eating like you should on top of exercising like a fucking maniac, that's not good. It's not healthy."

That purse of her lips appears before she says, "I'm fine."

"Don't lie to me, damn it!" I release her face and roll onto my back again, throwing my arm over my face. Has she been like this since the night we ended? Always struggling with a nonexistent weight problem because her brother was a fucking idiot who thought it was funny?

"What makes you think I'm lying, Winston?" It pisses

me off that she's curious about this and deflecting from the issue at hand.

"You have a tell," I snap. She wiggles on top of me and moves my hand. "You are the prettiest when you're healthy, Maddie. You don't look healthy to me right now," I say before she can utter a word.

"Can we just drop it?" she whispers, kissing my jaw, trying to distract me.

"No."

Maddie sighs, moves back to her side of the bed, and covers up. "Good night then."

"Maddie," I start.

"Good night, Winston," she repeats more forcefully.

I sigh. "Night."

This conversation is far from over. Once finals are over, she'll be out of reach until spring semester. I could hope that Dave notices, but I doubt he really understands what's going on with her. After tonight's conversation, I'm concerned. Maybe I should wait and see how things go once we get back. If things are the same, then I'll have to force Dave to talk to me.

CHAPTER 21

NEIL

IT FEELS LIKE so much has happened. Christmas is coming up. Thanksgiving, which was awesome, has already passed. I had the day off, so while everyone went home, I stayed at the house, relaxed, caught up on homework, and texted Audra. She and her parents traveled to her grandparents, so I was left here all alone. Can't say I didn't enjoy it either. It was much appreciated down time.

Audra has officially become my girlfriend, though the guys still don't know about the baby. They will soon enough if things go as planned. Things with Audra have been good. We've been going to childbirth classes. We're doing well in school, and we go out here and there. She's even going with me to dinner on Sundays sometimes.

We're supposed to go out tonight since we haven't seen each other much because I had some games during the week. Between losing last night and missing her, I'm ready to see Audra. Plus, tonight, I plan on asking her to move in with me. I'm over here early as usual.

"Neil? That you?" she calls from down the hall as I shut the door behind me.

"Yeah, babe." Yep. I can call her that now.

"Come here please."

I walk down to her find her in the bathroom. Her hair is down, sleek as it hangs around her shoulders. She's wearing a sweater that shows off her belly, but she hasn't put her pants on yet. Audra gives me a smile and kiss when I enter the room.

"Could you do me a huge favor?"

"What is it?"

She looks down at her legs. "Will you shave my legs for me again?"

I laugh. "You ask me that every time we go out. Do you think I'll end up saying no?" I ask, motioning for her to step in the tub so we can wet her legs like every other time I've done this for her.

"I don't know. I'm sure you get sick of it. I mean, I do and they're my legs."

"I don't mind, Audra. You know that."

"And that's why I lo-" She stops so suddenly that I look up at her, not even realizing what she was going to say until I do.

I keep my mouth shut, not wanting to make her uncomfortable if she's not ready to say that yet. Hell, I don't know if I am. There's still that small, irrational fear in the back of my mind that if I ever utter those words again, something terrible will follow. We are quiet as we follow through our steps to shave her legs. We're almost done when I clear my throat. With her almost admission, I'm jumping the gun on my plans, but I can't help it.

"There's something I've been meaning to talk to you about." I cut my eyes over at her as she places a hand on her stomach.

"You have?" Her voice is too quiet, and it hits me that she may think I want to leave with her slip of the tongue.

"I want you to move in with me."

Audra's eyes widen. "What? Why?"

I give her my best 'are you serious' look. "Babe, I stay here more than I do at my own place and your bed sleeps like shit. We're practically living together as it is. I just..." I pause, noting that she looks a little freaked out, something I was not expecting. At all. "Think about it, okay? My place is bigger, my parents won't make us pay rent because I'm not now, and I'll talk to the guys. It might be easier and better once the baby comes if we were living together, that's all I'm saying."

She doesn't say anything as I finish working on her legs. We're about to raise a baby together and she's freaked out over living with me? Why? The longer she's silent the more instances over the past month pop up. Any time I try to take charge in any way, she stiffens a little and usually snaps at me like she did at the doctor's office that day.

"Hey, you know what," she starts, trying to sound cheerful. "You haven't hung out with the guys in a while and I haven't with Mimi or the girls. Why don't we do that instead?"

Audra's canceling on me? After we've had this planned all week? After I shaved her legs? My heart sinks, which kind of surprises me if I'm honest. I was looking forward to going out, but if she doesn't want to, then we won't.

"Yeah, okay. I guess I'll go then." I give her a soft, short kiss and add, "Text me later."

She says she will, but for some reason, I doubt her. As I drive home, it hits me that my mistake was asking her to move in with me. I couldn't leave things alone and now, things aren't right between us. If she doesn't want to, then that's fine. As long as she and the baby are healthy, that's all that matters to me in the end.

When I get to the house, the guys are in the kitchen, talking. They all stop when I walk in.

"I thought you had plans tonight," Bo says.

"Plans get canceled. What are y'all doing?"

"Just decided we're going to the bar tonight," Winston states.

"Want to come?" Grant asks.

"Yeah, I think I will."

It's a bit early, but we leave anyway. We're all hungry and some of the other guys on the team will be meeting us there. By now, the guys know I'm dating someone, but that's it. They don't know anything more than that. So it doesn't faze anyone when Bo starts asking questions after the waitress, Liana, has taken our orders. Pretty name. I haven't seen her here before, so she must be new.

"Well, what happened?"

I take a swig of my beer. "I get there and she's not quite ready, which isn't new. I may have asked her something important, and then she suggested she go hang with the girls and I hang with y'all. So, I left."

Bo nods, like that makes complete sense. It doesn't, dumbass. That's what I want to say, but I don't. I don't want to talk about her, so I look at Grant and Winston.

"Where's Lucy and Maddie?" They would usually be with them, but I guess not tonight.

Winston laughs. "They ditched us earlier for each other."

"Yeah, apparently Maddie," Grant glares at Winston, "needed to go do something and Lucy had to go too."

"Don't look at me," Winston tells him. "Lucy's the one who decided it was better than going out with you tonight."

Grant rolls his eyes as two guys walk up to our table. "Hey, Patrick, Jonathan. Guys, these jackasses are two of Lucy's brothers." He laughs, and I'm surprised the guys chuckle. From what I've heard, they aren't all that nice when it comes to their sister.

I zone out of the conversation as they begin to talk, and I eat. What they say doesn't matter to me. Maybe it would if I wasn't so concerned about Audra. I want us to work, damn it. I haven't wanted anything as much as this in a long time, but that doesn't mean shit if Audra doesn't want it too.

"Let's play a game," Bo interrupts my thoughts as he nods at the pool table.

I should have known it was a bad idea because as soon as he breaks, he starts talking. "You asked her about moving in?" I nod curtly. "She said no?"

"She didn't say anything," I correct, feeling like it should matter more than it probably does. "Next thing out of her mouth was to cancel our plans, which I guess suffices for a no."

"Have you started freaking out yet?"

I want to take my pool cue and jab him in the gut. "No," I semi-lie and Bo leaves it at that. Like I said, all that really matters is that they are healthy. If Audra doesn't want more than what we have now, then that's fine. Even if I want more. I can survive either way. I just wish Audra would be up front with me about what she wants. She can tell me what she's thinking about everything, but this.

We don't talk for four more games with me drinking beer after beer after beer. Thoughts of Candace and my current situation with Audra swirl in my mind, fueling the drinking. And it doesn't miss my attention that Lucy and Maddie show up, heading straight for Grant and Winston with big smiles. My eyes scan the room as Bo takes a shot, landing on a girl I've slept with a time or two before. When was the last time I had sex anyway? It feels like a lifetime ago.

"Don't even think about it, Neil," Bo's voice cuts through my thoughts, making me turn to him. He glances at the girl to show me that he saw me looking. "Don't do anything stupid."

"Fuck off, Bo." I shove my pool cue at him much harder than I meant, and he stumbles backwards into a passing waitress. I stalk over to the table, ignoring all the eyes on me as I throw some cash down to cover my food and drinks and start walking out of the bar.

Like I would have actually gone after the girl! It pisses me off that he thinks I would do that to Audra, whether she ever found out about it or not. She's carrying my baby girl! I love her! And he thinks I would throw away the simple possibility of being with her like I want because she shut down on me today? Just for a piece of ass?

Fucking bastard.

I don't have to listen to his shit because I can get the hell out of here.

My phone rings and I answer it angrily, "What?"

"Neil?" Audra's voice sounds on the other end.

"Neil!" Bo calls from behind me.

I ignore him. "Hey, babe. Sorry about that," I say much nicer.

"Everything okay?"

"Neil!" Bo yells again as I unlock the doors to my car. "Don't you get in that fucking car!"

"Try to stop me!" I holler back, getting into the car with the intentions of getting away from him for a few to cool myself down.

"Neil, what's going on?" Audra asks with worry.

"Nothing," I reply, locking my doors and cranking the car to get warm.

"Why are you calling me?"

"I just got home. Are you sure you're okay? You're slurring."

Bo slaps an open palm on my window. "Neil, you're drunk. Get out of the damn car. You aren't driving."

"Watch me." I level my gaze at him. I wasn't going to drive anywhere, but if he won't go away, then I might as well leave.

"Neil," Audra brings me back to her. "What happened with Bo? Please don't do anything stupid," she echoes, which seriously pisses me off.

I slide the gearshift into reverse.

"Neil!" Bo bangs on the window again. "Put it back in park! Now!"

Audra panics when she hears Bo, her voice rising with fear. "Do it, Neil. Let him take you home. Please," her voice cracks and I know she's crying.

"Fuck!" I hit the steering wheel in frustration because

I didn't want to make her cry. It pisses me off though. She wants to call now? In the middle of this when I should've been with her instead? Bo is still pounding on the window, but all I hear is Audra.

"If you drive and you're drunk, you and maybe even someone else is going to get hurt. What if you die, Neil? What am I supposed to do without you? Let him drive. Come stay with me tonight."

"I'm not drunk."

"Yes, you are!" she snaps. I hear a long exhale, and then she stabs me in the fucking heart. "You lost Candace. Don't do anything that would make me lose you. I'm not supposed to do anything risky and you aren't allowed to either, Neil." I barely hear her whisper through her tears, "I need you. *We* need you."

I move the gearshift back into park. Bo stops hitting my window for now, and I realize I drew a crowd outside. Okay, only the guys, but still.

"I'm sorry. He'll drive me over there, okay?"

"Thank you. Call me if it takes longer than it should."

I agree and hang up. All my anger is gone now. I'm the fucking bastard. Unlocking my doors, I get out of the car and once I close the door, Bo shoves me against the car, my collar in his fists.

"You're a fucking idiot! What the hell is wrong with you?"

"Get off of me!" I push him backward. "If you would've left me the fuck alone, I would have sat in the damn car."

"She was on the phone, wasn't she?" He shakes his head. "You're a selfish piece of shit, Neil." Selfish? "Good luck being a fa-"

I lunge forward and punch him in the jaw before he even finishes. He throws one at me, getting me right in the eye as Winston and Grant rush over.

"Enough!" Winston yells once they've separated us, pushing me around to the other side of the car. "Get in the car and shut the fuck up." He roughly shoves me into the back seat before slamming the door. I watch as Lucy and Maddie walk with Bo to Maddie's car and then, Winston and Grant get in with me.

"You going home or somewhere else?" Winston curtly asks.

"Somewhere else." I give him Audra's address.

The car is deathly silent on the drive. When we get there, Grant asks if I'm good to walk to her apartment myself. Yes, I am. I'm not that fucking drunk, thank you. I do walk slowly to her building, though, because the ground is covered with stupid snow, and I don't want to fall. I'm already sore from the couple of hits Bo managed to get me with. Time seems to move in slow motion as I lift my hand to knock on Audra's door. I don't know why because I have a key somewhere.

I'm patting my pockets for my key when I realize that Winston's driving my car, so he has my key. Audra opens the door with puffy eyes and wet cheeks. That sight kills me, making me feel even worse than I already did.

She gasps. "What happened to you?" Her fingers reach up and gingerly touch around my eye.

"I'm sorry." I flinch, but it isn't from her touch. I can hear myself slur.

"You should be. Come in, so I can get something for your eye."

"No, it's okay," I tell her as I walk to her couch. I

don't deserve anything to make me feel better. Audra ignores me and walks into the living room seconds later with a bag of frozen peas. She sits sideways in my lap and puts the bag over my eye carefully, watching me. "I'm sorry," I say again.

"What happened? I've never seen you like this."

I close my one good eye. "Nothing, babe. I don't want to talk about it."

"What if I tell you why I didn't answer earlier? If I do that, will you talk to me?" Her voice is so soft, so caring. I don't deserve it. Not tonight, at least. "Neil, look at me." My eye opens and she sets down the bag of peas, cupping my cheeks. "You scared me tonight. You owe me an explanation. So if I tell you, are you going to tell me?" When I nod, she kisses me.

She rests her head on my shoulder and starts talking. "I overreacted and froze when you asked me because the last guy I dated was controlling. He wasn't always like that, but the longer we dated, the more he tried to take over my life and everything I did. When I ended things, it didn't go so well. I looked a lot like you do right now." My hand balls into a fist on her back, but I don't say anything. "It started with little things, so every time you mentioned wanting me to do something or anything like that, I panicked a bit. I know you aren't like that, but I reacted like you were anyway. Being pregnant doesn't help with my crazy thoughts either. I'm sorry, Neil."

Unclenching my fist, I rub her back. "I wish you would have told me sooner, but it's okay that you didn't."

Audra smiles. "You seem too perfect sometimes. Glad to know that you aren't." She chuckles as she picks up the frozen peas and puts them back over my eye. "Your turn."

"I was dumb."

She laughs. "I knew that already."

I crack a smile, happy she's not too pissed at me. "I overreacted with your non-answer and started drinking, which I don't usually do because I'm not the smartest person when I do. I was thinking about you and Candace and then Bo said some shit." I shake my head.

She runs her fingers through my hair. "What did he say?"

For half a second, I debate telling her before deciding I might as well. "All I did was notice a chick and he saw me. He told me to not even think about it and not to do something stupid. I didn't want her and it pissed me off that he thought I would mess things up with you. It went downhill from there."

"You really had me worried, Neil," she whispers.

"I know, and I'm sorry for that and for making you cry. Do you forgive me?"

Audra nods. She's quiet for a moment before she says, "You only noticed her? You didn't want her?"

"Babe, no. I noticed she was there, like I noticed when Maddie and Lucy showed up. I want you and baby girl, who still needs a name, by the way." She rubs her belly and looks down at it. "Do we need to go stand in front of the mirror again? I think I need to add 'really' in front of 'huge and ridiculous knockouts' to make it 'really huge and ridiculous knockouts'."

Audra smiles. "No, we don't. I was thinking about how we still haven't decided on a name."

"Let's go lay down and brainstorm then."

Once we change and climb into her bed, I go to pull

her to me, but Audra shakes her head. "What's wrong?"

Her request is simple. "Will you talk to her? She hasn't been as active today as usual."

When I nod, Audra sits up, and I move to lay my head in her lap. "Hey, baby girl," I whisper, kissing her stomach. "Everything okay in there? Maybe now is a good time to tell your momma if you like the name I've picked."

Audra perks an eyebrow at me, but smiles. Baby girl is moving. "What name?"

"Liana. Liana Lawson. I haven't figured out a middle name yet."

"Where did you get that name from?" she asks.

"Do you like it?"

"Actually, yes, I really do."

"There was a new waitress at the bar tonight. That was her name and I thought it sounded pretty. We need a middle name now, if you truly like Liana."

Audra smiles. "I do. I like your last name with it too. We can't pick a middle name that starts with O, though."

I frown in confusion. "Why?"

"Her initials would be LOL."

Laughter erupts from deep within my chest. I can't help it. Between earlier and now, it's erasing the tension. Plus, it's hilarious. I don't think I would have even thought of that either. Audra starts to giggle with me as I sit up and lean forward to kiss her. Kissing her is something else. It's like a little piece of heaven, and she gives it to me every time. Her lips are plump, soft, and pure magic. I love kissing her because things seriously feel better afterwards.

"Baby girl has a name?" I whisper against her lips.

"Ask me tomorrow or in a week, just to be sure I don't change my mind."

She takes one of my pillows as I go to lay down. Audra turns onto her side and slips the pillow between her legs. I face her, my eyes getting heavy already.

"What are you going to tell the guys?"

I peer through my eyelashes to look at her. "What?"

"If I move in, what are you going to tell the guys?"

"My parents can help find them a place, or two of them can share a room if they want to stay and then the baby can have a room. We'll figure something out."

She nods as I turn to lay on my back. Audra moves closer to lay her head on my shoulder. I trail my fingers from her shoulder down her back, my only available path with my arm bent at the elbow. The place is quiet, and I can't help but smile at the thought that it won't last much longer before the silence is replaced by the cries of baby girl.

THE FIRST THING that happens when I wake up is a recollection of last night. Ugh. God, I'm a bastard. I can feel Audra's ass against my hip and her back against my side. I'm still on my back, and she's facing away from me on her side, but she's still pressed against me.

"Babe?" I rasp, realizing my throat is dry as fuck.

"Hmm?"

"I'm sorry." Last night's apologies don't count because I was drunk.

Audra rolls over. "You've said that a lot. You can fix me breakfast, if you still feel really bad about it." She smiles, gives me a kiss on the cheek, and then leaves for the bathroom.

"I would have done that anyway," I call after her. I

get up and go to the kitchen to start cooking. Then I realize what she said before we went to sleep. The legs of the chair scrapes against the floor and a glance over my shoulder shows me her presence. "You're moving in?" No need to beat around the bush.

Before she can answer, there's a knock on her door. Who the hell is here? Audra gets up and returns with her parents. I've never met her dad, and I'm so thankful that it's winter because that means I'm wearing pajama pants and a t-shirt for a change.

"Neil, if I had known you were here and making breakfast, I wouldn't have brought any for Audra." Her mother sets a bag of food on the table and then turns to her husband.

"It's okay. I'm sure she'll eat everything still." I chuckle and manage to make both her parents laugh too. I turn off the burner and face her father, holding out my hand. "Nice to meet you, sir."

"You too. It works out that you're here," he says, taking a seat.

Audra comes and fixes her a plate. I stay standing near the stove because she only has three chairs at her table. Once they are all seated, Mr. Garcia angles himself towards me.

"Audra said she didn't want to travel for Christmas this year, especially since she saw everyone at Thanksgiving. We would like to have dinner with you and your parents."

"Um, yeah, I could arrange that. They haven't met Audra yet, and I'm sure they want to." Her parents exchange a look. I don't know what it means though. Truth is, I haven't talked to my parents much since I told them.

Mom texts me, wanting updates on how Audra is doing, but that's about it. Maybe I need to work on my relationship with them before they meet her parents.

"Since y'all are here," Audra starts, "might as well let you know that I'm going to move in with Neil. Oh!" She wipes her mouth with a napkin and looks at her mother. "What do you think about Liana, Ma? For the baby's name?"

"It's pretty. Where did it come from?" She smiles.

"Neil met someone with that name."

"What's wrong with this place?" her father asks, being the first to comment on her moving in with me. I can't tell for sure, but I don't think he really likes me.

Audra shrugs. "We talked about it and decided that was best for us. He's over here most of the time anyway."

"You'll sleep better in my bed too, babe," I say without much thought as to how it may sound. All eyes land on me and I add, "Your mattress sucks and mine doesn't. Hopefully, you can sleep more soundly than what you have been." She nods. "Um, is there any particular time you would like to have this dinner? So I could let my parents know?"

"Whenever is good for them," Mrs. Garcia answers.

CHAPTER 22

Grant

THAT SOFT CLICKING never fails to make me smile. I'm sitting in the library, studying, and Lucy has apparently arrived. Now, I'm waiting for that whine of disappointment when she realizes I've noticed her.

"Grant," she sighs. "You ruined it."

I lift my head to look at her walking towards me. "That's not a nice thing to say. I can't help that I have good hearing."

She sits down next to me and shrugs. "I guess." Her fingers fiddle with the camera hanging from her neck before she says, "I have a question."

"What's that?" I ask, closing my textbook to give her my full attention.

Lucy's face transforms with a rather serious expression. "Will you go somewhere with me tonight?"

"Sure. What favor are you wanting to cash in this time?" I tease.

She frowns. Uh, oh. "I'm not asking for a favor, Grant. I meant as a date." Oh. "We haven't technically been on one yet and I say we both need some fun before finals. We could go do our run first and then go."

"That sounds like a good plan." A slow smile makes its way onto my face as I lean back into my chair and fold my arms over my chest. "Where are you taking me on this date, Lucy?"

She rolls her eyes. "Don't make me change my mind."

I lean over, grab the leg of her chair, and pull her closer to me. Lucy tries not to smile as I hook a finger under her chin to make her lean towards me. "Would you really do that to me?"

She nods. "I would." Lucy gives me a soft kiss. "But I won't. Not this time anyway."

Smiling, I put my books away. "Let's go run then." As we walk over to the gym, which has a small track inside, I take her hand, deciding to tease her one more time. "If you're taking me, does this mean I don't have to drive?"

"Sure, we could walk," she laughs.

We have a locker here, so we already have clothes waiting for us. Once we change and stretch, we start our jog. We are perfect partners for this because we both run at the same pace. With how regularly we're running, we are getting a bit faster, but not much. It's not our forte, that's for sure. I love that she's trying, though. Especially when it was a pretty much whim decision because Maddie asked her, and she's never done it before. She could've said no, but she didn't. And she's putting all this effort into making sure she does it to the best of her ability.

My lungs are on fire when Lucy finally decides we're done. Hers might be too because her chest is heaving as she tries to take deep breaths.

"Remind me again why we do this?" Lucy asks.

"I'm doing it for you. You're doing it for Maddie."

She smiles, and I'm confused as to why as she grabs a handful of my shirt and tugs me flush against her. Lucy gives me a kiss and murmurs against my mouth, "You're sweaty, Grant."

I laugh. "So are you. Sure hope you plan on showering before our date. I don't want to go out with a stinky, sweaty girl."

Lucy wrinkles her nose and shoves me away from her. "You're so mean. Go get ready and then come pick me up, okay? And bring all your goalie stuff."

"Why?" I ask with confusion.

"You'll see."

I agree before leaving her to go do as she wants. Why in the world do we need my gear? She probably wants to take some shots afterwards. When I get back to campus, I go to Lucy's dorm and some chick answers with a bright smile.

"Hey, is Lucy here?"

"Yeah," she says. "Just a second." She disappears and seconds later as promised, Lucy is standing at the door.

"Hey, Grant."

"Hey, Lucy. Ready?"

"Yep!" She takes my hand and starts pulling me down the hallway.

"Excited?" I laugh. "What's the plan? Might help if I knew where I was driving, you know."

"I'll let you know when to turn," she giggles.

"You are enjoying this way too much," I say as I open the door of my truck for her.

She grins. "I know."

So as we leave campus, Lucy does indeed let me know when to turn until she leads me to a restaurant across town. Even from the outside, it has an old-fashioned southern feel to it, and I wonder how Lucy knew about this place. When I glance at her, she's wearing a smile.

"Whenever my grandparents come up to watch one of my brothers' games, this is their favorite place to eat. I thought you might like it too."

"Let's find out." We rush inside to escape the freezing cold. Once we're seated and our food comes, I ask, "Are you ready for Christmas break? Does your family have any special traditions?"

"Nothing special. I just really want to go see my grandparents. They're getting older and not as healthy. I go see them every break." Lucy's voice softens. "They took care of us and raised us after my parents died, so I want to make sure I visit, especially since their health seems to get worse after every visit. They are doing well right now, though." She attempts to give me a smile, but it falls too quickly to be a real one. "What about you and your family?"

"We travel for Christmas to get a break from everything. We're going to the Bahamas this year."

When she laughs, I'm lost, but I smile anyway. "Good. You could use some sun." I look down at the skin on my hand since my arms are covered by my long sleeved t-shirt. I'm not really tan, but I'm not pale either. The color is somewhere in between. I've never given it much thought before. Lucy laughs again. "Grant, I was kidding! You look fine, promise."

"Fine? That's how you reassure someone?" I shake my head with a grin. The girl is something else.

"What can I say? I have a spectacular way with words."

As we discuss finals, I realize that this is probably one of the last times I'm going to be able to spend a decent amount of time with her this year. After finals, we're both leaving until next semester. It's still on my mind as we leave, and I drive us to the rink. Lucy hasn't said what we're doing yet, which makes me notice she didn't bring her camera. Maybe I was wrong.

It's not until we're at the player's bench that I say, "Okay, Lucy, what are we doing here?"

"Well," she starts, her cheeks flushing a deep scarlet, "you know that I like photographing you when you're in the net and I've been thinking that I want to experience that. Being in the net like you are, I mean." She reaches for my helmet, looking down at it while turning it over in her hands. "What do you say?"

I take my helmet from her and put it on her head with a smile. "I say you look pretty damn hot right now."

She laughs and blushes, shaking her head at me. We get my pads and gloves on her and then I put on a pair of skates, grab an extra stick and a bunch of pucks before we step onto the ice. Since Lucy hasn't ever been skating, I let her go without them for now. It'll be a little easier for her to keep her balance this way.

"Are you sure you want to wear all that? You would be fine with just the glove and helmet."

"Full experience, Grant," she reminds me.

"Okay." I line up the pucks in a row and smile when she crouches, ready in case I slap one towards her. She acts like she knows exactly what to do when I haven't told her anything. "Try and glove the shots or let it bounce off your arm."

She nods, so I do my best to aim and shoot one at her. It's not often than I'm on this side. It's a pretty soft shot, but she misses. It takes her a few more times, but she finally gloves one. After about twenty minutes of her attempting to block various shots, she tells me she's done.

"Let's take all this stuff off."

I guide her back to the bench and remove all my gear. "Do you want to learn how to skate?"

"Yes, please." She puts on the extra pair, and I tie the laces for her. "You know, I don't think I could ever be a goalie," Lucy says it like it's something she would consider one day. "I wanted to flinch so many times and the puck wasn't even coming at me that fast. I thought you were fantastic before, but now, I think you're pretty amazing."

I help her to her feet, wrapping my arms around her waist. "Thanks. You're a pretty talented photographer. I never really paid attention to things like that before."

"Looks like we both introduced new things to one another." She places her hand on the back of my neck, pulling me closer for our lips to meet. "Now, teach me how to skate."

"Whatever you want, Lucy."

Her grip on my arms tells me how nervous she is about falling. We move slowly as she gets more comfortable, my comments staying on the task at hand.

"Okay, go a little faster," she says confidently.

I skate backwards with a little more speed, but it's a

tad too fast for Lucy and she starts to fall forward. Lucky for her, I have as good a grip on her as she does on me, so she doesn't fall. I almost expect her to be embarrassed, but she starts laughing.

"Sorry, I pictured it in my head and it looked funny." She shakes her head and takes a deep breath. "Something tells me a face plant would have hurt so much worse than if I had fallen backwards. Good thing you saved me from that." Her grip with her right hand tightens as she lets go with her left to move her hair out of her face. Between her laughter, her smile, and every damn thing about her, she's beautiful.

"I'm going to miss you," I sigh, pulling her against me so I can wrap my arms around her.

Lucy's lips fall into a frown. "Miss me? Where are you...oh, you mean because of Christmas break?"

"Yeah. I don't know what I'm going to do without you around, asking for favors."

"I'll make a list of all the things I want you to do while your gone then."

I chuckle and give her a kiss before resting my forehead on hers. "Like what?"

She thinks about it as we glide over the ice. "Well, first, I want you to come back."

"I can definitely do that for you," I laugh.

"You could bring me something from there, take pictures, be sure to miss me, and have fun with your parents. Nothing out of the ordinary."

We come up to the net, and I lift her up to sit on top of it, placing myself between her knees as I hold onto her waist. "I can do that. Do you remember what you told me the last time you were here?" She wrinkles her nose and shakes her head. "You said, and I quote, 'And no funny business'."

Lucy giggles, trailing her fingers over my chest. She's in a laughing mood tonight, not that I'm complaining. Happy and carefree are two emotions that fit Lucy. "I don't think I've said that tonight," she whispers. She wraps her arms around my neck. "You said you were going to miss me, right? Maybe you could show me what I have to look forward to when we get back?" Her words are so softly spoken, and her cheeks are ridiculously red. I love that she's being subtly suggestive, and it still makes her blush.

"Is here okay for you or are you going to make me take you back to the house?"

Instead of answering, she presses her lips to mine to show me what I'll be missing in the Bahamas.

CHAPTER 23

Winston

MADDIE HAS BEEN avoiding me since that night. She'll answer texts, but that's it. She claims she's too busy studying for finals. And now that finals are over, she's headed home a day early. Before the game tonight, I decided I needed some peace and quiet to think, so I came to the rink. At the sound of footsteps, I look over my shoulder to see Neil. His eyebrows lift in surprise.

"What are you doing here?" he asks the question I was thinking.

"Need to get away. Girl problems. You?"

"The same," he says, sitting next to me on the bench. Neil rarely speaks of his girlfriend, so I'm a bit surprised he even said what he did.

Before I hand him a beer from the six pack I bought, I

ask, "Are you going to act like a dumbass again?"

He shakes his head, and I give it to him. We both take a drag, and before either of us can say something else, more footsteps sound. Grant appears seconds later, looking much like Neil did.

"Girl problems?" Neil questions as Grant takes a seat on the other side of me as I hand him a beer.

"Not really."

Neil swallows a sip and says, "I can bet that mine is worse."

I give him a sideways glance and laugh, shaking my head at the seemingly absurdness of it all. "Are we seriously about to discuss this?"

He nods. "You're up first."

"I'm in love with Maddie," I say simply.

Grant and Neil chuckle. "We know that," Grant says. "What's the problem?"

I sigh. "She's my best friend's little sister, he's not talking to me, and I need him to. Have you noticed Maddie's lost a bit of weight?" They nod. "Long story short, I need to make Dave talk to me, so I can talk to him about that."

Neil slaps my shoulder. "Then it looks like you better be calling him until he answers."

"Yeah, and if he doesn't answer, find another way to get up with him," Grant adds.

"That's what I've been trying to do." I turn to Grant. "No problems at all?"

"Nope. What can I say? Lucy's amazing." A sly, stupidly happy grin lifts his lips.

Neil laughs. "You shouldn't even be allowed to drink then. Looks like it's my turn?"

"Yeah, Neil. You said you had girl troubles too," I say.

He shakes his head and takes a deep breath. Then he mutters, "I'm going to be a dad."

My jaw falls to the floor as Grant and I openly gape at him. Wow. That's huge. "Holy shit," I voice my thoughts.

"Yep," he agrees before drinking more beer.

"That's why you're working?" Grant asks.

He nods. "Yeah, gotta do something. And in-between, I'm with Audra. That's her name." He sighs again. "I'm in love with her, but not really sure how to tell her. We've been sticking to the pregnancy for the most part. It's a girl," he finishes with a small smile, looking genuinely happy.

"Wow," Grant breathes. "Why haven't you said anything to us before? Does Coach know?"

"Yeah, I told him soon after I found out. I just...I don't know. It's a big deal and I didn't want to hear any shit I guess."

"We wouldn't do that, you know that, Neil," I tell him. "Congrats, I guess?"

He grins. "Most definitely. Thanks."

"Congrats," Grant adds.

"Thanks. She's due in February." February? That's two months away. Neil clears his throat and keeps talking. "I've been meaning to talk to y'all anyway. She's moving in with me over break. You can stay as long as you need. My parents could help you find a new place or you could stay and deal with having a baby in the house until the semester ends. My room is big enough that the baby's stuff could be in there, but Audra's really hoping to have a nursery. So, someone might have to give up their room and share."

Ugh. That would be fun. Not only to share a room, but to have to be mindful of a baby? Our sex lives would go down the drain so fast, that is if Maddie ever comes around again. It'll have to do until the end of the spring semester at least. Neil drains the rest of his bottle and stands.

"Think about it over break and let me know what you're doing when you get back. I need to see her before the game. Thanks for the beer, Winston, and I hope you get up with him soon."

"Thanks."

He leaves and Grant shakes his head. "Who knew, right? A kid. Wow. Are you going to stay?"

"Maybe, but only for the semester. It'll be fun," I deadpan. "I'll get another place for next year. You?"

"Was thinking the same. Bo will probably stay too. Are we a bunch of idiots for staying anyway? A baby is going to drive us all crazy. Can you imagine trying to do homework or sleep?"

"We can handle three months of it, I think. Unless..." I trail off with my sudden thought.

"What?"

"The Kennedy boys stay off campus, right? Wonder if they have extra rooms they'd want to rent out?"

Grant seems to think about it. "I could find out. Worse comes to worse, we could talk Bo into moving out with us and us getting a place together. Neil did say his parents would help."

"I really don't want to live with a baby, so let's work on this over break."

He nods. "What's the story with Maddie? She hasn't

been around lately, which neither has Lucy, but I figured Maddie would since you were helping her study," he says after a lull of silence.

I sigh. "I don't really want to talk about it."

"Okay, well, let me know if you do. Or if you want, maybe you could talk to Lucy and she could try to talk to Maddie as her friend."

"Thanks. We'll see how things go over break. We should put the beer away. It is game day after all."

I THINK THE beer might have fueled the three of us. We're on fire tonight, lighting the lamp every chance we get, leaving the other team with zero hope of winning tonight. Neil seems to be floating on air, something he's been lacking lately, and I faintly wonder if it's because he's told us about the baby. He's been dominating the ice, so whatever happened, I'm thankful for it. Hopefully, it'll still be here once we return from break.

The door to the locker room opens, all of us in various stages of undressing and a bit rowdy from the win, but it's silent when the door swings closed with a thud. A few of us glance and then we're all looking. There's a pretty, pregnant girl standing just inside the locker room. This must be Audra.

"Neil?" Her eyes scan the room until they land on him. He was facing his locker, not paying attention to anyone else, but he swivels fast when he hears her. Neil looks mildly surprised. "I...Can I talk to you outside for a second?"

"Yeah, babe," he says easily, walking towards her. Neil is halfway to the nervous girl who's rubbing her stomach when he realizes we're all watching him and her. He faces the room. "Seriously? Stop staring. She's a girl, not an alien." Neil turns to her again, about to usher her out of the room.

"Sorry, Neil. I guess I should have waited until later," she says, realizing that we're still watching them. How could they not? Neil's girlfriend is pregnant! No one even knew she existed until last month and the girl looks like she's been pregnant longer than that, so of course they are all staring at her.

"No, it's fine. C'mon."

They disappear onto the other side of the door, and we all exchange glances. Bo, Grant, and I are the only ones who don't seem surprised because we all knew.

"Woah," Vincent speaks first. "Why hasn't he said anything?" he asks Bo.

"I don't know."

Neil reenters the room with a smile, but it goes slack when he sees we're very much the same as before. "Might as well get this over with, huh?" Everyone nods. "That's Audra. She's my girlfriend. In case you weren't staring at her long enough earlier to notice, she's pregnant and having a girl. That cover everything?"

They nod again and that's that. With the fall semester officially over, everyone is ready to get out of here. I am too, and on the way to my car, I try calling Dave, but he doesn't answer. I leave a voicemail anyway.

"Hey, I need to talk to you about Maddie. Call me back."

Something tells me I'll be leaving lots of voicemails until he answers or until I think of a better way to force him to talk to me.

CHAPTER 24

NEIL

AUDRA SHOWING UP last night wasn't exactly how I planned on telling the rest of the team, but it worked out fine. It was a day when she had a night class, so she was already on campus and decided to go to the game after she finished her final. With the snow and all, she decided to wait for me, so I could follow her home. She was tired of waiting though and was on the brink of leaving already since she wanted to stop by the store too. She wanted to see me though, so she barged right on into the locker room.

Now, I'm sitting in her living room while she's getting ready for work. My phone rings and it looks like I'll be asking my parents today. I wasn't planning on calling them until tomorrow.

"Hey, Mom. How are you and Dad?" I say once I answer.

"Good. You and Audra?" she asks.

"We're fine."

"That's great. I wanted to call and check in since the semester is over. How did you do in your classes?"

"Pretty good. I think I did well on my finals too. I'm glad you called." I take a deep breath, knowing this could go either way. "I wanted to see if you and Dad would like to have dinner with us and her parents? Then you can meet her. I've been wanting to talk to you and Dad anyway."

Mom's pause of silence tells me most of what I need to know. "Neil, you know your father. He still hasn't gotten over what happened."

I clench my jaw. "That's why I want to see you both. I want to apologize for the things I did and said."

"I can try talking to him," she offers, but it's not good enough.

"Mom, do more than try. I don't know what y'all want from me. All I can do is say sorry." After a calming breath, I quietly speak so Audra won't hear me talking. "The first person close to me in my entire life to die was Candace. Your parents and Dad's parents either died before I was born or while I was really little. I don't remember them. So yeah, it was fucking hard to deal with when I lost her. I didn't know how to cope and my method was a shitty one, but I did the best I could, Mom.

"I know it's not a good excuse for being stupid and saying crap to y'all, but you have to get over it at some point. I'm going to be a dad soon. If my baby girl ever did like I did, am I supposed to be civil towards her? Like she's not even my kid anymore?" My throat gets even tighter. "Don't you want to be a part of her life? How can you do that if you are barely a part of mine? I don't know what else to say."

She sniffs, but if she's crying, I don't feel bad about it. I need her to care. "I know, son, and I get it, I do. It was hard for us to see you go through that, but I think it was even harder to see you turn to them instead of us. Don't take it the wrong way, Neil. I was happy that you were healing, but I think we both sort of left the other behind. You see them every week and we're lucky to hear from you once a month if that. They've met her, haven't they?"

Seriously? She's jealous of the Lanier's? It bothers me and pisses me off at the same time. "They lost their daughter! They are like family to me and always have been. Of course I go see them. Not to mention Alice. I couldn't stop going when she was expecting to see me. I can't believe that's even something you're saying. Y'all were ready to abandon me when I told you she was pregnant. Don't act like this is all my fault. You were pissed and didn't want to help at all. Why wouldn't I turn to them, Mom? What did y'all do to even show support for Candace and me? You know what, fuck it. I'll come up with an excuse to get you out of it. Why don't you go ahead and cut me out of your lives completely and let me know what I need to do to own the house."

"Neil?"

I look over my shoulder at hearing Audra's voice. The look on her face tells me she's heard more than a fair share. "I gotta go," I interrupt my mom and hang up. Audra comes over and sits sideways in my lap, wrapping her arms tightly around neck. "Don't say anything, babe," I whisper into her hair. "Don't say anything yet." I let her comfort me, waiting to see exactly what she is going to say. My hand runs up her back, into her hair, and then I find myself hugging her back. "Thank you."

"You're going to have to help me get up, you know. I hate to leave, but if I don't, I'll be late."

"We don't want that," I tell her, pulling away so I can kiss her. "We can talk later and I'll tell you the full story." Audra nods, satisfied for now, and I help her stand. "Did you pack your things, so you can come to my place afterwards?"

"Yes, my bag is on the bed if you'll carry it over for me. Make sure you lock my doors and turn off all the lights and-"

"I know what to do, babe."

She smiles and kisses my cheek. "Right. Sorry. I'll see you later then."

Once she's gone, my shoulders sag as I sigh. I swear. My life seems to unravel even more in some areas and come closer together in others, and it's happening all at the same time. Instead of getting right to cleaning, I go crawl back into bed and sleep for a bit.

AFTER CLEANING UP both our places, I feel like I could use another nap. However, I still have laundry to do. Audra should be here any minute, and she's going to want me to talk, which is fine. I really want to relax for a bit, so hopefully, she does too. Just as I'm about to sit down on the couch, there's a knock at the door. Surely, Audra wouldn't knock. This is her place now too, even though she hasn't moved in yet.

"Mom? What are you doing here?"

She's standing at my door, hugging her coat tighter,

trying to stay warm. I don't want her here. Not now, especially since Audra just pulled up. Mom glances over her shoulder, but faces me again.

"Can I come in, Neil?"

"Oh, uh, yeah." I move aside for her to enter. "Let me go make sure she doesn't need any help. Make yourself at home." Leaving her inside, I hurry to Audra.

"Who's that?"

"My mom."

"Oh, should I go?"

I shake my head. I'll be damned if I'm about to make her leave. "I don't know what she wants, but you're not going anywhere but inside."

"Okay," she nods, her hand going to her stomach. "I brought dinner. It's in the passenger seat."

"I'll get it then."

She waits for me to grab the bag of food before taking my hand and walking with me inside as snow starts to fall. That simple act, of waiting so she can walk in with me, does wonders. I don't know why, but it does. My mother is waiting right where I left her. Guess she didn't feel comfortable making herself at home. Audra squeezes my hand as Mom gives her a tight lipped smile.

"Mom, this is Audra. Babe, this is my mom."

"Nice to meet you," Mom says, but even I can tell she doesn't mean it. Her words are too clipped, too formal.

"You too," Audra replies, turning towards me. "Want me to go put the food in the kitchen?"

"Yeah." I hand her the bag and she walks off. It's not until she walks around the corner that I realize she's never really been past the living room, so she doesn't know where the kitchen is. "What do you want, Mom?" I ask, guiding her into the living room. "I'm not really in the mood."

She wrings her hand and suddenly, I realize she's nervous. I've never seen my mom appear anxious before. Not like this anyway. "I don't know why I came other than on the phone this morning, you sounded like the son I remember. I want to understand, Neil, and I want to be around to meet my granddaughter."

"Does Dad know you're here?" My parents are pretty hard to separate. I mean, they are usually a joined force that doesn't deviate from each other on their view of something.

"Yes. He had to leave for a trip, so he couldn't come."

"There's enough food if you'd like to eat with us." We both turn at the sound of Audra's voice. "Well, Neil has extra to share," she jokes with a smile.

God, I love her. I face my mom. This could either be a turning point towards progress, or she can take a step backwards by declining her offer.

"That sounds nice," she answers.

"Hard to turn down a pregnant girl, isn't it?" Audra chuckles.

I laugh as we head towards the kitchen. "You need to let that go, babe. Sometimes, people say yes because they mean yes. Not because they don't want to tell you no."

"Well, I choose to believe otherwise, so leave me alone." Audra already has three plates on the table. "Oh! I forgot the drinks."

"I'll get them."

They sit as I fix everyone something to drink. It's not until after our plates have food on them and we begin to eat that Mom starts talking. She glances at Audra, who is keeping her eyes on her plate for the most part.

"I, uh...I've been thinking about what you said all day. You shouldn't have to apologize, Neil. We should. We weren't there for you like we should've been, but the Lanier's were and they still are. I'm thankful for that. I think that you continuing to go after her death, in part because of Alice, shows the kind of man you are. So, I am sorry we weren't there for you and I'm sorry that it's taken this long for you to hear that. Your father feels the same, and we would love to have dinner with your family," she finishes, looking at Audra.

There is a part of me that doesn't believe her, but then there's a larger part that simply wants to move on. All I can manage to say in return are two words. "Thanks, Mom."

After a brief pause, Audra smiles widely and shifts the conversation. "Would you like to see the latest sonogram?" My mom nods, and Audra adds, "Well, show her, Neil."

I reach into my back pocket for my wallet and pull it out, handing it to my mom. She studies it for a moment before asking, "Does she have a name yet?"

"Liana, but we're still figuring out a middle name," Audra answers. With that, I'm out of the conversation as Mom and Audra start talking about the pregnancy. I'm a good listener while they talk and talk and talk. By the time my mom decides it's time to go, I've already washed our dirty dishes. I want to groan when Audra asks, "Are you sure you'll be okay driving back?"

Luckily, Mom says, "Yes. Neil, I'll let you know a date soon. It was so nice to meet you, Audra." They hug and my mom turns to me, giving me one as well. She kisses my cheek, tells me she loves me, and then she's out the door. Things seem better. They feel better. All I can do now is hope she wasn't lying when she said Dad was on the same page.

Audra turns to me with curious eyes, but I shake my head. I take her hand and silently lead her to the living room. She sits at one end of the couch before I grab the remote and lay down, resting my head in her lap. Her fingers weave their way into my hair as I turn on the TV.

"Are we going to talk about that?" Audra questions.

"Not tonight. I want to relax for a bit."

"Okay."

I turn the TV to *The Big Bang Theory* and we watch the marathon for about two hours before I break our silence. "How was your day, Audra?"

"Weird to say the least," she chuckles softly. Her legs move underneath my head as she lifts her sock covered feet up onto my coffee table.

"And how was Liana's day?"

"Normal. Ooh," she pats my shoulder repeatedly. "Up, Neil. Get up." I sit up and she stands. Audra disappears down the hallway. "Oh my God! Which door is the bathroom?" she yells with frustration.

"Third on right," I call back, trying not to laugh but not able to hold back a chuckle.

When she returns with her hands on her hips, she says, "Okay. I think it's time I get a tour. Plus, I'm ready to shower and change out of these clothes anyway."

I show her everyone's rooms, the bathrooms, the laundry room, which room I think would be good for the nursery, and then the master bedroom. Her bag was sitting on my bed, waiting for her. While she's grabbing her things, I get her a towel and such for her shower. I even turn the water on for her.

"Neil?" I hear from my bedroom.

"Yeah, babe?"

"I need one more thing."

"What's that?" I ask as I walk back into the room.

"You."

What? The corners of my mouth slightly fall and my brows bunch together. Me? What is she talking about? I'm right here. Once I'm standing in front of her, she leans forward to kiss me softly. Those are the kind of kisses that make me want more from her because they are so simply sweet and full of...love? I don't know, but I sure do love them.

"Thank you," she mumbles sincerely against my lips, watching me carefully.

"You're welcome. Go shower before the water runs cold."

Audra nods and steps around me to go to the bathroom. While I change and then go back downstairs to the couch, I wonder what Audra will do with her furniture. We already have everything here, so she wouldn't need to bring all of that. Maybe her place was already furnished when she moved in. I'm not sure when she's going to make the move, but I figured it would be during our break. We need to do some more shopping, but Audra wants to wait until after her baby shower. At least, that way, it'll give me time to paint the baby's room, if she wants it painted.

With the end of the year, I can't help but think about next year. It's going to bring so many things. My first child, Audra's first Mother's Day, my first Father's Day, and our baby's first of everything. As for hockey, I'm too old to be drafted, but I'm an unrestricted free agent. According to my agent, there's a good chance I could get signed this year, but do I want to? Should I? Would I? Audra's going to finish her degree. I'll finish mine, and then we'll be looking to find jobs that those degrees were earned for. On top of that, we're going to have a baby to take care of. We would need time to be more settled before a change like that. It's now or never in my eyes. I won't be playing for school anymore, and if I don't get signed, then I'm done. It'll be time to move on. But what if I do? Do I want that life?

My thoughts are halted as Audra comes in, sits next to me, and rests her head on my shoulder. I place my hand on the inside her of left thigh. "You look like you were thinking about something," she comments.

"I was." Instead of mentioning hockey, I ask, "Was your apartment fully furnished? I was trying to figure out what you planned on doing with all the stuff if it's all yours."

"It's not all mine, so don't worry." After a pause, she lifts her head to look at me and says, "I'm ready to try out your bed. This day seems to have lasted far too long."

I turn off the TV, stand, take her hand, and we walk up to my room. We crawl into bed, getting comfortable with me on my back and Audra on her side like usual. I lift my arm up to rest my head on it, staring at the ceiling. I'm tired, but I'm not sleepy.

"When are you moving in?"

"Whenever. I'll need to be out by the end of the month though. What did the guys say?"

"They're going to let me know what they're doing once they get back."

She doesn't respond for a long time, but when she does, it's certainly not what I was expecting. "This doesn't seem too bad, does it? Us here together?"

"Was that what you were expecting?" There's no malice in my voice. Audra's comments don't bother me nearly as much as they did before. Now, I know that her intentions are usually nicer than the words that end up leaving her mouth.

"I didn't really know what to expect. You're nothing like I thought you'd be. We're just...I think we're going to be good together, that's all."

"We already are, Audra."

CHAPTER 25

NEIL

BETWEEN CHILDBIRTH CLASSES, Audra moving in, working, and the holidays nearing, I don't know how I have any time at all. Audra has been sleeping a lot better in my bed, but I know that's all due to the mattress and not who may own the bed. We're supposed to be having dinner with our parents tonight, and I'm almost looking forward to it. First, though, I need to get my present shopping done.

This past Sunday, Alice told me exactly what she wanted. She even got Mrs. Lanier to print off a picture of it, so I wouldn't buy the wrong one. Last year, I asked what she wanted and accidentally bought the wrong kind. Alice hasn't forgotten, so I laughed when she handed me the picture.

I need to figure out what I'm buying Audra too. She asked if I was going to decorate for Christmas and I told her no. It didn't seem like a big deal to me. However, that's unacceptable, apparently.

"We at least need a tree, Neil. It can be a tiny one, if you don't want a big one, but we need a tree." Her eyes started to shine with unshed tears. "How can we be in the holiday spirit otherwise? Are you going to be like this with Liana, Neil? Is she going to grow up in an undecorated house for Christmas?!"

She was getting so worked up about it, we went and bought a small artificial tree that day. She let me know real quick too that Liana would need a real tree in the future. I'm pretty sure she's starting to lose it. I nod my head and go with it though.

It's not until I've bought everyone's present, including a little stuffed duck for Liana, that I know what I want to give Audra. I was heading home when I passed a spa place. She loves my little massages, and I've seen her nails painted a few times. After the baby is born, she could take a spa day for herself and come relax. So I buy her a gift certificate.

"Whatcha got there?" Audra asks as I walk into the house.

"Presents." Thank God for gift wrapping services. I don't have the skill, patience, or time for wrapping presents. It works for secrecy too.

Coming home to Audra brings out a new emotion. It's strangely satisfying and for a moment, I barely hesitate when I go to kiss her. Being honest and, for lack of a more manly term, following my heart has never been an issue for me. But this is an entire new level of commitment that I've never had to deal with. Candace and I were young and never got the opportunity to reach this point in our relationship.

It's scary as fuck knowing that not only am I with this girl, but she's living with me and carrying our kid. We're bound for life no matter what happens between us. It's crazy to think about in such a large span of time. Am I ready for this? Probably not as much as I'd like, but as scary as it seems, I'm ready for it and I want it so badly. I wonder if Audra thinks about these things too.

I set the presents underneath our tree and turn around, almost running into Audra, who was peering over my shoulder.

She even tries to look surprised that I've caught her looking. "Did you give your parents the directions to the restaurant?"

"Yes."

"Did you tell them what time?"

"Yes."

"Did you-" she starts, rubbing her belly.

"Babe, everything is set. I didn't forget anything." Audra smiles with relief and a touch of embarrassment. I ignore it and bend down to kiss her stomach. "Hey, baby girl. Tell your momma to leave Daddy alone."

Audra laughs. "Fine. Go get ready then. I do know that you need to that."

I chuckle and shake my head at her. She's right. I want a shower and a change of clothes before we go tonight. My nerves are higher than usual. All of us are getting together, plus the roads are supposed to freeze tonight. I don't want to drive in it, so hopefully, this dinner won't last too terribly long.

After my shower, I dry off, hang the towel, and realize I didn't grab clean clothes. Without a second thought, I swing the door open and walk into my bedroom.

"Oh! Sorry, Neil!" Audra covers her eyes with her hands, and I laugh. She's sitting in the middle of the bed with her back propped up on pillows that are leaning against the headboard. "Stop laughing!" she squeals as I go over to my closet. "I know it's nothing I haven't seen before, but I...don't want to ogle."

I freeze and slowly turn to face her. "You don't want to ogle?" A smirk rises on my lips. "You find me attractive, Audra?" I tease. "You know this body is all yours, right?"

She peeks through her fingers and groans. "Get dressed already. Let's not think about all that right now when we're about to go meet our parents."

After grabbing my clothes, I walk over to her, setting them on the bed as I slowly start to get dressed. Quietly, because I don't want to upset her and I don't want her to think I'm only saying it for me, I say, "Sex *is* still an option, Audra."

As I slip on my t-shirt, the final piece of clothing, she drops her hands into her lap. "I don't want to. Big difference in being horny and actually feeling like having sex."

"Okay."

Audra scoots over to the edge of the bed and sits so her legs are dangling off. She reaches for me, pulling me closer as she wraps her arms around my waist and rests her head on my chest. "I need to change, but I wanted to give you a hug first."

"Why?"

"Well, I was in here because your bed is so ridiculously comfy and I wanted to relax before we left. But..." she drags, looking up at me with a smile. "I think I could use a back massage later. A hug might soften you up since I'm really only asking because I want one. Not because my back is hurting."

"Hmm," I hum, pretending to think about it. "We'll see how I feel after dinner."

"Okay," she nods.

Audra gently pushes me away so she can stand. She's about to walk off, but I grab her hand, feeling the urge to state the obvious. "I'm kidding, babe. You know I will."

"I know," she winks.

I roll my eyes as she goes to change. When she's finally ready, we walk out of the house, hand and hand, and leave for the restaurant. Audra's parents are already there and waiting when we arrive. I watch as they hug their daughter, smile, and then her mother hugs me before her father shakes my hand. Before we can sit, my parents walk in. Mom hugs me, but they shake everyone else's hand during introductions. I try to figure out if Mom was right about Dad as we all take a seat.

The waitress holds off conversation for a few minutes as we order drinks and look over our menus for what we want for dinner. Mr. Garcia seems like the take charge kind of guy, so it doesn't surprise me when he speaks first.

"Thank you for coming. We wanted to meet you since we're all going to be connected with this baby. My wife and I thought it would be nice to know you."

"Yes, you're right," my mother starts, but my dad cuts her off early.

"I'm surprised the Lanier's aren't here too," he says dryly.

And there it is. Audra's parents look confused as my mother chides him. It takes everything in me not to sigh.

"Who are they? Why should they be here?" Mrs. Garcia asks, looking between me and my father.

"Oh? Neil hasn't told you?" he says.

"Excuse me, Mr. Lawson," Audra starts, quite frankly surprising me by saying anything at all. Her stare is as cold as the weather outside as she bores her gaze into him. "But that is Neil's to tell. Not yours. If you don't want to be here, then leave."

"Audra," Mrs. Garcia begins, probably about to chide her daughter.

"No," I interrupt. "Sorry, Mrs. Garcia, but Audra's right." I turn to look at my parents. "We're not here to focus on our problems, which Mom assured me were no longer issues. So, if you don't want to know the other half of my daughter's family, then leave." Facing my mother, I add, "If you want to stay, you can. You can sleep at the house and I'll take you home in the morning." This is fucking ridiculous. One simple dinner, people. That's all they wanted. I feel Audra's fingers slip between mine while we wait for an answer.

Dad finally shakes his head after what seems like forever. "Okay, I apologize, son, and to you as well," he finishes looking at Audra and her family.

"Thank you," Audra says. "Neil said you two own a realtor company?"

That starts our parents discussing their businesses for a while. Turns out, Audra's parents are looking to open another restaurant and my parents may be able to help them look for a place. We're about midway through our meal before talk turns to hockey, thanks to my dad.

"Are you still going to pursue the NHL, Neil? There's no need in keeping your agent if you aren't."

"Agent? What is he talking about?" Audra asks.

"Neil could be signed this year to play with the NHL. He has an agent who will hopefully be working on a contract in a few months. There's no telling where in the States or in Canada he'll end up. If he pursues it, that is."

At the mention of other places, Audra absentmindedly starts caressing her belly. Thanks a lot, Dad. "I don't know what I'm going to do yet," I answer quietly. "I don't know what I want." I turn to Audra. "That's why I haven't mentioned it to you yet. I haven't figured out what I want."

She's not happy if the frown on her face is any indication. "That might be a good reason to talk to me, Neil," she says softly. "We can discuss it later, though."

"Have you figured out a middle name yet?" Mom asks to change the subject.

"Well," Audra glances at me, a sign that she's found one she likes, but hasn't mentioned to me yet. "Neil was joking around one night and mentioned Grace. Liana Grace Lawson sounds pretty, doesn't it?" Our moms nod. "Do you like it, Neil?"

I lean over to kiss her temple. "Yeah, babe. It's perfect. Plus, her initials won't be LOL."

Audra laughs and that makes the night so much better than it was.

WHEN WE FINALLY make it home, Audra props her feet up on the coffee table and sits down on the couch with a sigh of relief. I lay with my head in her lap, feeling much the same way.

"That went pretty well, don't you think?"

"Yeah," I answer, closing my eyes.

Her fingers play with strands of my hair. "I hope she has your hair."

"Mhm," I hum, feeling sleepier.

"When are we going to talk about hockey?"

"Later."

"Ooh! Head up."

I lift my head as she stands, probably going to the bathroom. I lay back down.

"Neil," a voice whispers in the distance. "Neil. Wake up!" she says louder, shaking my shoulder to jar me away. Audra is hovering over me, looking a bit aggravated. "About time. Come on, let's go to bed," she finishes nicely.

As we change and get ready for bed, I realize I never gave her what she asked for. "Babe," I start as we slip between the sheets. "Did you still want a massage?"

"No, it's okay. You need to sleep a bit before you go into work anyway."

"Fuck." I reach for my phone having forgotten to set my alarm. After I set it, I finally relax, closing my eyes once more.

"Good night, Neil," Audra whispers.

Turning my head, I open my eyes. She's seems so far away even though she's only on her side of the bed. "C'mere." Once she's cuddled against me, I continue, "Everything will be okay, so don't worry, alright? We'll talk soon. Promise."

CHRISTMAS DAY IS finally here. Audra really loves the holiday. She could barely fall asleep last night as if Santa himself was about to climb through my window and surprise her. I was nearly asleep when she shook me awake again because we didn't make cookies. Not even kidding. So then I had to not only go bake cookies with her, but I had to quickly run to the store to buy what we needed to make them. We ended up eating all of them before we went to bed. It was more fun than what I'm making it out to be. Probably because I need more sleep.

It's five in the morning and Audra wants to do presents. Seriously.

"Babe, don't you want to wait until later? It's one present. Two, if you count Liana's. The sun isn't even up yet. Why are we?" I roll away from her, intent on going back to sleep.

"Neil Lawson, get your butt out of bed right now." She pokes me hard in the back.

"This is crazy, Audra."

"Please. We're already awake."

Yeah, because she woke me up. "Fine," I give in, knowing that she won't stop otherwise.

She actually giggles with excitement. "Let's fix a cup of hot chocolate first. Good thing you bought some last week." Only because she insisted.

We head into the kitchen and start fixing us some hot chocolate. I leave her to finish as I go gather the presents together and put them on the middle cushion on the couch. Audra walks into the room with our cups just as I've grabbed a blanket for us since it's a little chilly in here. She puts the cups on the end table as I sit and then pull her into my lap, so she sits sideways. I lay the blanket over us and Audra hands me my cup. After we both take a sip, Audra places them back where they were.

I reach for only one present and hand it to her. "This

is for baby girl. I had them wrap it anyway."

She unwraps it as if she's an excited kid who has a big box to open. Upon seeing the stuffed toy duck, she says, "Aw, it's so cute. Once the guys get back, we can start on the nursery and put it in there." Audra gives me a kiss and then sets it aside. "Your turn," she tells me before drinking more of her hot chocolate.

I grab the one she bought for me. When I tear all the paper away, I can't manage to find words. She bought skates that are sized for a kid.

"It's more symbolic than anything. It doesn't take a fool to realize you love hockey and I think it would be amazing for you to pass that on to Liana. If she wants to be an ice skater or a hockey player like her daddy, then I'm all for it, as long as you're there if she gets hurt. Show her that it's okay to fall down, to get hurt, but to make her tough enough to get back up and keep going. You said you would, remember?"

Swallowing hard, I nod. "I remember," I whisper. She's given me something that I don't even know how to put into words, but it makes me fucking emotional. She took what I said and made it beautiful, made it a gift for me to give and teach to our daughter later. It's probably the best Christmas gift I've ever received. "Thanks, Audra," I kiss her cheek and then hand her the last present. Her eyes light up even though it's only a card. She rips open the envelope, and as she sees what it is, I say, "This is for after the baby is born. Whenever you want to relax, you can grab a friend and go."

Audra stares at the card for a moment and then lifts her head to look at me with glassy eyes. "You..." She glances at the gift certificate again. "You thought about me for after our baby is born? Neil..." A tear spills over, and I wipe it away. "That's so thoughtful. Thank you." She presses her mouth to mine, softly at first, but when I part her lips with my tongue, she wraps her arms around my neck. Audra pulls away entirely too soon and whispers, "I'm glad you are her father. I couldn't have accidentally picked a better man for the job." Her lips quirk up into a smile.

"Thank you for saying that. Now, drink your hot cocoa so we can go back to bed."

Audra laughs, but does what I've told her. I don't think I'll ever tire of that laugh.

CHAPTER 26

Winston

WE'RE TWO WEEKS into the new semester, and nothing has changed with Maddie. Although, she is hanging around me again, and she doesn't look like she's lost more weight, but she hasn't gained any either. Audra has made herself at home in the house and Grant and I are moving in with Lucy's brothers this weekend. Since this is Bo's last semester, he decided to stick through until the end. For now, we're sitting at the table in the kitchen, eating breakfast.

"Hey, Grant. Let me borrow your phone."

He slides it over the table, and I pick it up. After putting my dirty dish in the dishwasher, I sneak off into my bedroom. I dial Dave's number and what do you know? He answers.

"Hello?"

"Don't hang up. This is serious."

Dave sighs. "What in the hell do you want?"

"Don't you listen to your voicemails?"

"Not yours. What is it?"

"We need to talk about Maddie," I tell him.

"I don't want to hear about any trouble you two-"

"Don't even start that bullshit, Dave. You need to listen to me because I need your fucking help. Maddie needs your help. I told you this shit is serious, so quit acting like I'm calling you to complain."

He's quiet for a moment before he speaks again. "Okay. I'm listening."

"Do you remember our senior party? Maddie showed up and we all ended up telling her to go home. You used to tease her by calling her Fatty Maddie."

"Yeah, she was a little chunky because of how short she is."

"Well, that fucked her up, Dave. That night is why she started running and exercising."

"What's wrong with that, Winston?"

"Seriously? Did you not see Maddie at all over break? She doesn't eat enough and definitely not enough for how much she's exercising. It's worse now that we're dating, but she won't listen to me, Dave. When I bring it up, she shuts me out and says that she won't go back to being Fatty Maddie."

"Shit," he mumbles.

"Exactly. All I want is for her to be healthy and she's not. If she keeps this up, it'll be so much worse."

"I'll try talking to her. Apologize for teasing her and I'll tell Mom and Dad. If she won't listen to us, then maybe she will to them."

"Thanks," I say, feeling better. I hope it makes a difference. We hang up and I go give Grant his phone back. If I don't hurry, I'm going to be late for class. Christmas with my family went pretty well. I told them I was dating Maddie and they were a bit surprised, but overall happy. I text Maddie in between classes, but I don't hear back until after lunch.

"Winston!" a pissed off Maddie yells as I turn to see her stalking towards me. When she reaches me, she shoves me as hard as her little body can, but it doesn't do much damage. "You told Dave?! Now my entire family is all concerned over nothing! How dare you!"

"Calm down."

"No!" Her voice quiets down, but there's no denying the anger. "You do *not* get to talk about me to my brother. He is not your best friend where I'm concerned, so you are not allowed to speak to him about me, especially when you don't know what the fuck you're talking about."

"Maddie." I reach for her, but she steps away.

"No. I have to go, but I figured there was a little time to let you know that I'm pissed." She turns and walks away as fast as she can.

Fuck. I run after her because I know her schedule, and she doesn't actually have a class to go to. I reach for her elbow, wrap my fingers around it, and tug just enough so she turns around to face me.

"Let me go," she softly demands.

"No. We're going to talk. Right now." I usher her towards the parking lot to my car. Once we're inside, I angle myself in my seat to face her. Her arms are crossed defensively and she's staring straight ahead. "Maddie, you wouldn't talk to me."

"That doesn't mean you can tattle to my family."

"Yes, it damn sure does. Just...tell me the way you see it then because I'm wondering if I'm part of the problem." Maddie quickly looks at me, surprised. "You seemed fine before we started dating again. You ate, you exercised a normal amount of times every day, and you were healthy. Once we were back together, you went into overdrive or something. If you're more conscious with me, then I don't want to be with you. I don't know how many times I have to tell you that you're gorgeous the way you are for you to believe me. So, if I make it worse, you need to let me know."

She glances at me again and sighs. "I know it isn't the reason why, but it was almost as if you wanted me to leave because I was fat, like Dave said. I didn't want to risk that ever happening again in the future with anyone else. And maybe you are right. I went a little overboard, but I want to make sure I don't lose you again," she finishes in a whisper.

"I wouldn't ever leave you because of something like that. You should know better, Maddie. All I want is for you to be healthy."

"Well, thanks to you, my parents want me to go see a therapist. I don't have a problem, Winston." I open my mouth to interrupt her, but she beats me to it. "All I did was what I wanted to do. I ate a little less and worked out a little more. It might not have been the smartest move, but I wasn't starving myself. I mean, it sounds like it, but I still ate." There was some struggle with her words, and I watch her for a moment as I collect my thoughts on how to respond. "I took what I was already doing to the extreme, I know that," she adds.

"You should still go to a counselor, Maddie. Talk to someone about how you feel, someone who could really help, and start being healthy again."

She nods, a tear falling from the corner of her eye. "I ate four donuts after Dave and my parents called," she blurts out.

"With chocolate icing and sprinkles?" Those were her favorite. I'm not sure why she's bringing it up though.

Maddie nods her head again. "I haven't had one in years and after Dave called, I kind of broke down and bought some. Then I was angry and disgusted with myself that I caved, which is when I found you. I was on my way to the gym."

"I'm glad you ran into me then." I reach for her hand, intertwining our fingers.

"I missed you," she whispers, looking down at our hands. "Do you really think I should go see someone?"

"What do you think?" This needs to be something she wants, I think. If I say yes, then her answer will be the same.

"Couldn't hurt, right? I doubt everyone will leave it alone unless I go anyway." She gulps and her leg starts bouncing a little. A steady stream of air exhales from her lips.

"It'll be fine. Promise. How about we go see that movie tonight that we saw the preview for the last time?"

"Yeah, that sounds like fun." She leans over to kiss me. "I do need to go this time, though. Let me know when you're picking me up."

Grant

"HEY, GRANT," LUCY smiles as she takes the seat next to me in the library. She reaches over, grabbing the back of my neck, and pulls me closer. Lucy presses her lips to mine with purpose and a lot of unhidden want. She's amped things up since break, not that I'm complaining in any way. Her cheeks are flushed when she settles back into her seat.

"Well, hello to you too," I grin, making her laugh.

"I figured I better get it all out now before you go live with my brothers."

"Are you sure you're okay with it?" She told me she was, but maybe she's changed her mind.

"Yes, of course. Are you sure you're ready to live with the looney Kennedy brothers?" she teases with a smile.

"As long as I have the beautiful Kennedy sister, I'll be fine."

Lucy blushes, but rolls her eyes. "I don't see that being a problem."

"Good." After a moment, I add, "You know, there's one favor I didn't do and you haven't mentioned it."

She scrunches her nose up. "Wouldn't it be rude to ask how come you didn't bring me anything back? And it's not like you have to do everything I ask. I'm sure this isn't the first time you couldn't do something for me."

I raise an eyebrow at her. "Really? When have I ever turned you down?"

"Well, there was when..." her voice trails as she thinks. And thinks some more until her eyes widen and her lips part. "Grant Faison, why haven't you ever said no? I must be like the bossiest, neediest person ever. Why do you always help me when I ask?"

"Because I want to and I don't mind one bit."

"Yeah, but it has to be annoying after a while."

I shake my head. "Nope. I enjoy it, but we're off track. I did bring you something back from the Bahamas." Her eyes light up with excitement, even though she stays quiet. "I left it at my parents and they've taken forever to mail it to me. That's why you haven't gotten it yet. It should be here today, though."

"What is it?" she asks curiously.

"If I tell you, that'll ruin the surprise, Lucy. You can ride with me to the house after practice, if you want."

"Luce." We turn to see Patrick walking towards her. He looks anxious, which makes Lucy stand. "I need your help with something. Now."

"Oh, okay." She looks down at me. "I'll catch you later, Grant." It's hardly out of her mouth before Patrick is pulling her away.

I swear, I don't think I'll ever get used to their relationship. It's all loyalty and dropping everything for one another without a second thought, much less a complaint. That's just one more thing to admire about her. She loves how close they are and all they do for her and with her. It's an amazing thing to see. And I wouldn't be me if I wasn't wondering what has Patrick all concerned. Knowing them, I won't ever find out either.

"BABE, WE'RE GOING to be late for class if you don't decide soon."

We decided to stop by to pick up paint after her doctor appointment. Audra told me she knew what color she wanted the nursery to be painted, but we've been here for an hour now and she's changed her mind every time we go to get the color mixed. She originally said a purple and gray theme, like I'm a decorating/painting expert. But that turned into purple, blue, green, yellow, and all the shades in between.

"What do you think?" she asks, taking a moment to look away from the pallet of colors.

"I think that since the walls are already gray, you should decorate with purple stuff."

She frowns. "Are you saying that so you don't have to paint?"

"No, that's not why. That makes the most sense to me, though."

Audra looks back at all the colors before nodding. "Okay, we'll do it your way. No painting, all decorating then."

Thank God. A decision. Hopefully, the last one. "So, we're leaving?" I ask, just to be sure.

"Yep. Let me go to the bathroom first." On our way to the bathroom in the front of the store, she glances at me. "We haven't talked about hockey yet, Neil."

"I know." Time seems to be flying by and we've been

a bit busy, so it slips our minds. Which is just a shitty way to say I've been avoiding it. "We both don't have to work tonight, so we'll talk over dinner, okay?"

She nods. I still don't know what I want to do, and I've been hoping that I could come to my own conclusion before talking to Audra. That might not happen and maybe I need to talk to someone other than my agent to figure it out. Hopefully, Audra is that someone for me.

Winston

"HOW BADLY ARE you guys going to miss us?" I joke. Bo, Grant, Neil, and I are all in the house, but not for much longer.

"None," Neil laughs. "I'll still have to deal with your asses for hockey."

"I'll miss ya," Bo inputs. "At least, y'all don't cry." Neil sends him a glare, but doesn't say anything.

"If you get interest, are you going to sign?" Grant asks the one question we've all be wondering since we found out.

"Yeah, what are you thinking?" I say.

"I don't know. I've played my ass off for four years and I don't want it to be all for nothing, you know, but I have to think about Audra and the baby, too. We're supposed to discuss it tonight. Did you ever get up with Dave about Maddie?"

I nod. "Things are looking up."

"Good."

My phone beeps with a text.

Maddie: I haven't had a greasy burger in a while. Dinner? :)

"I gotta go, boys. Maddie's a callin' and she wants a burger." As I stand, Bo suggests some burger place he and the guys on the team are always raving about and I text her that I'm on my way. Maybe we'll skip the movies tonight and go eat all the things she had forbidden herself to eat. I don't know a lot about eating disorders, and she may not be suffering from one, but there is definitely something going on that needs to be worked on. There's an undeniable issue that Maddie has with food and exercising, so hopefully we can get her through it with the help of a counselor.

She's standing outside when I pull into the dorm parking lot, and she carefully runs to my car before sliding in. "It's frrreaking cold," she chatters.

"Why were you waiting outside then?" I ask, turning up the heat.

"Because I didn't think it would be that bad and by the time I decided to go back in, you were here." She tightens her jacket around her and turns towards me.

I lean over the console and kiss her like she's expecting. "Where do you want to go?"

"I didn't have a place in mind. I figured you would know somewhere to go."

So we head across town to the restaurant that Bo suggested. Hopefully, it's as good as he said. Maddie seems quieter than usual as we wait for our food. I reach for her hand, which hasn't left her lap since we sat down. She's usually touching me in some way, but not tonight.

"What's wrong? Thinking you should have gone with a salad?" The surprise in her eyes is a gut punch of truth. "Talk to me, Maddie," I add softly.

"I haven't talked to anyone about this in three years. I thought that maybe I could throw it all away like it hasn't been..."

"A struggle?" I fill in for her. She nods. "We used to be able to talk about everything."

"A lot has changed," Maddie reminds me.

"You know what hasn't changed? My love for you. Has that changed for you?" She shakes her head. "Then get over here."

Maddie gets up and slides into my side of the booth. I wrap my arm around her shoulders, pulling her closer as she rests her head on my shoulder.

"Talk to me, gorgeous," I whisper, kissing the top of her head.

She grabs a handful of my shirt at my side before tilting her head up at me. "Is it too late to order that salad?" I nod because I want her to try, at least. "I don't want the burger anymore."

"It's like a salad. There's lettuce on it," I try, making Maddie laugh. "What if we order a small salad and have that with the burger?"

"No, that's fine. All or nothing, right?" she says, taking a deep breath.

"For us, yes. For this, it doesn't have to be that way."

Our waitress places our plates in front of us and Maddie stares at the burger. "Let's see how it goes," she finally says, glancing at me. "And let's talk about something else."

We take the first bite at the same time, and I start talking about anything and everything.

"Neil's girlfriend, Audra, moved in. She's pregnant, which is why Grant and I are moving out. Since you are my girlfriend, I expect that I won't have to hear about the 'super hot Kennedy brothers' anymore, especially now that I'm moving in with them?"

Maddie laughs, wiping the ketchup from the corner of her mouth. "Only occasionally," she teases. "It works out anyway, doesn't it? Because Neil graduates this year, right?"

"Yeah, him and Bo both. I still can't get over that he's having a kid." I shake my head at the thought.

"Yeah," Maddie nods in agreement. "What's the story with Bo anyway? He's single, isn't he? He seems to keep to himself. The most expression I've ever seen from him is that night at the bar when he and Neil argued and fought."

"As far as I know, he's single. He keeps to himself," I shrug. "He and Neil both are private people, for the most part. I mean, look at how long it took for Neil to tell us about Audra."

Maddie takes a swallow of her drink, and I peek to see that her burger is almost gone. "So..." she cuts her eyes over at me, "are you and Dave friends again?"

"I haven't heard from him since this morning. He's been pissed for a while, so he should come around soon."

"I think he misses you."

I look at her curiously. "Why do you think that?"

"Over break, he didn't ask about you, but he didn't tell me to shut up when I was filling my parents in on you either. I tried to talk to him about how he was being ridiculous. He listened, but didn't say anything one way or the other. So yeah, I think he misses you. How could he not? You've been best friends for forever. He's just too stuck up his own ass to say anything."

My eyes widen as Dave appears at our table as Maddie finishes. "Well, thanks for letting me know how you really feel, little sister." He slides into the other side of the booth.

"What are you doing here?" she asks. "How did you find us?"

"You weren't at your dorm and your roommate said you were out with your boyfriend. I went to the house and some guy told me where I might find y'all. You've been ignoring us all day since we called, and I was worried. I just wanted to see my sister."

Maddie seems stumped by his presence and his words. Can't say I blame her. They've never been close, obviously, but despite anything he's said, Dave loves his little sister. He glances between us, waiting for Maddie to say something. She pushes her plate over to him, all that's left are her untouched fries. "You can have the rest of those. I already ate a burger."

"Thanks. I didn't mean to crash your, uh," he looks at me, "date."

"It's fine. Maddie must have missed you since she was talking about you," I joke.

She rolls her eyes and steals a fry from my plate. "Whatever. We were running out of things to occupy my mind." We're quiet for a moment as we realize why she needed a distraction, so she could finish eating her burger. Maddie puts her half-eaten fry back on my plate and goes for my drink since we're waiting for the waitress to refill hers.

"I always knew Winston was boring," Dave says with a forced laugh.

"Shut the hell up," I chuckle.

Maddie leans her head on my shoulder, officially done with food. I rest my hand on her thigh, and she immediately holds my hand. "Are you staying the night?" she asks.

"Yeah. It's a long drive back, so I'll leave in the morning. I have a hotel not too far from here. I just...wanted to see you. If I had known that you took what I said to heart, or hell, paid me any attention, I would have never said it, Maddie. I feel terrible. I'm sorry. I never thought it would-"

"It's okay," Maddie interrupts. "You feel bad because you were a dick and your little sister actually listened to her brother." Her voice drops to a whisper. "You made me pay attention to what was already there." She takes a deep breath and looks at me. "I'm tired of talking about this. Can we go?"

"Yeah, of course." We've missed the movie, so we'll have to catch it another day. I wave the waitress over for the check as Maddie looks everywhere but at her brother, who seems at a loss for words. I fish my keys from my pockets and give them to her. "Go get the car warmed up." Maddie happily takes my escape without so much of a goodbye to Dave. "I'm going to make her stay with me tonight, if it makes you feel any better," I tell him once she's gone.

"Would have never thought my sister going home with my best friend would make me happy." He does looked relieved.

"Don't worry about what she said. She barely talks to

me about it, so don't be surprised that she doesn't want to talk to you."

"That makes me feel so much better," he mumbles as the waitress takes my card. "Has she said anything about Mom wanting her to see a professional?"

I nod. "I think she'll go, too."

Dave shakes his head. "I always worried about some ass hurting her. Never thought it would be me."

"Neither of us knew how much it bothered her, Dave. I mean, I knew she hated it, but I thought it was because you teased her in front of everyone, and I definitely didn't think she was that worried about her weight. We were both idiots," I finish as I stick my card back in my wallet.

"Do you think she'll be okay?"

"Yeah, I do, but she needs time for that to happen. I should go." I turn to leave, but he stops me.

"I'm not angry anymore, if it makes a difference. I was pissed about all I didn't know, what you didn't tell me, more than anything."

"Yeah, I figured that was it. You've always been needy that way."

He laughs. "Shut the hell up and go take care of my sister."

CHAPTER 27

Grant

I ALMOST THOUGHT Lucy was going to bail on me after Patrick came for her at the library. She canceled our run, so I thought for sure she would. But she texted me saying that we were still on. The package with all I brought back for her is in my back seat. She's walking out of the building as I park.

"What are you doing?" I ask when she climbs into the back seat.

"Leave the truck running and get back here with me," she answers, looking curiously at the box. I move into the back, placing the box in my lap. "We don't have to go anywhere." Lucy slides over to me and sinks into me. "I missed you," she whispers, wrapping her arms around me.

"Everything okay, Lucy?" Last time she hugged me

like this, she had disappeared for a few days after staying with me and having Patrick come get her.

"Yeah, still thinking about why Patrick came for me." She looks like she's unsure if she wants to share it with me or not. Lucy takes a breath and decides to fill me in. "You know that Corey can't play anymore, right? He's been having a hard time dealing with it, more than we thought, and we had to go see him. Well, more than I thought. Patrick and Jon knew. They are always so strong for me, it bothers me when I see any of them struggle. It made me not want to waste time going somewhere before I could do this." She briefly squeezes her hold on me, lifting her head to look at me. I lean down to gently kiss her, wanting to make her feel better. When I pull away, she smiles, her cheeks starting to blush.

"Do you want to talk more about it?"

"Not tonight," she answers.

"Well, here," I say, releasing her to place the box in her lap. "Open it."

Lucy wastes no time, but her hands still as she sees everything in the box. Staring at the contents, she mumbles, "Something means one thing, Grant."

"I couldn't decide and every time I saw something that I wanted you to have, I couldn't resist."

I watch this quiet, independent force of a person that is Lucy, run her fingers over what's in the box. There's a few t-shirts, a necklace, a keychain, and even one of those old film cameras that are sold for tourists, filled with pictures I took for her that she can develop. Some shells and sand from the beaches are in a bag, and Lucy seems mesmerized and appreciative of it all, particularly the camera.

"There's one left," she says, noticing that one more

picture can be taken on it. Lucy looks over at me. "Take one with me."

I turn on the overhead light as Lucy presses herself into my side and holds the camera out. We smile and she presses the button, releasing a soft click. She places it back into the box and sets it in the empty seat next to her.

"Thank you, Grant." She closes the space between us to kiss me.

"Anything for you," I murmur against her lips.

Lucy pulls back at my words, almost looking confused. "Have you always been this way? You've seriously done that since you met me, even with the very first favor. Why?"

I think about what she's asking. Even though I've known my lack of saying no, I never thought about why. My mind flashes back to when I met her, and I try to explain how I saw it. "At first, you seemed nervous and I didn't want to be mean. Plus, I was curious about you. When I found out who you were, who your brothers were, I wondered what it was like to have them for siblings. The more I saw you, the less the thought of saying no passed my mind. You were you..." I repeat what she once told me.

"I couldn't have been any other way. You gave me bits and pieces, left me with questions, and were a person I wanted to be around. I wanted to do your favors, to see life like you do, to see the way you thought and behaved, to see your relationship with those around you. I wanted you in any and every way you would let me have you. So yeah, I was more than happy agreeing to do whatever you asked of me."

Lucy's blue eyes search mine, almost frantically, and I wonder what she's thinking. The words that leave her mouth next are so carefully spoken I could almost believe they've never been strung together in the same sentence before. They've never meant anything to anyone else, never existed before this moment because that's how special those words are to be leaving Lucy's mouth, directed at me. "I love you," she says softly, but clearly.

She's left me speechless. The only thing I can do is kiss her. To press my mouth to hers, glide my tongue between her lips and try to make my kiss speak what my voice seems to have forgotten how to do.

"And even now, you overwhelm me," she whispers when I pull away, resting my forehead against hers.

"You do?" I ask, ignoring her statement. "You love me?" My mind is trying to figure out what I ever did to create such an emotion in her. I'm overwhelmed, just like she is, but for different reasons. Or maybe they are the same.

Her lashes fall and rise before she smiles. "Yes. Don't you love me?" Lucy's cheeks are softly colored with a blush.

"Yes, I do." I kiss her quickly. "I love you so much." I press my lips to hers again, wanting to taste every inch of her.

Lucy rests a hand on my thigh and gently uses the other to push me away. Her eyes are bright with a playfulness and a desire stronger than I'm used to seeing from her. "Maybe we should go eat and then go back to your place." She sees the questions in my eyes and laughs softly. "Don't ask questions now, Grant. Unless you want to say no?" Lucy raises her eyebrows at me.

"Of course not," I answer, making her laugh again. "I'm pretty sure that word isn't even in my vocabulary."

We go back to the front seats and continue with our plans, knowing what is to come later.

NEIL

"HOW DO YOU not know what you want, Neil?" Audra asks for the umpteenth time.

"I don't know," I sigh. "I mean, I've worked towards this for a long time, yeah, but things change. There's Liana and we're together now, so there's you too. I don't know if I would want to get signed, if that opportunity came." We're running in circles with this conversation. Audra obviously has an opinion, but she's holding back for a change. "Be honest with me, babe. What would *you* want me to do?" I've told her about the traveling, the moving to whatever city that hosts the team, and it feels like bad karma to discuss something that might not even happen.

Audra glides her hand in a circle over her belly, looking down at it before lifting her head to meet my gaze. "I think our daughter would want her daddy to go after his dreams. When she grows up, do we tell her that she stole your chance? That you felt like you couldn't? You can, Neil. Players are doing it right now. They have families. What's stopping you from doing the same thing?"

I reach for her hand and pull her over so she can sit sideways in my lap. We stayed in for dinner since everyone else would be going out. "First of all, she wouldn't have stolen it. I know I could."

"Then what's stopping you?" she repeats.

She gazes at me, and I take a deep breath. I hate voicing my fears, but when it's Audra, it's not as bad. "I could miss so much with Liana while she's growing up. It's bad timing for her first year. And what if something were to happen while I was at a game? I don't want to come home to something bad ever again when I could prevent the being away while playing part."

Audra plays with the hair at the base of my neck with one hand with sad eyes. "You can't keep worrying about what if's, Neil. Here," she takes my hand and hovers it above her stomach, "if she moves, then you will play if a contract comes your way. If she doesn't, then consider your hockey days numbered. Now, ask her what she thinks." She puts my hand on her belly.

She seems so serious about it that I laugh, but say, "What do you think, baby girl?" I feel a kick before I can even finish.

A grin rises on Audra's face. "Looks like we have an answer."

"We couldn't let her pick her name, but we let her decide our future?"

"Technically, I decided and then she helped you decide. She was moving around before I put your hand there."

"God, I love you," I laugh as I kiss her temple.

It's not until Audra quietly replies, "I love you too, Neil," that I realize exactly what I said.

My heart nearly bursts on the spot with her words. The last thing I wanted after Candace died turned out to be exactly what I needed. I needed someone to love, care for, and be there for. I didn't really need for someone to do that in return. I just needed to be able to do all those things for someone else again because for a long time, I didn't think it was possible. Audra's that person for me. She's even managed to help me heal. Not to mention that she's giving me a daughter, and she loves me too.

"C'mon. Let's put our dishes away and go lay down. My back is bothering me, too. Will you please put those hands to work?" she asks, giving me a small kiss, as if I need an incentive.

"Of course. You can go on up, if you want. I can take care of these." I nod towards the plates.

"No, I can help."

So we put away our dishes, and I give her a massage before we lay down for bed. Life is looking pretty damn good, if I say so myself. Baby girl will be here soon, and as I fall asleep, I pray that she'll be healthy. I can't wait to meet her.

Grant

"GRANT," JON CALLS out. "Luce is here."

So far, living with her brothers hasn't been too bad. We're all learning how to be around each other when we're here. There are still things I don't understand about them, but that's their business, not mine. Plus, I actually see Lucy a bit more because she'll come to see her brothers, and I'm already here as well.

"Hey," I greet once I find her and her brothers in the kitchen.

Lucy smiles and kisses me quickly on the lips. "Hey."

"What did I tell you about that?" Jon frowns at his sister.

She shrugs. "I'll kiss him if I want. You should be grateful that we're not making out in front of you."

Jon groans as does Patrick, but Patrick's turns into a laugh. "Don't you have a 5K to run?" he asks. "Grant, make sure you beat her time for us."

Jon shakes his head. "Make sure she doesn't get dehydrated. That's what you should be telling him, Patrick." A small smile does appear on his face. "But definitely beat her time."

I glance at Lucy, who rolls her eyes. "Grant's not leaving my side, so he can't beat my time. And he will take care of me. Won't you?" She turns to face me and takes my hand.

"Of course."

Jon and I are still getting used to each other, but for the most part, things are good between her brothers and me. It's good to be around them when Lucy isn't around. I get more insight into their personalities instead of the overbearing, overprotective brothers that they are around Lucy. They trust me more, and they are even kind of fun to be around. It's just hard to tell whenever Lucy is here.

"Let's go do this," I say, pulling her to the door before we're late.

"C'MON, LUCY," I breathe. "Almost there." We have half a mile left of this fucking 5K. It's really not so bad because we've been running for a while now, but Lucy's slowing down a bit.

"How much further?"

"Half mile."

Her pace picks back up and soon, we're crossing the finish line. We weren't the fastest or the slowest, but we finished. Lucy bends over with her hands on her knees once we're out of the way. I take her hand, making her stand upright, and I pull her to me for a hug, even though we're both hot.

"I'm so proud of you," I whisper.

Before she can respond, Maddie shouts, "Lucy! You did it! And you too, Grant."

Lucy pulls away to face Maddie and Winston. The girls hug and I say to Winston, "You piece of shit. You should have run too."

He grins. "I know how to tell Maddie no. Maybe you should take notes and learn a thing or two."

Maddie slaps his stomach, but laughs and I roll my eyes.

"I don't need to tell Lucy no because I actually like doing things with her."

"Are y'all going to bicker or can I get some water now?" Lucy says as Winston opens his mouth to respond. Without waiting for an answer, she takes my hand and pulls me over to the table with snacks and bottles of water. Once she's rehydrated, she smiles at me. "Thanks for doing this with me. I'm proud of you too."

"Think you may want to do another?"

She laughs. "No. I don't really like running, but now I can at least say I tried." Lucy takes a step closer to me with a wide smile, so I wrap an arm around her waist. "You're sweaty, Grant."

I chuckle. "You do know that most people find sweat gross, right?"

Lucy shrugs. "Sometimes, it is. I love you," she adds, lifting her chin a bit as she leans in to kiss me.

"I love you too."

Not much has changed since we first slept together.

We've gotten closer, and Lucy will tell me those three words every chance she gets. Sometimes, I think that she learned to tell her loved ones that often because she knows they might not always be here. She reserves it for those who deserve it, and then she says it with every parting, and any other time she wants to remind you of her love.

Our future together looks bright. We have another year of college together before I graduate and Lucy has one more after that. Instead of going to see her grandparents, she's going home with me for spring break to meet my parents. I can't wait for them to meet her. I kind of wish we were having a big family reunion so I could show her off to everyone.

"Hey, we're going to eat. Want to come?" We turn at the sound of Maddie's voice.

"Of course," Lucy answers, tugging me towards Maddie and Winston.

She can drag me anywhere, ask me to do anything, and I'll always go and do whatever she wants. It's worked for us so far, so why stop? I can't help but wonder what the next few years will bring. I'm looking forward to it because the future seems even more exciting with Lucy by my side.

Winston

MADDIE HAS BEEN seeing a counselor, working through her issues. Things got worse before they got better. It was like acknowledging it made her even more conscious, and she snuck around to overexercise. We argued a lot over it, too. I would catch her at the gym, drag her away, and it always ended with her being angry and hurt. After a huge argument and her passing out from having not eaten enough on top of being dehydrated, Maddie started being more cooperative.

She scared me to death, enough that I didn't want her running the 5K today because she would've stop training for it then. We compromised instead. She stopped exercising at the gym and only ran a certain amount four days a week, and I had to be with her. Maddie didn't like me shadowing her though. I had to start running with her so it would feel more like I was doing it with her and not watching her.

Since the incident and since Maddie has accepted that she needs help, she seems happier and most definitely healthier. Her sessions are better, more helpful, and she took me with her for a few sessions. It allowed me to understand her better, even though I never spoke a word. She wanted me there as a quiet support, so I was. After that, she felt good going on her own, and she didn't want me there anymore.

With the 5K over, her exercise routine will cut back to three times a week, including running because of how much she ran. The counselor has even introduced her to another person with similar struggles, and they workout together in a healthy way. Her new friend and counselor often support her in ways I can't because I don't understand. I always know when she's going to talk to either of them because Maddie says, "I want to talk to someone who gets it, Winston." One day, she'll hopefully feel like I "get it" enough for her to talk to me more than she does.

It's working for her, and that's all that matters.

She's also learning that she can eat whatever she wants, in moderation as she constantly reminds me, and still be fit. Skinny is a word she doesn't use anymore. So is fat. Maddie wants to be fit and healthy instead. Her mindset has finally turned, and she is learning how to adjust to that kind of lifestyle.

The Kennedy brothers haven't been bad roommates either. Grant and I teach kids hockey at a local rink, and it pays the bills for us. If I thought Neil and Bo were private, they have nothing on these brothers. They share nothing of importance, only small talk about sports usually, but it works. I'm not buddies with them or anything, so I keep to myself most of the time. Grant can be the social one of the two of us.

"I kind of want an ice cream," Maddie says thoughtfully, glancing at me. We've just finished lunch with Lucy and Grant. Desserts and junk food are the hardest for Maddie, so anytime she says she wants some, I give her the same answer.

"We can split one, if you want."

"Mm, I think I want one too," Lucy adds. With Lucy ordering one, it helps Maddie do the same. Sometimes, it's hard for her to even say she wants one, much less order it herself. It makes me proud to watch her order us one to share. "Are you coming to the game tonight, Maddie?"

"Yeah, my brother is coming up to watch, and I'm going with him."

Dave and I have slipped back into our friendship, but the details of my relationship are off limits at the request of them both. She doesn't want me telling him, and he doesn't want to hear most of it. Maddie hasn't really spoken to him since he showed up last month, but she wants to make amends between them and go back to normal.

We only have a few games left this season, and instead of getting that end-of-season tiredness, we're more pumped than ever. Coach has been giving us great pep talks, Neil has been playing even better than he has all season, and we feel unstoppable. It's a good feeling to have with the season coming to a close. What's even better is that Maddie is mine, she's healthier, and I still have my best friend.

MADDIE AND DAVE hug awkwardly. She asked me to stay, in case she needed a quick escape. We're about to all ride over to the game together and Dave just arrived.

"Can we talk first?" Maddie asks him.

He glances behind her to me where I'm leaning against the driver's door to my car. "Yeah, of course."

"I want us to go back to normal. All of us," she adds, looking back at me. "You're still my brother. You don't need to be cautious over what you say. Be sincere and nice and we'll be fine. I want you to stop treating me like a kid. Be my brother, Dave."

He nods. "Okay. I'm sorry. I'll work on it."

"Thank you." Maddie steps so she can see us both. "Now, you two need to stop being weird when we're all together." She's right that he's weird, but me? I didn't think I acted any differently. "We're not going to have sex in front of you, Dave. He's not going to burst into flames if you hold my hand, Winston. You're best friends. Stop all your extra thinking and be that. Stop thinking of me as the sister when you're around each other. Be best friends, okay?"

I glance to Dave, who smiles. "I always knew you were bossy," he teases.

Maddie laughs and I add, "She calls the shots, that's for sure."

"That's more like it," she says.

It'll take some time for us to find a normal for all three of us, but it'll happen. Maybe Dave and Maddie will have a better relationship than before too. We're slow going, but all we're looking for right now is progress. Dave hugs Maddie one last time to officially make up for all the wrong doings. With a smile, Maddie takes my hand and says we better get going.

BO PLOPS DOWN next to me on the couch. We haven't really talked since that night we fought. He hasn't been with me to see the Lanier's but once or twice when Alice said he better show up.

"I'm sorry," I tell him. "I was an ass and drunk."

"I'm sorry too. You aren't selfish, or at least, not in the way I intended. You're going to be a great father, Neil. I've always known that from watching you with Alice. So yeah. Sorry for what I said."

I nod, clearing my throat. "This mean you'll be her uncle Bo?"

Bo grins. "Someone has to teach her how a winger is better than a forward."

I laugh. "Thanks."

Liana is supposed to be here any day now, so you can imagine how anxious I've been. Audra seems calmer than me. She's driving me almost to insanity, though. She's ready for Liana to come, and she seems more emotional than ever. From the time I talk to Bo to the time I leave for my game, I've almost made her cry three times and each time, I said something nice! I'm beyond ready for this game tonight. It can let me escape just for a bit.

Coach builds us up for another win, reminding us of our jobs on the ice. As soon as he gives the order to get on the ice, my phone rings. The guys glance my way at the sound. It's Audra, so I answer.

"Babe? What's up? The game is about to start? Everything okay?"

"Neil," Mrs. Garcia says. So wasn't expecting to hear her voice. "She's gone into labor. She asked me to tell you that she knows it could still be awhile, but-"

"She's crazy if she thinks I'm staying here," I breathe.

Mrs. Garcia laughs. "That's not what I was going to say. She wants you here as soon as you can get here. She's panicking a little and said she absolutely will not have this baby until she talks to you in person."

"Okay, I'll be there soon." When I turn away from my locker, the entire team is staring at me. None of them have left the room yet. "I have to go. Sorry, Coach."

He smiles. "Don't worry about us. You've led this team all season. They are strong enough to win without you here, thanks to you. Keep us updated." Words of congrats spread through my teammates before Coach booms, "Alright, let's go! We have a game to win and Neil has to go officially become a dad."

I grin. Baby girl is finally on her way.

ALL I CAN manage to think about is how beautiful my daughter is. Liana Grace Lawson entered the world at 7 pounds 2 ounces. Right now, she's sleeping in my arms while her momma sleeps. The nurse will probably come for her soon. My parents and the Lanier's will be stopping by in the morning and Audra's parents will be back too, I'm sure.

"There's the new dad," Bo's quiet voice comes from the doorway. Almost the entire team is with him, as well as Lucy and Maddie.

"What are you all doing here?" I whisper.

"We came to tell you that we won, to check in on everyone, and to congratulate you," Winston says.

"She's beautiful," Grant tells me.

"Thanks," I smile.

"She looks like every other baby I've ever seen," Vincent comments.

I hear someone hit him in the stomach, and I softly laugh.

"She's so cute," Lucy says, peering over Bo's shoulder.

"You're in a different world now," Bo tells me. "She already has you wrapped around her finger," he adds with a grin.

"Sure does," I nod. "Thanks for stopping by, y'all. It means a lot."

They congratulate me again before leaving. The nurse comes for Liana, and I look down at her one more time. So unbelievably beautiful. I don't want her to leave my arms ever, but she'll be back. My perfect baby girl. All the things I'll teach her as she grows up flash through my mind. How to walk, talk, and skate barely scratch the surface. It hits me as hard as if I were punched in the gut that I truly have a family now. The Lanier's, the Garcia's, my parents, Audra and now Liana are all part of my family. My life is going to be amazing, and it's all starts with my baby girl. I really hope her first word is Daddy.

AS ALWAYS, I need to thank my wonderful beta readers for giving me their time to provide fantastic feedback for my guys. Thank you Andrekia, Heidi, Louise, Lucy, Michael, and Rachel.

A huge thanks goes to one beta reader in particular. Thank you, Heidi, for help my struggling self give this book a title that I'm in love with and fits perfectly.

Thanks to Kim C. and Jessica P. for choosing the names, Winston and Maddie, for me to use in this book!

Kathy from K² Editing, thank you for working with me, my deadlines, and for those little comments you leave while editing.

I really need to thank Alisha from Damonza for designing a cover that met my wants and couldn't be more perfect. Thank you for always being a pleasure to work with and for being so accommodating.

Lastly, I need to thank Mary Smith. You're my best friend, my writing BFF, and you get me. You're not only helpful with my everyday problems, but you help me with my writing worries.

About the Author

LINDSAY PAIGE IS the author of the Bold as Love series, *Don't Panic*, *You Before Me*, and *Bracing the Blue Line*. She is also the co-author of The Penalty Kill Trilogy. She has three passions in life: reading, writing, and watching hockey, especially the Pittsburgh Penguins. Among the pile of books to read, stories to write, and games to watch, Lindsay is also focused on completing college.
Lindsay resides in North Carolina and is inspired by world around her and the people in it. Many of the aspects in her books stem from her love for hockey and her struggles in life and with anxiety, as evident in *Don't Panic*.
She is currently working on numerous solo works and a couple of projects with coauthor Mary Smith as well.

http://authorlindsaypaige.blogspot.com/
https://www.facebook.com/authorlindsaypaige
www.twitter.com/lindsaypaige11

Printed in Great Britain
by Amazon